candygirl

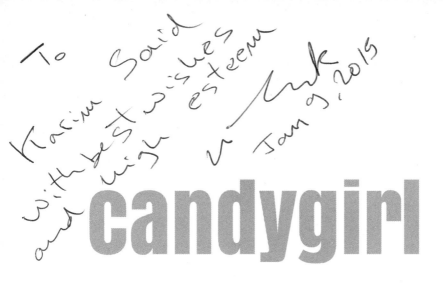

candygirl

M.M. Tawfik

Translated by the Author

The American University in Cairo Press
Cairo   New York

First published in 2012 by
The American University in Cairo Press
113 Sharia Kasr el Aini, Cairo, Egypt
420 Fifth Avenue, New York, NY 10018
www.aucpress.com

Dar el Kutub No. 2227/12
ISBN 978 977 416 559 7

Dar el Kutub Cataloging-in-Publication Data

Tawfiq, M.M.
        candygirl/ M.M. Tawfik; translated by M.M Tawfik.—Cairo: The American
    University in Cairo Press, 2012
        p.   cm.
        ISBN 978 977 416 559 7
                1. Arabic fiction   2. Arabic fiction—Translating into English
        892.73

1 2 3 4 5   16 15 14 13 12

Designed by Andrea El-Akshar
Printed in Egypt

chapter 1

Giza, Egypt
Monday, January 8, 2007
Sometime before the afternoon call to prayer

Upon exiting the bank, Dr. Mustafa Mahmud Korany—a.k.a. the Cerebellum—pauses for a moment. Tucked under his arm is a portfolio that contains what remains of his life savings. He has just closed the CD and cleaned out his account. The sum did not exceed fifteen thousand pounds by much, and all the time he had thought he was well off. From behind eyeglasses that cover half his face, he scans the area with nervous glances. Al-Tahrir Street flows in its usual turbulence, under the gaze of dull gray buildings sprinkled with the signs of doctors' offices and a variety of businesses. In the middle of the road, people walk in their thousands and vehicles spar like chariots in a Roman coliseum. Snatches of a Nancy Agram song emanate from one of the shops.

Hundreds of eyes intersect with his, redoubling his fears, almost driving him out of his mind. How is he to distinguish between an inquisitive youth and a scout for a criminal gang? How can he tell if that person in the café, observing him from behind his newspaper, is a plainclothes policeman or an agent for the CIA? One thing is for sure: danger lurks in every corner. It aims weapons at him from the rooftops. It is ready to pounce on him from behind tinted car windows.

Right now, his only wish is that the minutes or hours that separate him from his rendezvous with the most beautiful woman in the universe would elapse quickly. If only he could shut his eyes and reopen them to find himself back in his hideout in Cairo's underworld. He absolutely needs to get away from the official city, to get back to his room on the roof of a crooked house, in a slum whose name he doesn't even know.

His one desire is to get back into the arms of candygirl.

His body suddenly jolts forward. A shove from behind has thrown him a few steps ahead. He looks back in terror. Facing him is an elderly gentleman wearing a tarboosh. The Cerebellum's slender body shudders beneath his jacket, which is several sizes too large. He makes an effort to contain his anger. The man just stares calmly back. The serenity in his face dissipates the Cerebellum's rage, without the man needing to utter a word of apology. The Cerebellum quickly forces himself to focus on the danger that is growing by the second. He heads for the Dokki intersection, leaving the old man behind.

He walks as fast as he can, looking back every few steps. He bumps into a fat woman, who shouts in his face. With a distracted mumble of apology, he dashes ahead. He catches sight of his speeding body mirrored in the shop windows. Scrutinizing the reflections in the glass, he tries to ascertain if he's being followed, but only sees people coming and going in customary gloom.

Rounds of confrontation separated by moments of apathy: how better to sum up the everyday lives of Egyptians?

Suddenly he freezes.

He had already caught a glimpse of it among the displayed shoes in a shop he just passed, but now the image of the gallows is crystal clear, floating over there among women's Islamic dresses. The nightmare that has surrounded him throughout the Eid holiday is now following him in the streets, peering at him from the shop windows.

He had spent the holidays gargling like a just-slaughtered sheep. The hangman's noose felt tighter around his own neck than it probably felt to the defeated dictator. The holiday elapsed at a snail's pace, like a nightmare. But, like all crises, it passed. So today, the Cerebellum has hit the streets, eager to accomplish his desperate scheme. The plan of his final escape is to sever whatever remaining links bind him to the official world, to drop under the American radar forever.

Motionless on the sidewalk, peering at Islamic costumes in a shop window, he refuses to curse his bad luck. Years ago, he came to accept that the moment he agreed to link his fate to that of a butcher called Saddam Hussein, he had staked his future in a game of Russian roulette. But his anger today is directed inward. Why has he allowed hope to trickle into his soul? How could he have passively watched as a sense of stability built up incrementally over the past few months? Who had given someone like him the right to fall in love, to become emotionally involved with the likes of candygirl?

When will he stop being so naive?

He fooled himself when he thought his life could ever regain the normality he had yearned for. Rats like him hide in their holes out of fear, not to cozily enjoy their stability.

Will he never learn?

He toys with the ivory dice he carries in his trouser pocket. Chance controls everything. The law of probability governs the universe. One throw of the dice took Saddam from the palace to the grave. The Cerebellum acknowledges that he never felt the slightest compassion for the Iraqi despot. He was not even sorry to see him hang from the gallows. The man deserved no better fate. But this is not about Saddam the person. When mountains collapse the world loses its constants. He pictures scenes from movies about prehistoric times: angry volcanoes blow up the mountains, earthquakes shake the plains, the earth opens up to swallow mighty dinosaurs as they stampede in panic. A mass extinction, as the scientists like to describe it. Could this be what the Arabs are facing today . . . the onset of a mass extinction?

The aroma of frying falafel hits him. If he were a normal person, he would get himself a couple of sandwiches, one fuul and one falafel, with maybe some pickles and eggplant stuffed with garlic paste on the side. But he is a scientist on the run, one of the pillars of the defunct

Iraqi nuclear program. He possesses forbidden knowledge, the kind that condemns its owner to sexual violation at Abu Ghraib, or silent assassination anywhere else in the world. But now he must control his runaway imagination and leave the vicinity of the bank as quickly as possible. The bank, after all, is his last point of contact with official Egypt, his last station along the road of government documents and international information networks, the last location he can be traced to. As quickly as he can, he must plunge into the Cairo underworld and merge with the masses before some Mossad agent can catch up with him.

The Cerebellum starts to hurry away, but once again he freezes. The same man who had pushed him at the bank's entrance is now blocking his way. He is an elderly man with a radiant face, smiling now, beautiful in a way that is difficult to define. A crimson tarboosh decorates his head, brand new as if just out of the factory.

"Ah, my good man . . . you were just on my mind." The man speaks through a toothless mouth.

Surprise ties the Cerebellum's tongue. Why does the man address him like an old friend, though he's quite sure he's never set eyes on his face before? And why did he make no allusion to the fact that they had just met in front of the bank, and that he had pushed him with neither excuse nor apology? And, most importantly, why is he following him? What is really perplexing him is that the old man's reflection did not appear in the shop window. He is quite sure of that, because he carefully studied the mirror image of the street behind him to see if he was being shadowed.

Fear starts to seep into the Cerebellum's heart. He does not respond to the man's comments, but tightens his grip around his valise. After all, it holds all that is left of his life savings.

"You remember the ten dinars you loaned me on the seventh of March, 1955?" The man speaks in a quiet voice, low-pitched but crystal clear.

"At exactly 10:20 p.m.," the old man goes on, when the Cerebellum—out of sheer amazement—does not respond. Then he produces a worn leather purse from his pocket and counts out ten shimmering gold coins. One by one, he drops them into the Cerebellum's breast pocket.

"There you go . . . now we're even, my friend."

The man is wearing an elegant brown suit, a silk shirt, and a striped tie. His shoes are brown and white in the fashion of an old Abdel Wahhab movie. The Cerebellum is certain that he has never loaned this man money. He has never even met him until today. But what blows his mind is that the date the man mentioned is the very day he was born. In fact, his mother— God rest her soul—told him he was born at night, a little after ten.

"Stay in touch." The old man turns around and, with surprising agility, speeds away.

The Cerebellum has no idea how much ten gold guineas—or dinars, as the man called them—are worth. But he has no doubt they would fetch a fortune. The old man must have made a mistake. Well, at least he is not a pickpocket or a gang boss. He certainly presents no threat. Despite the Cerebellum's dire financial straits, he has no doubt that he must give the man back his coins. He follows, shouting:

"Hajji . . . one moment, please."

Rather than stopping, the man doubles his pace. Maybe he's hard of hearing and can't hear the Cerebellum's call. But where did he get this amazing stamina?

The Cerebellum is surprised by the enormous effort he is forced to make in order to catch up with the man. He pauses for a split second at the Metro exit. He has the opportunity to disappear into the bowels of the earth, this very instant, to shake off any possible surveillance. It is definitely in his best interest to go down the dusty stairs. His personal security dictates it. He'd be wise to put this madman behind him and hold on to the coins. Who knows, they may turn out to be worth something after all.

But he simply cannot get himself to do it. All his life, he has never acted dishonorably and he is not about to give up his principles. He is determined to return the dinars to their rightful owner, come what may. Yes, come what may. Before resuming his trot behind the man, like a schoolboy, he takes a last glance at the Metro exit.

Abruptly, the old man changes direction and turns left into a side street. The Cerebellum follows, but when he reaches the corner, there is no trace of the man . . . he is gone, like a pinch of salt disappearing in soup.

The Cerebellum looks around. Then he decides to search behind a closed cigarette kiosk. From behind the kiosk, he thinks he has caught a glimpse of the man walking into a nearby building. He heads toward it and penetrates the darkness of the foyer. After the bright sunlight in the street, the building's darkness makes him squint. He waits for his eyes to get accustomed to the dark. The sudden transformation has confounded all his senses.

In the foyer's dark, humid atmosphere, he is gripped—for the first time ever—by a sense of total disorientation, as though a thick mist has enveloped his inner compass. He is no longer sure where he is coming from or where he's heading. His life's journey seems pointless, controlled by rules and laws he is not—despite his broad knowledge—getting any closer to deciphering.

Is it possible that he has allowed himself to stumble into a tight trap, one from which there can be no escape? He should have disappeared inside that Metro exit when he had the chance, dug deep into the bowels of the earth in the company of millions of others. He should have simply dissolved in the human mass that is the Egyptian people, and enjoyed the sense of security that comes from belonging to a flock. That was his chance to distance himself from danger, once and for all. But in a split second, he made his crucial decision. He chose to follow the tracks of the mysterious old man, to give him back what was rightfully his. And now, he must face the consequences. . . .

In any case, what is the use of running away?

He almost bumps into someone rushing in the opposite direction. At least he can see clearly now. It is a girl. At the last moment, she manages to steer clear of him. Before he can fully grasp the situation, she is in the street, in her blind rush to some unknown destination. Her hair is a curtain of black velvet floating behind her. But what surprises him most is that the girl's features seem so familiar.

Can it be her?

The mere thought that it might be her in the flesh produces shivers all over his body.

"Didi. Wait!" He forgets all else and rushes after her.

The girl is gorgeous. Her beauty causes an earthquake in the street, an explosion that sucks all the oxygen from the air. Her magnetism leaves pedestrians—men and women alike—gasping for breath. The Cerebellum finds himself trotting after her. What if candygirl were to come face to face with this bombshell? Would she feel jealous? He does not think so. His lover knows only too well that there is no place for someone else in his heart, that his feelings toward Didi will never go beyond compassion. It may even be that his affection toward her stems from a dormant paternal instinct, a virtual fatherhood that can never see the light of day, like a blind man's longing for color, or a cripple's sensation of the ground beneath his recently amputated foot.

He calls out Didi's name as loudly as he can. She does not respond. Like her, he darts into the middle of the road, pushing out of the way a fat man carrying a paper bag. Oranges roll onto the asphalt. No time for apologies. By a miracle, the Cerebellum dodges a speeding taxi. The girl's red sweater is an easy target to follow. And this worn-out bull suddenly finds himself at the heart of a Spanish corrida.

He tightens his grip on his valise and runs as fast as he can. But Didi is in her prime, and he is over fifty. By the time the girl reaches al-Misaha Square, he finally realizes he is not going to catch up with her. Just then, something unexpected happens: two men pounce on her. One of them—a well-built type—grabs her from behind, raising her in the air. The girl tries, unsuccessfully, to kick and hit back.

What is happening? There must be some mistake.

He thinks that the two men have stopped the girl out of a sense of civic responsibility. They probably assumed she was a pickpocket on the run, and that he was pursuing her to reclaim a snatched watch or wallet. By the time he reaches the two men and the girl, he is feeling sick and gasping for breath. He starts to urge them to let her go, but is interrupted by screeching brakes.

An SUV comes to a standstill a few meters away.

The Cerebellum's unexpected appearance has taken the two men by surprise. He observes a cloud of uncertainty float inside their eyes for a split second. But they are quick to realize that he is a weak man, a regular guy protected by neither armed gang nor effective security force. The smaller man grasps him by the arm. His grip is like steel. Then he speaks calmly: "Are you two together?"

The Cerebellum nods without hesitation. He is still struggling to catch his breath.

"Then come with us."

The Cerebellum notices that the other man is pulling Didi into the car. When she steps up her resistance, he lifts her completely off the ground. The girl cries out in distress. A small crowd starts to gather, but no one intervenes. The Cerebellum tries to pull free of the man's grip, but the guy is stronger. He shoves him, without difficulty, into the waiting Pajero.

The car speeds away.

Didi starts to shout hysterically. Frantically, she pulls at the door handle, but it will not open. The Cerebellum's mind is unable to grasp what is going on. He is not even able to get emotionally involved. His inner computer has shut down. He finds himself following the chain of events from a spectator's seat.

The hulk who carried Didi in is sitting between them in the back seat. His head almost touches the roof. The other guy, with the dark wraparound sunglasses, has jumped into the front seat, next to the driver.

The brute next to Didi produces a knife and passes its blunt side over the girl's cheek.

"Why don't we quiet down? No one would want to see this beautiful face disfigured," he says calmly.

Didi freezes.

"Someone wrote down our license number." The driver speaks from the corner of his mouth because of a cigarette glued to his lower lip.

"Switch the plates at the next lights," the man in the front seat replies with the confidence of a doctor handing out a prescription. Then he turns to the Cerebellum.

"Is this the dough?" He points to the Cerebellum's portfolio.

The Cerebellum ignores the question. He tightens his grip on the portfolio, although he has no idea what this is all about. The man next to him thrusts his elbow into his side and snatches the portfolio.

"What's this, Mister . . . fifteen three? We've got a smartass here."

"That is all there was left in my account." The Cerebellum no longer knows if this is dream or reality. His side hurts like hell. He is worried his kidney may have suffered some massive injury.

"Do you realize how much this princess would fetch if we sold her to one of those networks?" the thug says. "She can easily survive five years of delicious labor . . . and believe me, she'd make some guy a mighty happy owner."

His insolence is nauseating.

The driver's cigarette smoke has conquered the car. It adds a visual cloud to the fog that envelops the Cerebellum's mind, intensifying his agony as he struggles to catch his breath. Despite his stupor, he realizes that things are getting more complicated. He needs to understand what is going on. He needs time to think. He must figure out how to make use of his vast knowledge—his so-called genius—to get himself out of this jam. Where do Napier's logarithms or Mersenne's fifth number fit in this equation? And the Platonic solids, the magic squares, and the puzzle of the Tower of Hanoi, what good are any of them at a time like this?

The asthma hits him hard. He felt it coming. It always strikes in fits. Whenever he ignores the warning signs, he has only himself to blame. He can no longer breathe. With shaking fingers, he feels in his pocket for the inhaler. He pumps a double dose into his throat. But his mind is working overtime. It clicks like a Geiger counter closing in on radioactive material. All of his thoughts orbit around this mess he has landed himself in. How can he help innocent Didi? How can he save his own skin?

"Why don't we all . . . calm down?" he gasps. "And would someone . . . be kind enough . . . to tell me . . . what's going on." He stutters, gulping for that damn impossible air.

Charlotte, North Carolina
Monday, January 8, 2007
0755 EST

"Good morning, Alpha." Martin takes off his tweed blazer and hangs it on the coat rack in the corner, next to his coworker's worn-out size XXL bomber jacket. He's early today. His shift won't officially start for over an hour, but anticipation has chased away his sleep.

"Morning, Gamma . . . you chose a good day to come in early. You're in for a pretty exciting day." Alpha seems to be in an uncharacteristically good mood.

Martin felt off balance the instant he entered the room. But he's gotten used to that. He's learned to live with this feeling ever since he started working here, over three years ago. He's not quite sure if it's related to his metamorphosis from Martin into Agent Gamma upon crossing the center's doorstep, or a result of the electromagnetic radiation emitted by all this equipment. Or it may simply be that the oscillating artificial lighting is playing havoc with his vision.

The transition from the certainty of daylight to this room's tentative luminosity is inevitably depressing. The center is windowless. It is lit by four neon lights in the ceiling, in addition, of course, to the glow of the three giant screens that occupy an entire wall, and the five tabletop plasmas. Within the center, there is no way of distinguishing night from day. Maybe that's why Alpha calls this place the Ghost Center.

"Any news?" Martin asks, trying to contain his excitement. A gut feeling tells him something big is about to happen.

The inner section of the apartment is made up of this operations center, a toilet, and a kitchenette. The outer section is a full-fledged residential apartment. The bedroom closets are crammed. The washer contains soiled shirts and underwear. The fridge is packed. The dishwasher is pregnant with dirty dishes. The TV is timed to turn on at intervals. This apartment is part of a comprehensive undercover plan, which includes false names for its inhabitants, fabricated life stories, and correspondence addressed to them from time to time. The neighbors never suspect anything out of the ordinary is going on.

The real technological marvel, however, is the magic passage that separates the two sections. It reminds Martin of *Goldfinger*, *Dr. No*, and the other James Bond movies that fueled his childhood fantasies. The secret entrance is located in the outer apartment's bathroom, next to the washbasin. After a sensor recognizes the person through an electronic chip embedded under his skin, the entire wall slides sideways, exposing the passageway. Nowadays, access is limited to Agent Alpha and Martin—Agent Gamma, as he is known here. Until about a month ago, they had a third coworker. But his coordinates have been deleted from the central computer's database, and now the COBRA Center is made up of just the two of them.

"Actually, there's good news and there's bad news . . . would you rather I start with the good?" the fat man replies, after a provoking silence.

Martin nods. He knows Alpha will do whatever he wants to in the end. After all, he's the boss. Besides, communication between the COBRA Center and the mother agency is almost nonexistent, so he always has the final say.

"The good news is: Mickey Mouse has surfaced at last. As we expected, he went to the bank to withdraw some cash."

"And the bad news?" Martin has never seen Alpha worried by any kind of news. When he enters this place, he simply leaves all human emotions behind. Maybe he parks them on the pavement, together with his Harley.

"Mickey Mouse withdrew everything, which means he's not going to visit the bank again. Obviously, he's trying to disappear in the Cairo crowds." Alpha palpates his enormous belly with both hands as he speaks, as though he's measuring a change in its size. "This is our last chance."

Martin is quite aware of the difficulty of tracking down their subject. He's single and has no known relatives. They've never located a lover or even a friend, and he doesn't belong to a political party or group of any kind. He doesn't even have personal vices that could give him away, like gambling or drugs or women. With his tiny body and commonplace face, he can easily melt into a Third World crowd.

Alpha points at the central screen, which shows a bank entrance in a Middle Eastern city. A policeman dressed in black stands next to a doorframe metal detector. He looks on apathetically as the customers walk in without even emptying their pockets. The red lights on the top of the frame keep on flickering, but no one seems to care. A stream of pedestrians flows on the sidewalk in front of the bank. The picture is taken from a good angle, exposing all from above. Martin knows that the camera is fixed to a rifle with a silencer that one of their agents is aiming at the bank. He assumes that the agent is looking down from a window across the street.

"We're not going to fail this time . . . especially since our guys have already taken up their positions." Martin has endless faith in their agents, supported as they are by the command and control capabilities at their disposal. When they built the Ghost Center, they gave its operators the option to make use of all the intelligence agencies' capabilities, without even needing to expose their presence to these agencies. Martin has access to all the networks to obtain whatever information he needs. He can use satellites for surveillance and to send coded instructions to COBRA's agents on the ground. In short, they can run their operations from this modest apartment with the capabilities of a giant intelligence agency.

"It's not that simple," Alpha says. "Cairo's overcrowded conditions could confound the best-planned operations." He picks up a handful of popcorn from a large bowl in his lap and mechanically deposits it in his mouth. On the counter in front of him is a giant plastic Coca-Cola cup. It occurs to Martin that he's never seen the fat man without some kind of fast food in his vicinity, which he munches with the impulsiveness of a cartoon character who breathes fast food instead of air.

After years of painstaking effort, their eureka moment happened three months ago, when they managed to track down Mickey Mouse's bank account. After that, it was not difficult to follow the money trail. By studying the account's activity over the past few years, they managed to chart a precise pattern for the subject's banking habits. In fact, it wasn't all that complicated, as the man had deposited all the savings he'd gathered from years of work in Iraq in the form of CDs in this particular branch of the Arab Bank. His banking activities during this period—ever since he escaped from Iraq in July 1999—were limited to a visit every six or seven months to withdraw a fixed sum of five thousand Egyptian pounds.

Martin sinks into a comfortable computer chair next to Alpha, who's crammed into an identical one. Although he hates to admit it, the fat man got it right when he dedicated a surveillance team to watch the bank during working hours. Martin had questioned whether the subject would continue this pattern of behavior until his account was completely cleaned out. He reasoned that a scientist with such a high IQ would find a way to make money and set aside the remaining balance for emergencies. He had not, however, objected to keeping an eye the bank, just in case. That's why he had come in this morning bubbling with excitement. But now—after Alpha's predictions have, again, been proven right—he's overcome with animosity toward this Mr. Know-It-All.

Although his shift doesn't officially end till nine, Alpha is free to go anytime, since Martin is already here. But he seems to be in no hurry to leave.

The right-hand screen shows a black-and-white photograph of the subject. The picture was taken from one side, almost in profile. Obviously, it was shot from a distance, while the subject was in motion. He cannot make out whether the background shows Egypt or Iraq. This distorted photo has been watching over the Ghost Center ever since he joined. Was it meant to better acquaint the members of COBRA with their eccentric target? Or simply to motivate them to track him down, like hounds once they've become familiar with their prey's scent?

Martin observes the subject's innocent, childlike face. His glasses are too big, yet behind them the one eye that is visible in the picture is alert, radiating intelligence. His ear is too big and protruding, justifying the nickname Mickey Mouse, except that his buck teeth are more like those of a rabbit. Maybe they should have called him Bugs Bunny.

Mickey Mouse suddenly appears in the bank's entrance, as if obeying a telepathic order from Alpha's eyes, which have been focused on the middle screen. The subject freezes an instant as he studies the street. Martin can visualize their agent's finger creeping to the trigger. Ten more seconds and it'll all be over.

Martin's pulse sends tremors across his seat. A momentary silence imposes itself upon the Ghost Center, but is soon broken by Alpha crunching a new mouthful of popcorn. The subject suddenly jolts forward. Has he been hit? Not possible; he would have fallen back. Then Martin realizes what has happened. An old man, standing just behind the subject, pushed him at the right moment. Had the agent pulled the trigger, he would have killed the old man instead. He's wearing a red Turkish hat, beneath which his features are fuzzy. Martin wasn't aware that such hats were still in use. The subject turns to face the old guy, but no words are exchanged. Before the agent can get the job done, Mickey Mouse lunges to the right and his small body disappears from the screen.

The left-hand screen shows people coming and going on the sidewalk. This camera, Martin guesses, is built into the eyeglasses of another agent posted next to the bank's entrance. It produces a posterior shot of Mickey Mouse. The agent is now following him. With a quick click of his mouse, Alpha moves this picture to the middle screen. It is replaced on the left-hand screen by a random flow of cars. This is an attempt by a third agent to catch the subject from the other side of the street. His fat coworker clicks again and replaces this picture with one taken from a higher angle. Their man in the window has managed to track the subject through his sniper scope.

The target is in a hurry. He easily squeezes his small body through the crowd. The pictures on the left and middle screens start shaking. Alpha keeps munching popcorn. His gluttony increases by the day. He takes a long gulp of Coke, then double-clicks. For the first time since Martin has been here, the target's photograph disappears from the right-hand screen. It is replaced by a map of Dokki, the Giza neighborhood where all this is happening.

Alpha holds the mike and speaks in his calm, indifferent voice:

"COBRA 3 . . . redeploy to the corner of al-Tahrir Street and Dokki intersection."

"Roger," the loudspeaker replies.

Unit 3 appears as two adjacent green lights. Immediately, they start to move on the map. This unit must be made up of two agents in a car. Their agents appear as green lights on the map because—like Martin— they have chips implanted under their skins, enabling satellites to chart their coordinates anywhere on Earth. Martin taps his keyboard without waiting for Alpha's instructions. It is time to direct the satellite's powerful lens to track their subject. It's easier said than done, but he's well trained. The challenge of tracking an individual via satellite stems from the fact that the angle of vision is perfectly vertical, showing only the tops of people's heads and shoulders. This makes it difficult to distinguish particular individuals. Luckily, they have ground-based surveillance today, which makes the job much easier.

Martin follows the satellite picture on his laptop. He fixes the cursor on the Metro exit and waits till Mickey Mouse passes next to it. The satellite's picture is in black and white, which distinguishes it from the colored images of ground-based cameras. Martin follows the subject on the wall-mounted screens. At the right moment, he focuses on the laptop. In a matter of seconds, the satellite's lens shows Mickey Mouse's head with its small bald spot. He fixes the indicator on the subject and left-clicks the mouse. Then he leans back and takes a deep breath. From now on, the satellite will automatically track the subject, who appears on the map as a red light, surrounded on all sides by their agents' green dots.

The subject stops suddenly in front of a shop window. What does the fool think he's doing . . . window shopping? When all's said and done, people's awareness is so flawed, no matter how knowledgeable they may be. Ultimately, everyone makes mistakes. This is the golden rule of intelligence agencies. An officer's job is all about careful observation and patience. Mickey Mouse—like all rodents—will ultimately fall into the trap.

The sniper's scope shows the target well within range. But once again, pedestrians get in the way. Martin curses the Third World and its crowds. The agent will have to wait for a clean shot. The crunching of popcorn fills up the universe. What a lucky break: the subject is still glued to the shop window. Funnily enough, this shop only sells women's clothing. He obviously doesn't suspect he's under surveillance. This shows how professional and well-trained their agents are.

For a split second, the crowd clears. The subject is now smack in the center of the sniper's crosshairs. Martin flexes his finger as though he's pulling the trigger himself. The end is near. Alpha sucks noisily at his Coke through the straw. His years of work are about to pay off. But suddenly, the old man with the Turkish hat blocks the screen. He's saved the subject for the second time today. Who is this clown? Could he too be following Mickey Mouse, possibly to claim a debt or ask for some favor?

The central screen, taken from the vantage point of the agent on foot, shows the old man drop a few coins into Mickey Mouse's breast pocket. Then the old man turns around and walks away. For a second, the left-hand screen affords an unobstructed view of the subject. But he quickly moves out of the screen. The camera in the eyeglasses of the agent on foot shows the subject rushing after the old man, waving for him to stop. Alpha shakes violently in his chair. His head is bald and pink, like a basketball. What's left of his long red hair, on the sides and back of his head, is tied up in a ponytail, dangling over his collar. He has a thick red bush of a beard, like a Muslim terrorist. A flake of popcorn, caught in the man's beard, catches Martin's attention. The pictures on both screens shake intensely, and it's impossible to distinguish the subject. But Martin can still trace him on his laptop, courtesy of the satellite camera.

"The subject has moved out of the sniper's range," Alpha says as he strokes his beard. He discovers the corn crumb and mechanically deposits it in his mouth. Then he speaks into the mike:

"COBRA 2 . . . prepare to redeploy."

The sniper's picture shuts down. He will now join his mobile unit. With a click of the mouse, Alpha replaces his picture with that of the satellite on the left-hand screen. The subject suddenly veers left into a side street and hides behind a cigarette kiosk. He must have realized he's being followed. At least he doesn't suspect he's being tracked via satellite.

"All units . . . the subject is behind a cigarette kiosk in the side street . . . do not approach. I repeat: do not approach. Give him some breathing space," Alpha whispers into his mike.

"Roger."

Martin starts to wonder where the expression 'Roger' comes from, but he's quickly distracted by Mickey Mouse's suspicious maneuvers. The subject walks away from the kiosk and quickly enters one of the buildings, moving out of range of the satellite's vision. Could he have figured out he's also under surveillance from space?

"COBRA 2 . . . redeploy immediately to al-Misaha Square," the fat man barks.

Before Martin can figure out Mickey Mouse's plan, he's already back in the street. The satellite shows him pushing people aside and jogging alongside the cars. He must have uncovered the entire operation. But how?

The central screen's picture vibrates violently. The agent on foot is in hot pursuit. There's no sense in hiding any more. The game is being played out in the open.

"COBRA 3 . . . redeploy to Galaa Square." The fat man talks mechanically.

"COBRA 1 . . . redeploy to Orman Gardens." This unit is made up of one person on a motorbike.

Rather than tighten the noose around the subject, Alpha is redeploying his units in a wider circle to ensure that Mickey Mouse will remain under surveillance even if he manages to break free.

The image on the central screen is still shaking. But at least the subject has reappeared inside it. The agent is gaining on him. He's almost got him. Martin knows that the agent will stick the tip of his umbrella—fitted with a syringe that injects a deadly toxin—into the subject's body. Then the agent will immediately disengage. Death will occur by heart attack within fifteen minutes. No one will ever suspect anything other than natural causes. This is, by far, their preferred method, much more useful than the sniper's bullet, to which they only resorted out of fear that they might lose the target for good.

Suddenly, the picture shakes even more violently and the asphalt swallows the screen. Then it goes completely dark.

"The agent has tripped. He's fallen to the ground," Alpha says in amazement.

The picture reappears, showing people's legs approaching. The agent must have pulled himself up and is now sitting on the pavement. Pedestrians have gathered to help. The screen shakes again as the agent stands up. Martin checks the subject's position on the left-hand screen. He has almost reached al-Misaha Square.

"Everything is under control . . . no need to worry," the agent says, panting, through the loudspeaker.

"The old man with the tarboosh pushed me. I'm certain he did it on purpose," he adds in a whisper, then resumes his pursuit of Mickey Mouse.

On the right-hand screen, the green lights are racing in every direction. The left-hand screen shows the subject talking to two men and a woman. A Land Rover or Pajero comes to a stop next to them. They all climb inside. This has the makings of a well-drawn plan. The escaping vehicle appears on the left-hand screen. Martin was right: it is a Pajero.

"The subject has obviously got himself some professional help." The words stumble from the corners of Alpha's thick lips. He digs his hand into the popcorn bowl, but finds it empty.

"Whatever the outcome, it's always fun to watch a car chase in the streets of Cairo. Unfortunately, the overcrowded conditions may not necessarily play in our favor." Alpha takes his last gulp of Coke and stands to leave.

At last, Martin finds himself in charge of the operation, as it enters its most critical phase.

chapter 2

Giza, Egypt
Monday, January 8, 2007
Soon after the afternoon call to prayer

"To cut a long story short . . . the pretty miss here is into acting," the man with the spaceman sunglasses says after a long silence. Then he turns to face the Cerebellum in the seat behind him.

This comes as no great revelation. As far as he knows, she has actually played a minor role in some sitcom. Didi, after all, is the sister of the late Ahlam Shawarby, the movie star who got herself murdered a few years back. The man's statement, however, does little to explain what is happening right now. Yet the Cerebellum is somehow pleased with himself; at least he has succeeded in starting a conversation with the man. Despite his smaller size compared to the gorilla sitting between Didi and the Cerebellum, he is the older of the two and displays an air of authority.

"So you do this with every amateur actress in the country?"

"We're a respectable business, Mister. A collection agency. Our mission is of national significance." The man adopts a businessman's tone. As though kidnapping has become a respectable line of work these days. Maybe that's really the case, who knows? Perhaps the problem has more to do with the Cerebellum himself, who lost touch with Egyptian reality years ago.

"You could have fooled me." The words spill out of the Cerebellum's mouth unintentionally.

"Let's say someone owes you some real money . . . would you stand a chance of getting it back, if you had to go through the courts or the police?" the man asks calmly.

"No . . . I might as well kiss my money goodbye," the Cerebellum replies after some thought.

"So how do you expect the country to function then? Don't they say that the private sector is the locomotive for development? Well, Mister . . . *we* are the private sector."

"So the problem is that Didi owes you money?" At last things are getting clearer.

"I swear to God, I never borrowed a penny from anyone," the girl intervenes.

"But you guaranteed the producer," the bully in the middle thunders like a jet engine.

"I signed some papers. He tricked me, that's all." The girl's beauty warrants her forgiveness for any sin she may have committed.

"That doesn't concern us. Our job is just to collect. Once you've paid up and our contract with our customer has been fulfilled, you can always hire us to get your money back," the boss explains calmly. His sunglasses remind the Cerebellum of U.S. Marines in Iraq.

"We're being tailed, Doctor," the driver says abruptly.

"Are you sure?"

"A professional surveillance operation . . . so far I've spotted two cars and a motorbike . . . the one gives way to the other." Wisps of smoke escape from the driver's mouth and nostrils as he speaks.

"Plainclothes cops?" the Doctor asks.

"No. Intelligence, at the very least."

The Doctor turns to the Cerebellum with an intense look. "Who exactly have you been talking to?"

"Did I get a chance to talk to anyone?"

"But you two weren't walking together . . . you were following her. Who the hell are you, anyway?" The man takes off his sunglasses and stares at him. His eyes are fiery slits. The Cerebellum does not doubt for a second that, despite his calm appearance, this guy would gouge out his eyeballs without a second thought. Yet, although quite aware of the precariousness of their situation, he is unable to focus. The absurdity of it all anesthetizes him. He throws a quick glance at Didi. She is stiff as a statue.

"To be precise, I am on the run . . . important people are after me." The Cerebellum decides that telling the truth is his best option.

"And what's your business with the pretty miss here?"

"We had not met in years. I mean, we just met today, by chance . . . but she is an angel. It is her beauty that is always getting her into trouble."

"They must be pretty important people." The man stares at the Cerebellum as if trying to glean information about the pursuers from his face.

"Believe me, you do not want to know who they are."

"Fine . . . but now you've got us involved in your problems." The man conceals his eyes again behind the sunglasses.

"Why don't we just throw him out of the car?" the driver says calmly. He has not sped up since he announced they were being followed. The Cerebellum had expected a Hollywood-style car chase.

The Doctor produces a cell phone from his pocket.

"Yes, sir. Sorry to disturb you. But we seem to be facing some complications . . . a kind of tail," he whispers into the phone. "That wouldn't work, sir. They seem to be professionals . . . okay."

He puts the phone back in his pocket, then turns to the driver.

"Maneuver number five."

The driver nods and draws strongly on his burnt-up cigarette, which he treats like an extension of his thin lips. He says nothing.

"We can't just throw him out. His friends wouldn't leave us alone. They'd want to know what business we have with him," the Doctor says.

Finally, the driver throws his cigarette stub out of the window, and immediately pulls another from a packet in his pocket. He places the cigarette between his lips but refrains from lighting up.

The Doctor turns to the Cerebellum, "Your debt has just doubled, Mister."

The Pajero cruises past Cairo University. The area is not nearly as crowded, or as noisy, as he would have expected. Classes obviously haven't resumed yet after the holiday. Instinctively, the Cerebellum's gaze turns to the left, toward the Faculty of Engineering. For a moment he recaptures that delicious mixture of anticipation and awe that overcame him when his youthful figure first entered its historic gates. It seemed as though the horizons were opening up, as though he had just dived into a sea of limitless knowledge. That day, he may well have summoned up the excitement of Hero of Alexandria some two millennia before him, when he set out to calculate the value of $\sqrt{81-144}$, and thus opened up the floodgates to the discipline of mathematics.

A cluster of modern structures cram the faculty grounds, defying the classical dignity of its original buildings, upsetting their harmony. It crosses his mind that he has not set foot in this place in over twenty years—this cauldron in whose stew he was formed, this boxing ring that has witnessed round after round of the crucial contests of his life. He is overcome by an unexpected sense of relief when the faculty buildings finally slip out of his field of vision.

The car shudders over the uneven asphalt. The road has settled, leaving the manholes sticking up, in mockery of all the knowledge that has impregnated the faculty's lecture halls for almost a century. The professors of the past, having taught generations of engineers, must surely be turning in their graves, fuming, he imagines, at what has happened to this country. The Pajero's momentum has succeeded in putting the faculty out of sight, but its ghosts still pursue him. The specters of victory and defeat; his academic exploits that made the nickname 'Cerebellum' stick, and the fudged relationships with the opposite sex—or lack thereof, to be precise—which, in turn, confirmed that label, to the extent that it has come to sum him up in the world's eyes and, sometimes, in his own.

He suddenly recalls the Doctor's last sentence. The sum he owes has doubled. But when did he owe these ruthless people anything? Through his simple statement, the man transferred responsibility from Didi to him. He even doubled it. The Doctor added a debt that was never borrowed to start with, just like that. The truth has been disfigured, reason thrown out of the window . . . in this country only brute force remains. The strong impose their every whim. As for everyone else—the silent majority—the best they can hope for is to be permitted to groan with pain.

As the car approaches Giza Square, the Cerebellum notices that the traffic is getting denser. Yet the driver suddenly hits the gas and embarks on a series of maneuvers to pass the vehicles ahead of him. The man has not lit his cigarette yet. He is content to let it dangle from his mouth, as though glued to his lower lip. But the smoke from his last one still fills the car. The Cerebellum holds tightly to the front seat to avoid leaning on the brute next to him. He notices that Didi is clinging to the handle on top of the door next to her. No one says a word. The Cerebellum is surprised by his own composure. He feels like a neutral observer, as though all this were of no concern to him, as though his very life were not under threat, whether or not the pursuers succeed in catching up with them. Matters are beyond his control and he can only wait and see what fate will throw in his way. The American car chase he had expected is finally underway.

The Pajero cuts across the square, makes a U-turn beneath the flyover, then intersects the incoming flow from Manial. It is besieged by angry horns. The car plunges into one of the crowded alleys on the opposite side of the square. A smell of sweat attacks the Cerebellum's senses. Its source, he suspects, is the gorilla next to him, but he dares not look in his direction. Once inside the alley, the driver is forced to slow down in order to tackle cyclists, pedestrians, and parked cars.

"How's it going?" the Doctor asks.

"There's one bike still on our tail," the driver says. He produces a cheap lighter from the glove compartment and lights up.

The Cerebellum wonders why the man did not use the car's built-in lighter. Unable to resist his natural curiosity, he leans toward the gangster next to him to get a better look at the dashboard. There is an empty socket, but no lighter, not even a matchstick. So even gangsters' cars do not escape pilfering, the petty theft that everyone on Egyptian soil must put up with. It occurs to him that Egypt has been consistently plundered since the time of the pharaohs, not by means of Chicago-style bank robbery, but through pilfering.

"Don't look behind. And that applies to everyone," the Doctor warns.

The terms 'amicable numbers' and 'sociable numbers' come to the Cerebellum's mind, though he can't recall their precise mathematical significance. The ivory dice inside his pocket press against his thigh. He has no idea what fate has in store for him this time, but he could sure use some amicable numbers today.

For what feels like an eternity, the Pajero zigzags from alley to alley. The houses are discolored and downtrodden, yet air conditioners protrude from their walls and satellite dishes gaze upward from the rooftops. Every now and then, the driver exchanges greetings with shop owners relaxing on chairs on the narrow sidewalks. The Cerebellum can no longer tell in which direction they are headed. His thoughts meander with the car's vibrations. How he misses candygirl's posts, short and sweet, like drops of honey. How he longs for her smile, more enigmatic than the Mona Lisa's.

This is the first time he has ventured outside his hideout in six months, a period that advanced at a snail's pace. But in this commotion, it seems to him as though all the action meant for that half year has been stored away in some mysterious fold of the universe, left to accumulate beyond the boundaries of his consciousness, only to be released into existence on this particular day, in a breathtaking sequence, like a movie played on fast forward. What a coincidence to have met Didi after seven long years, at the exact time when she needed him most. As for the old man who led him to her, the Cerebellum isn't quite sure whether to count him as human or jinn.

But all that is of no import . . . what *is* important is that he now has irrefutable evidence that his suspicions were justified, all these years. There are real enemies after him, determined to eliminate him. What's more, they have allocated enormous resources for this task. Now he knows for sure that his pursuers are not illusory. Whoever they are, they are certainly not manifestations of paranoia nourished by the solitude and fear he's been going through. And what is even more important is that, evidently, the pursuers will neither tire nor lose interest. Like hounds from hell, they are still on his track, more than seven years after his escape from Iraq.

He remembers the gold dinars, feels them weigh heavily in his breast pocket, like Aladdin's treasure sitting precisely over his heart. Will he use them to ransom the beautiful Didi today, or hold on to them for his own future needs? Now that these criminals have seized virtually all his worldly possessions, how will he be able to repay the debts that have piled up to both the grocer and the landlady, not to mention his meager living expenses for the coming months? Without any money, he will simply be unable to continue to lie low.

Then he reminds himself that the coins never belonged to him in the first place.

It is evident that these fiendish agencies—despite all the resources at their disposal—have, so far, failed to uncover his hideout. The Cerebellum takes a deep breath and relaxes in his seat. His hiding place is still safe and his pocket is stuffed with gold. All he needs, right now, is to disentangle himself from this mess, then to melt into Cairo's crowds.

"Azuz is ready and waiting." The Doctor's words pull the Cerebellum away from his thoughts. This can only mean that they are on the verge of a decisive step. He braces himself for "maneuver number five."

He examines the faces on the sidewalk, searching for this Azuz who is ready and waiting, but cannot find anyone who looks remotely like he might belong to a sophisticated gang, or for that matter any outfit worthy of the term 'organized crime,' as the Americans would say. Clearly, the tons of Hollywood movies he has been watching have affected his ability to interact with Egyptian reality.

Ignoring his own orders, the Doctor turns around and looks out of the rear window. Spontaneously, the Cerebellum follows suit. After a moment's observation, he bursts into squeals of childish laughter. The simplicity and effectiveness of maneuver number five attests to the genius of whoever planned it. The ingenuity of ordinary Egyptians will often outsmart the latest technology.

Unconcerned for the safety of pedestrians, the driver steps on the gas. Skillfully, he manages to reach the main road without causing casualties or even dropping the cigarette from his mouth.

"What's the verdict . . . all clear?"

"We've come out clean as a whistle," the driver replies, and the Pajero speeds on along the side streets of the Pyramids District.

"The bill has just hit the hundred thousand mark," the Doctor calmly addresses the Cerebellum, as he produces a small notepad from his pocket.

"You've put down fifteen thousand up front . . . which leaves you with eighty-five. When do you plan on paying up, Mister?"

Despite the speeding car's vibrations, the man with the Marines sunglasses holds up a fancy Mont Blanc pen, ready to register the Cerebellum's reply. He gives the impression that whatever gets into his notepad carries more weight than any legalized contract.

The man's question hits the Cerebellum like a ton of bricks. It awakens him from the stupor that had crept in on him, once the immediate danger posed by his pursuers—whether they belonged to the CIA, Mossad, or the blue jinn—had been dispelled. Now, the distinguished mafioso—a.k.a. the Doctor—wakes him up to the fact that his predicament has not actually diminished. In fact, it has multiplied a thousandfold.

Until this morning, he was a free man. He is burdened by neither woman nor child. And, with the exception of candygirl, he has no friends or relatives. The most he stood to lose was his life. A risk that did not amount to much, as, in any case, he was buried alive. Now he has suddenly become responsible for this beautiful girl, who has come, in his mind, to personify innocence and youth. Didi symbolizes everything that is beautiful in Egypt. Her bold smile embodies the country's bright future—if there is any hope left for a bright future, that is.

"Give us a few days . . . that should be enough . . . for Didi and me . . . to make the . . . necessary arrangements. . . . We will be in touch . . . in no time." The Cerebellum has made up his mind that his first priority is to free the girl from the gang's clutches. But his asthma will not go away. The suffocation is setting in.

"That's cute . . . really cute," the Doctor says. "Did you honestly think I'd be holding my baby . . . then go out and look for it?"

The car has reached Faisal Street. It makes a right turn, heading back to Giza. The tone of the Doctor's reply leaves him uncomfortable, though he cannot understand exactly what the man is trying to say. He fumbles in his pockets for the inhaler. Instead, he finds the two dice. He waits for an explanation but the man is not forthcoming. He simply holds his fancy pen just above his devil's notepad.

"We're professionals. We like our arrangements to be clear-cut. So what do you say, Mister?" the Doctor says impatiently, after a long wait. The Cerebellum wonders if the man is really a doctor, or if he even holds a PhD.

"Say something." The bodyguard digs his elbow into the Cerebellum's ribs, which still smart from the last blow.

"All I'm asking . . . twenty-four hours . . . just so Didi and I . . . can get organized . . . we'll let you know . . . if we can pay up sooner. . . ." The Cerebellum makes a great effort just to catch his breath. He tries to be as noncommittal as possible, though he's not quite sure what they expect of him.

"Twenty-four hours . . . all right. As for the cutie, she stays with us. We'll take good care of her till this small matter is settled."

"We'll take *really* good care of the princess," the gorilla sitting next to him says with a broad grin. The smell of his sweat has become unbearable.

At last, the Cerebellum locates the inhaler. He sends a double dose down his throat.

"But sir—" he starts to object.

"It's a done deal," the Doctor interrupts. "Do you know how to use e-mail?"

Without waiting for a reply, he starts to scribble in his notepad like a doctor writing a prescription.

The Cerebellum reflexively turns to Didi. She does not return his gaze. Her eyes remain fixed on the back of the driver's head. She clings to the ceiling grab-handle as if it were the only thing between her and drowning. A sense of loss has been creeping up on him for the past ten years. Now it has reached the point of desperation. Where have his learning and expertise—his so-called genius—gone? What has become of the Golden Number, the Cunningham chains? What is the use of Archimedes's sand-reckoner anyway? Why hang on to reason in a world gone crazy? The driver's smoke is a merciless fog, enveloping his heart, making his eyes water, suffocating him with slow, sadistic relish. But why does the ferryboat come to mind now? Al-Salam '98. One thousand and thirty-three throats singing their pain as the waters submerge their vessel, as the sharks prepare to rip their guts apart.

The car's vibrations have become unbearable. The driver takes the turn with Hollywood-style tire screeching. The smell of tobacco invades his sinuses, takes his breath away. What can he do to save the innocent Didi now? How would Biceps, his avatar, react in a situation like this? He would paralyze the giant with one decisive blow from his elbow to the neck, just below the ear. Then he would shove the Doctor's head right through the windshield. After that, he would strangle the driver and force the Pajero to come to a standstill in the middle of the road. Biceps would have done all this in the blink of an eye. In less than no time, he would have turned the entire situation in his favor, and innocent Didi would be saved. But Biceps is over there, not here. Besides, he is so radically different from the Cerebellum, who has nothing up his sleeve other than to double the flow from his inhaler and rack his brains for a solution that may not be there to find.

The cigarette in the driver's mouth has turned to ash. It will collapse any moment now. But thus far, it has maintained the original cigarette's form. There must be a message in that. Like the recording of the last few exchanges in the ferryboat's command cabin. A tragic, desperate message. The bodyguard's stench has become simply unbearable. The soul is being withdrawn from the Cerebellum's weak body. Cairo University's solemn buildings reappear on right. To the left is Bayn al-Sarayat District. Nausea finally overcomes him. He can no longer think. He wishes the earth would open up and swallow him. He desires a quick end to his life . . . a lifespan that, in the end, has embodied a nation's journey to ruin.

The Pajero comes to a standstill with a final screech of the brakes. The smell of burnt rubber fills the world. He is paralyzed by his nausea. The Doctor tears out the page from his shady notepad and hands it over to him.

"You can contact us by e-mail," he says in boredom.

The bodyguard leans over him and opens the car door. The Cerebellum tries to think of something to say that could turn the situation around. But nausea has tied his tongue. And the words of ghosts from the ferryboat's black box reverberate around him. The bodyguard pushes him violently and the entire world spins. He finds himself sitting on the sidewalk, watching the Pajero's rear end disappear into the fast-flowing automotive current. A coarse voice whispers in his ear:

"The boat is sinking, Captain."

Charlotte, North Carolina
Monday January 8, 2007
0907 EST

Martin has never been to Egypt. In fact, he's only traveled outside the United States once, on an official mission to the United Kingdom. Cairo, in his mind's eye, is a city out of the *Arabian Nights*: alleyways teeming with people and camels, merchants squatting on the sidewalks selling dates and spices, women in colorful silk saris that envelop their voluptuous curves, checking out the passersby with kohl-lined eyes. He wishes he were there right now, in the heart of Cairo. He'd give almost anything to take part in this breathtaking car chase, whose echoes come to him across the ether, rather than being cooped up in a secret chamber, windowless and soundproof, wearing his eyes out staring at lifeless computer screens.

A mug of coffee in his hand, he rotates his chair to the right, then to the left. Alpha departed soon after the end of his shift, and Martin was left to direct, on his own, an unmanageable chase on another continent. He takes a sip of the dark liquid, unperturbed by its steaming surface. The image on the central screen is hazy, constantly flickering on and off. He can barely make out the details. Still, he can distinguish that the vehicles on the streets are much more numerous than he'd expected, and so far there is not a single camel in sight. Their tracking team is made up of two cars and a motorbike. The black-and-white satellite image allows him to follow what's going on. But the crowdedness has made it impossible for him to manage the car chase. At this stage, it's all up to the judgment of the agents on the ground. He starts a game of FreeCell on the laptop.

As he was leaving home this morning, Amy reminded him that her birthday was the day after tomorrow. She woke up early just so she could see him, and, of course, to make sure he wouldn't forget about her birthday. On Wednesday, his little angel will turn five. The years have passed like hours. No, minutes. He remembers the day Amy was born as if it were yesterday. Susan was crying out in pain. He stood by her bed, puffing Lamaze-style. But rather than organize her breathing—as they had practiced together time and again—she started to curse him in the vilest language, and yelled at the nurse to boost her anesthetic.

Amy was born in the hospital at Crypto City, a small town in Maryland whose name appears on no map and whose telephone numbers aren't listed. At the time, he was a young agent for the NSA, where secrecy is a doctrine and a way of life. Even the priests and ministers have security clearances and their services are held in unbuggable rooms. In its obsession with secrecy, his ex-agency surpasses the CIA a thousand times. He was a promising officer, really, holder of a blue badge that allowed him access to the most restricted areas and an endless stream of top-secret information. It was more like a blue medal he carried proudly on his chest, living proof of just how trustworthy he'd become. Then he made a mistake of a personal nature, while on his sole mission for the agency abroad, and fell into the "What if?" trap. His idealized world collapsed.

Within hours of his return to headquarters, his blue badge had been withdrawn. They gave him a red one instead. All of a sudden, his job opportunities in Crypto City became limited to the cafeteria, the supermarket, and the beauty salon. Before he could say "Bobby Inman," his horizons had shrunk to almost nothing. Martin tastes, for a second, a familiar sourness in his throat, a feeling of injustice and humiliation. He follows the central screen from the corner of his eye. It only shows the posterior ends of various Cairo vehicles. He loses his game of FreeCell.

"I can see Mickey Mouse has gotten himself some professional help," he says out loud as he starts a new game.

Martin is used to talking to himself, a habit he developed from working long hours in complete solitude. But that's perfectly okay. The center is completely sterile. In layman's terms, it is immune to eavesdropping. During his orientation, Alpha told him that they'd used a copper shielding technique codenamed 'Tempest' to build the center. This featured double walls in which the exterior masonry was protected from the inside by an orange copper film, and the inner shell was also lined with copper mesh. The two layers were separated by five inches of sound-killing space. With such specifications, he insisted, all sound waves and electromagnetic radiation were either absorbed or reflected, and prevented from seeping through to the outside. Alpha went so far as to compare the COBRA Center to a black hole: the center received millions of messages and electronic pulses from all over the world, while not a single electron was ever allowed to escape.

"We can't let Mickey Mouse escape this time." Martin's voice resounds throughout the chamber.

This may be their very last chance to eliminate the subject. He's a shrewd guy, and he's become an expert at covering his tracks. Otherwise, how could he have evaded their electronic surveillance networks all these years? Had he attempted to travel through any port or airport, his name would have turned up on their computer. Even if he'd used a false name and a forged passport, they'd have located him within minutes, courtesy of their top-notch face-recognition software coupled with the millions of CCTV cameras all over the advanced world—in shopping malls, on the streets next to ATMs, even inside public transport. Needless to say, even dreaming about using a cell phone or a credit card would spell his downfall. But Mickey Mouse is a scientist. He's familiar with the technological means at their disposal, which is why he's been so careful to avoid using modern communications equipment. His only weak point—until today—was his need to withdraw cash from the bank, although at fairly long intervals.

The chase is getting more intense. The Pajero speeds up, with their three units still in hot pursuit. So long as he remains inside the car, the subject can hardly get away because the satellite will track the Pajero wherever it goes. Martin needs to go to the bathroom but he holds it in.

Susan has reserved a big table at a pizza parlor to celebrate Amy's birthday on Wednesday. She called the mothers of Amy's little friends to invite them. She got the little princess a nurse Barbie doll and hid it at the bottom of her closet. Since the party conflicts with his morning shift, Susan suggested that they give Amy her present early in the morning, before he leaves for work. Thank God for his loving, generous wife and his angel of a daughter. In a moment's recklessness, he almost lost all this, this treasure that he wouldn't exchange for all the money in the world.

He had kissed his blue badge goodbye and, in the process, almost lost Susan and Amy, all because of a blonde bombshell. It had happened when he went to England on a mission to RAF Menwith Hill, the largest NSA listening post in the world. On his last night before coming home, he went out looking for fun in the nearby village of Harrogate. It was one of those warm summer days, when the light lingers till well after ten. For some reason, he stopped the car on the way to the village. He parked on a hillside overlooking the base and contemplated its twenty-eight white domes that shone like silver under the sun's oblique rays. He knew that each of the domes—technically termed radomes—housed a satellite dish antenna trained on a satellite more than twenty thousand miles above. The volume of information they collected defied human imagination.

Martin was overcome by a sense of pride, a rush beyond anything he'd felt before. To think that he was part of this tremendous technological feat—even though the world knew nothing about it. These installations were the cathedrals of the twenty-first century, the apogee of today's civilization in terms of creativity, organization, and mobilization of resources.

When, at last, he reached Harrogate, he was in a state of euphoria, ready for the adventure of his life. An adventure called Veronica.

It was an escapade Martin is determined never to repeat as long as he lives. Yet he hasn't, for one second, regretted that night he spent with Veronica. And what a night it was . . . beyond his wildest fantasies. The feel of her skin still lingers, like a mist wrapping his body. And the visual delight of her breasts—full and slightly drooping with their dainty nipples—he's recaptured them in his imagination so many times that their image has taken root inside his consciousness. But beyond all this, the pungent whiff of her arousal has accompanied him ever since, adding color to his life, giving his existence a sensual dimension that's impossible to rationally define.

When the agency called him in for the investigation, he didn't even deny the charge. Instead, he said to the bald, stony-faced man sitting across the bare table from him, "Is there a man alive who can resist a blonde bombshell?"

The man explained in a lawyer's no-nonsense tone that the agency does not employ ordinary men, but intelligence officers, and that—while nothing in his remarks should be construed as an invitation to promiscuity—they may be willing to look the other way in some instances of personal indiscretion, provided the other party is beyond reproach.

Martin immediately retorted that Veronica was precisely that—beyond reproach. She was a nurse whom he'd met by chance at a pub in Harrogate—the Black Bull Inn, to be exact. Since he'd never set foot inside the pub before that night and hadn't even planned to go there, it was inconceivable that an enemy agency could have planted a blonde on the slim chance he might turn up. In any case, they'd only spent one night together, and had subsequently never made contact.

Martin will never forget the evil grin on the investigator's face as he said, "In these matters, security will follow the lead of medicine.

When you have sex with a woman, you're actually having intercourse with all her previous partners."

Then the bald man started to explain that, years before he met her, his blonde had had an affair with a Palestinian doctor—a coworker at the hospital. The investigation found nothing about either Nurse Veronica or her Palestinian doctor—a Christian, by the way—that was not strictly kosher, he pointed out with utter sadism. But all that notwithstanding, the agency couldn't possibly be expected to put up with even the slimmest possibilities of a security breach. The "What if?" rule always has the final say.

Martin rushes to the bathroom without bothering to shut the door behind him. The sound of his flow resonates in the toilet bowl. Then he returns to the operations room. Having satisfied himself that the chase is still ongoing, he stops for a moment in front of four circular clocks fixed on the top third of the wall opposite the screens. Beneath them, the respective time zones are marked: Tehran, Cairo, London, EST. The Cairo clock indicates 4:20 p.m. He contemplates a large poster beneath the clocks. The sun is setting in the background. The ground is covered in different hues of orange. In the foreground is a noose hanging from the branch of a tree, with the caption, "For Repeated Security Violations." The rush of water into the toilet tank stops. Martin nods and returns to his chair.

On the screen, the Pajero stops at the traffic lights. This is Giza Square, an intersection with some of the craziest traffic on the planet. The vehicle suddenly takes off while the lights are still red. Without the slightest hesitation, it lunges into the intersecting flow of cars. There's going to be a terrible collision. No, they get lucky this time. The driver's skill in crossing the square and reaching the opposite side stuns Martin.

"Son of a bitch!" The voice of one of their agents comes through the loudspeaker, announcing the failure of the two pursuing cars to maintain the chase. The agent on the motorbike, however, manages to weave his way through the torrent of cars and, in hot pursuit, penetrates the alleys on the other side of the square. Martin does not blame the agents in the two cars. He doesn't know any of them in person but, as a professional, he appreciates the need for due caution when operating in a foreign country, particularly when there's no prior coordination with the local agencies. He takes a sip of his coffee as it starts to cool down. Its taste is bitter. This may be a temporary setback, but the operation isn't over yet.

The screen shows drab, downtrodden houses, cars blocking the alleyways, and people crawling like ants in all directions, heedless of the moving vehicles. The Pajero's driver maneuvers right and left from one alley to the next. But in these narrow spaces, the pursuing motorbike has the upper hand. Martin hasn't lost confidence yet. He wants to go for another cup of coffee, but before he can leave his seat something totally unexpected happens on the central screen. As the Pajero passes a mirror maker's workshop, a giant mirror on dollies is pushed out all the way across the lane. Suddenly, the mirror turns into an impenetrable barrier in the pursuing agent's path, an obstacle that, nevertheless, reflects the approaching motorbike's image. The picture shudders violently before going completely black. The agent's scream confirms that the bike has crashed. One shrill cry, then there is silence.

Martin stares at the empty screen in shock. He hopes their agent wasn't seriously injured. But right now, that's a secondary concern. Mechanically, he checks the satellite image. He'll be able to continue to track the Pajero, but needs to quickly redirect the two remaining units, so they can catch up with it. Today's shift is turning out to be hectic. He badly needs that coffee. He decides that it's useless to redirect the two remaining units until the vehicle has resurfaced on one of the main streets, and he can establish its direction. Who knows? This could be a blessing in disguise. It's important that Mickey Mouse and his associates feel relaxed and secure.

When Martin returns with a steaming mug, the central screen is still blank. The satellite image shows that the subject is heading back toward Cairo University by a different route. Martin directs the two units to follow, but he knows that they are at least ten minutes away from the vehicle. One of the agents wants to know what has happened to his colleague, the biker. These agents think that their controllers have the resources of a CIA or an NSA operations center at their disposal. If they had an inkling that the COBRA Center wasn't much better than a dump, that for the time being it was manned by just two men working in shifts, they'd definitely get the shock of their lives, and lose that misguided sense of security. Before he can respond, the Pajero has parked next to the Cairo University Metro station.

Martin can make out from the satellite image that the guy who just got out of the car next to the Metro station is indeed Mickey Mouse. The subject loses his balance and falls to the ground. He rests on the pavement for a moment, then rises and immediately heads toward the Metro exit. Within seconds, the subject has disappeared into the bowels of Cairo, out of reach of satellite surveillance. Martin finds himself screaming like a madman. His profanities ring across the room, then, gradually, he regains control of himself.

He knows only too well that searching for one man in the middle of the Cairo crowds is like searching for the proverbial needle in a haystack. However, the subject's decision to seek assistance from a gang of professionals has introduced a new element into the equation. No, the game is not over yet. There's still hope. This group could not possibly be linked to the Egyptian authorities. Otherwise, Mickey Mouse would never have surfaced to start with. The subject must have allied himself to a criminal gang or a terrorist group or an intelligence agency belonging to a third country. A dangerous step, really. Sure, it complicates things. But at the same time, Mickey Mouse has linked himself to a large entity that's easier to track down. At last you've made your strategic mistake, Mickey. It will definitely lead you into our trap.

"Everyone makes mistakes, didn't you know?" Martin says aloud.

This thought makes him feel a little better. He smiles and starts a new game of FreeCell.

chapter 3

Giza, Egypt
Monday, 8 January, 2007
Evening

As the nighttime call to prayer resounds, the Cerebellum makes a turn into the crooked alley. The muezzin's voice is untrained. Its natural coarseness is exacerbated by static from the loudspeaker fixed to a balcony railing, next to a string of garlic, a net of onions, and three rows of clothing left out to dry. The laundry is made up of children's clothes, men's long-legged Upper Egypt–style underpants, undershirts, and one dark gallabiya. This apartment has no women, or else its inhabitants have an aversion to hanging out women's clothing in public.

For the first time since he decided to move to this neighborhood five years ago, Sheikh Barhuma's cracked voice instills in him a sense of relief. He realizes that he feels safer here than anywhere else on earth. In this slum, where the houses have no numbers and the streets remain nameless—at least officially. Here, where the alleyways are too narrow for cars to penetrate, and pedestrians are forced to zigzag between the garbage heaps, where people are practiced at maintaining their balance while they hop on the bricks strewn among the puddles of raw sewage. This neighborhood is a hybrid of rural and urban lifestyles, yet it is only meters away from Sudan Street and the official city. Here he has found shelter, along with thousands of others who eat and drink, love and procreate, fall sick and die, with not a hint that they ever existed in the official records.

A terrible stench, emanating from a garbage heap, attacks the Cerebellum's sinuses. Yet it does nothing to dispel the positive energy that he has just regenerated, after years of despair.

This alley bears no allegiance to the Egyptian state—that "ignorant despot," as it was appropriately termed by Gamal Hemdan. Its inhabitants do not recognize the American Empire, or its allies and vassals. They do not acknowledge its enemies, the pariahs, the sponsors of terror, the so-called axis of evil. They do not even give a hoot about the United Nations, with its bellyful of fluttering flags, resounding speeches, and Excellencies earnestly debating issues that no one else can comprehend. Here, to be precise, you find yourself in a parallel world, outside the official course of history, denoted by neither shape nor color on the map of the world.

This is a universe that consecutive governments have ignored, excluding its inhabitants and their activities from the records and statistics, and, by and large, doing their best to erase all traces that these people ever existed on the face of the planet. Ironically, the tragedy of these Third World slums is exactly what attracted the Cerebellum to this one in the first place, particularly when he realized that—by some miracle—electricity was readily available and that even access to the Internet could be obtained. Of course, he had no choice but to compromise on the delicate matter of running water and sewage. Like millions of human beings, he has been forced to survive without such luxuries.

He walks past the wide-open entrance to the Good Lady's house, pretending to have nothing to do with this crooked building with the unfinished facade. Its pink silt bricks and concrete columns and beams are all shamelessly bare, denied both plaster and paint. With steady footsteps, he treads the alley's muddy soil, taking care to stay in the shadows as much as he can. After a hundred meters or so, he stops abruptly and turns around. In this dark corner, he would be hidden from the sight of a potential pursuer. As soon as he has assured himself that all is safe, he quickly heads for the entrance of the Good Lady's house, unprotected by either door or doorman.

Whenever he approaches this house, whose builder threw the basic rules of engineering out the window, he never fails to marvel at fate's wicked sense of humor. Here he is, the genius of structural engineering, living on top of a less illustrious rival to the Tower of Pisa. Looking at the shack next door, one gets the feeling it is about to be smothered by the Good Lady's house. To be precise, it is a fellah's mud-brick house, left over from the days when this area was inhabited by fields, waterwheels, goats, and barefoot women carrying straw baskets on their heads, laden with farm cheese and country bread. A vestige of a time when poverty went hand in hand with contentment, when one lucky morsel fed a hundred mouths. That is, before the hordes of undesirables from the city crawled upon it like an army of termites, whose belligerence could only be matched by their avarice.

By contrast, the house where he lives—owned by the Good Lady— is narrow and deep, with the facade overlooking the alley no wider than four meters. Passing through its doorway, he has the feeling he is penetrating a shadowy tunnel. There is only one apartment on the ground floor, protected by burglar bars and a solid English padlock. He knows that the tenant is a merchant, who uses it as a warehouse. He has never seen it in actual use, although from time to time he hears men coming and going in the middle of the night, hauling merchandise onto Suzukis—the only motor vehicles small enough to access these narrow alleyways. The Cerebellum is not a hundred percent sure what the nature of this merchandise may be. He has his suspicions, though.

He heads toward the decrepit staircase that leads to his hideout on the roof. He treads with caution, in the dark, and freezes the instant the Good Lady's voice starts to shake the house like a tsunami engendered by all the world's oceans in tandem.

"Zakzuka . . . where have you gone, bitch?"

The Cerebellum is hyperventilating from the day's exhaustion. His breathing whistles like a gale storming through ruins. Lately, his asthma has become chronic. He wonders if his gasps will give him away.

"You should thank your lucky stars men will even look at you . . . with your resemblance to that American hag on TV."

For the first time today, the Cerebellum finds himself smiling. For once, he appreciates the Good Lady's sense of humor. Actually, he now recognizes a resemblance of sorts between Zakzuka and the world's most powerful woman, the American secretary of state, which he had not noticed before. Or to be precise, he had, in fact, realized it, but only in his subconscious, and the impulse had never crystallized into a concrete thought.

He concludes from the Good Lady's grunts that her patience is running out. But there is no reply forthcoming from Zakzuka. Taking his cue from the click of the Lady's lock, he resumes his upward journey. In his eagerness, he takes a couple of steps at a time. A sense of relief starts to sink in once he has safely crossed the first-floor landing. He has been spared any further bother, at least for tonight. But the Good Lady's armor-piercing voice grips the back of his neck before he can get through the next flight of stairs.

"So did you pull a lion or a hyena, Mister?" Only a fool would believe that there is anything good about the Good Lady. It is just a nickname, her trademark.

"It's a long story, my dear Lady . . . no need to worry your little head . . . I won't bother you with the details right now . . . but tomorrow's a new day." The Cerebellum tries to sound like a common man.

"By God, you're treating me to a symphony, Mister. You said you were going to the bank to get some cash so you could pay up, and now, after being gone all day, this is the best you can come up with? Tomorrow's a new day . . . why don't you play me a couple of new tunes?"

All of a sudden, light from the hall of her apartment floods the landing and part of the flight of stairs on which he is standing. The Cerebellum realizes that she intentionally kept her hallway in darkness, in order to catch him by surprise.

The Good Lady is wearing a delicately embroidered Moroccan burnoose that covers her short plump body from head to toe, giving the professional fortune teller—and mistress of other even less

40

respectable activities—the appearance of an imaginary spherical creature, or a fat woman in a cartoon.

The Cerebellum freezes. For the second time today, he racks his brains for one magical sentence with the power to resolve a complex situation, or at least postpone it till tomorrow. And for the second time, the words refuse to come to his rescue. But now, at least, fate intervenes to save the day. The stairwell rings with masculine footsteps, which the Lady interprets as belonging to some customer. This causes her frown to evaporate. She replaces it with a well-rehearsed expression of piety. In less than no time, she has adopted the air of a holy person in communion with unseen worlds, beyond the reach of mere mortals.

In spite of the darkness, he covers the remaining three flights of stairs in the blink of an eye. He reaches the roof quite out of breath. He locks up behind him and turns on the light, then rushes to the corner of his room that serves both as toilet and kitchen. But the bucket is missing. He forgot to bring it in. He rushes out to the roof's southern-most corner and comes back with it in disgust; he hasn't emptied it. He relieves himself with a full but intermittent flow, then heads mechanically to the laptop on a small metal table with rusting legs. He presses the computer's power switch, then opens the nine-cubic-foot fridge and stoops to get a plastic water bottle. He downs half of it in one gulp and looks at the remaining amount of water. He returns the bottle to the refrigerator, sinks into his cane chair, clicks on the palm icon, and waits.

The Cerebellum wishes for a quick escape, but the surrounding din will not leave him alone: a man curses his wife, a somber female broadcaster's voice reads the news, a baby shrieks in a prelude to an extended wailing session. A workman in a body shop attacks a fender in a string of tireless thumping. The very clamor of everyday life that he is trying to escape embraces him with a passion. Then it all dissolves into the background as the familiar website's comforting blue wallpaper appears. He types in 'Biceps' for his username and his real date of birth as password.

Quickly, the map of his private world opens up in front of him.

His double in the parallel universe—his avatar—is relaxing on a deckchair by the swimming pool. His muscles—the Cerebellum's virtual muscles—bulge beneath his red shirt, unbuttoned to the middle of his belly. Just looking at his virtual figure, which would shame the fittest of athletes, produces a tingle of excitement all over his body. The thick gold necklace glimmering on his chest, however, generates a hint of guilt. He feels like a schoolboy stealing a puff from a cigarette on the porch in the middle of the night, while his parents sleep. The Cerebellum has, at last, regained his idyllic form after long hours wasted in a lonely, meaningless world, teeming with danger. An existence whose injustice smothers the soul, where the stench of sweat mingled with cigarette smoke leaves everyone gulping for air.

Candygirl is stretched out on a deckchair next to his. She sips a strawberry milkshake—her favorite drink—through a retro candy-striped red-and-white straw. Her name is floating in the air above her head. Her orange hair fans over her bare shoulders and parts of her white dress, which reveals more than it conceals. Her breasts are the size of ripe Timor mangoes. His heart does somersaults at the sight of her delicious electronic figure.

candygirl said: u r late biceps

You said: Sorry, my darling . . . so sorry . . . I had to attend to some annoying business.

candygirl said: i worry that one day u won't wake up from ur slumber next 2 me

You said: Why would you say something like that, my darling? You are the most important thing in my life . . . but wait . . . I know how I can make it up to you. How about a night on the town? What do you say to the Latin Club?

The Cerebellum taps the keyboard with experienced fingertips. The words appear in English at the bottom of the screen. Biceps stands up. The Cerebellum rotates the angle of vision in order to enjoy the sight of his beloved's figure with her exaggerated curves. A forged steel fence, less than a meter high, surrounds the pool. Behind it looms a rocky cliff from which a silent waterfall cascades. Biceps rotates again to face the pool. The steam that emanates from it indicates that it is heated. Behind the fence, the sea extends to the edge of the screen. Its waves dance in monotonous electronic shudders.

candygirl said: love u coz u understand me sooo
well. u know how i love 2 dance

You said: And that the tango is your favorite.

Candygirl rises and approaches Biceps. She is so much shorter than him, even in her heels. This he always finds exhilarating. The Cerebellum actually chose the form of Biceps for his tall stature more than anything else, and particularly for the way he towers over the opposite sex, something he had missed in his previous life. He admires his avatar's long hair cascading over his neck but not quite reaching his shoulders. He expresses his masculinity through a mustache and a goatee.

candygirl said: what r we waiting 4 let's go

The avatars move their fingers as they talk to indicate typing on the keyboard, a few seconds before the words actually appear on the screen.

The girl walks into the villa. Biceps follows. In the living room, they are received by a familiar song with a catchy beat. A screen that covers most of the wall is showing the music video. The blonde singer is dancing to the rhythm. His darling faces the right-hand corner.

candygirl said: i m thinking 2 buy a sculpture 4 ths
corner what dya thnk

43

Without waiting for his reply, she walks out the front door. Biceps follows her across the lawn, then into the wide public space.

You said: Let's walk all the way to the club. Maybe
we can skip teleporting today.

candygirl said: u're acting weird these days biceps

You said: I would really like to look at the houses,
to say hello to our neighbors. I need to sense the
distances . . . to sense space. I want to be in touch
with the millions of people that share our world
with us.

candygirl said: its jst a phase we all go thru it
sooner or later its coz we need 2 assure ourselves
that our world is no less real than the material
world. still its a long way 2 the club

You said: At least, let us walk until I feel secure . . .
after that we can teleport to the club, if you like.

They stroll across a wide square covered in gray marble with brown streaks. To the right, a row of shops advertise their merchandise on large screens featuring smiling girls. On the opposite side of the square, the river's surface sparkles like a string of pearls. From his vantage point, Biceps can see the place just beyond the square where the river flows into the sea. People in the square go their ways, in every direction. Their names float in the air above their heads. Some hang around. Others hurry toward an unknown destination and quickly cross the screen's boundaries. On the riverbank, there is a garden with palm trees and red and purple flowers of exaggerated proportions. On the other bank of the river, high-rises and postmodern structures emphasize that this is a metropolis in every sense of the word.

You said: I hate the commercialization that is
creeping up on our city.

candygirl said: u r right honey but its a sign of the
times and anyways the shops provide us wth all the
stuff we need

You said: You are probably referring to the new
flower shop. I have never seen it here before.

candygirl said: genius u understand me better than
anyone else in the whole world

They walk past a man sweeping the sidewalk. Next to him in red letters are the words: "so far he has earned 8 units." It crosses the Cerebellum's mind that here is a job he can resort to, when the need arises. They hit the riverbank next to the ladder that leads up to a helical slide.

You said: Let us have some fun like little kids.

candygirl said: beneath ur muscles and manly features u r reeeally a little boy

The girl's avatar rocks with laughter. Her white dress flutters, arousing his senses. The Cerebellum presses the laughter button so that Biceps, too, can shake. Then he starts to climb the ladder until he reaches the mouth of the tube. As soon as she catches up with him, he throws himself in. He picks up speed with every turn of the toboggan. And candygirl is right behind him. Yes, the sensitive girl with the curvaceous body, the woman of his dreams. The excitement intoxicates him. There are musical notes in the background. This is happiness as he has never felt it before. Amid drumbeats coming from far away, he penetrates the river's calm surface. What a stimulating splash! The girl comes into the river next to him. The water caresses his face with mischievous sensuality. The drumbeats get more intense. He wants to hug her in the middle of the river, but he has not mastered the art of moving his avatar to that extent.

> You said: I feel like hugging you . . . you are the most beautiful and delicious girl in the world.

> candygirl said: i do that sometimes myself i hold my arms around my breasts and i can feel ur muscular body embracing me.

The Cerebellum tries to do as she says. He shuts his eyes and hugs himself. His pulse echoes, like drumbeats in his ears. Her body feels like Turkish delight against his chest. Their two masses almost fuse into one, each melting into the other. Her heartbeats produce small tremors across his body. She talks to him in erotic whispers coming from deep within. Suddenly, he realizes that the source of the sound is external. There is intense knocking at his door, coupled with a female voice with a permanently out-of-breath sensuality.

"Wake up, Mister Poet . . . please, wake up, Mister. Why do I always have to keep knocking till I'm out of breath?"

It took the Cerebellum a good six months after moving into the Good Lady's house to figure out he was living in a brothel. He was a little surprised, at first, to find this room readily available for a reasonable rent, despite the crushing housing crisis. Soon enough, he heard rumors of the Lady's supernatural activities and hints that she was even married to a prince of the jinn. So, naively enough, he reasoned that the room on the roof must be haunted. And as it happened, this was a condition that did not worry him too much. Previous experience had taught him how to cohabit with ghosts. In fact, he got a bit carried away in his first few days in the neighborhood. Despite his slight build, he would march down the alley with macho steps, a straight back, and a protruding chest. He imagined himself a knight capable of looking both ghosts and jinn in the eye, without so much as a wink; a modern-day Saint George on his white steed, challenging the unknown. So he adopted the role of a hero in a cartoon.

What a great way to sum up his life: sometimes a Greek tragedy, sometimes a slapstick comedy.

"What's with you, Mister Poet . . . do you have to live inside your computer all the time?"

Facing him through the open doorway is a woman in a veil that covers her whole face except her eyes. Her loose gown does not succeed in completely concealing her curvaceous contours. Two dark-skinned feet are exposed beneath her fashionable black leather slippers. Her toenails glitter in reddish-purple nail polish.

"Sorry, Condoleezza. I got carried away with my work." Out of courtesy, he gestures an invitation for her to come in, knowing full well she will decline.

"So you, too, are going to start twisting your tongue and call me by that confusing name." He cannot tell whether she is proud of her unusual nickname or if she is actually objecting to it.

"Who else calls you Condoleezza?"

Of course the Good Lady was the first to point out the—by now obvious—resemblance between Zakzuka and the U.S. secretary of state, but he doubts her linguistic capacity would allow her to actually pronounce the name.

"What's the matter . . . do you think you're the only one with an education around here, good sir?"

He had not intended to patronize anyone. He is too embarrassed to reply. Instead, he signals again for her to come in.

"Maybe you're forgetting the story about the man, the woman, and that other guy whose name I won't even mention." Her voice exposes her extreme youth, in stark contrast to her mature body.

"Well, I remember a time when you used to come in, and nothing bad ever came from it."

When he first got to know her, in 2002, she never hesitated to come in and lie on his bed in her revealing dresses. Back then, she was—and to some extent, still is—a child imprisoned in a woman's body.

47

"God has been kind to me, good sir. Do you think it's too much for me to hope for God's mercy?"

Liar! You are a bold-faced liar, Zakzuka. You have never really changed. The flowing clothes and the veil are just for show. Yet she is not really to blame. After all he has been through, the Cerebellum is in no position to judge anyone. He has learned to accept people as they are. Nothing can surprise him any more. Except, perhaps, his own self, for his unshakable naiveté.

Funnily enough, it actually took him months to discover the girl's profession. The men would come and go, while he isolated himself inside his cocoon, unconcerned with what transpired around him. Until one day, she casually asked him, "Would you like a freebie?" He turned the word around in his mind, trying to guess what she meant. Obviously, she did not mean a Frisbee, which could be of no possible use to either of them. Well, it did not take a genius to deduce she was offering him something for free . . . maybe some kind of cookie? But the look in her dark eyes, coupled with her naughty smile, convinced him that she was not referring to food.

"I give up." In the end, he was forced to admit defeat. So she broke out in laughter. "A turn for free, good sir. As the saying goes, if it's for free, take another one." Then she lay down seductively on the narrow bed, exposing a dark shapely thigh. Only then did the genius of his age grasp the truth.

"May the grace of God be upon us all. But we are like brother and sister, remember?" Today, he can rebut her in confidence, because he did not accept her offer that day. Nor had he ever consented to a carnal relationship with her since.

"By God, if I had milk in my breasts, I'd nurse you . . . then there'd be nothing for us to worry about." Her eyes glow like those of a naughty schoolgirl.

The Cerebellum holds back, taking care not to be the first to laugh. Ever since her religious rebirth, a few months ago, she has come to take these fatwas with utter seriousness. Indeed, he has experienced her angry outbursts at first hand whenever he questioned their logic.

Time and again, she has demonstrated her willingness to suspend her critical faculties once a religious edict has been issued by some sheikh or other. A case in point is the fatwa she is referring to now, which proclaims that if a woman breastfeeds a grown man, he becomes like a son to her, thus removing the stigma of the two of them being together in the same room without a chaperone.

But the feeling of unease she generates in him goes beyond the prostitute's superficial religiosity. In fact, he has never felt quite at ease with her, even before she clad herself in black. Her eyes carry a dangerous glint, even when she is being seductive. A latent aggression fills her to the marrow, a silent rage that throbs with her every move. He feels sorry for this young woman, but at the same time he fears her.

"I was only trying to say that there are matters more worthy of repentance." The Cerebellum is surprised by the cruelty of his remark, its crassness, in fact. He tries to justify his unexpected reply to himself by claiming it is for her own good. She is not even twenty and has her whole life ahead of her. But sympathy can never spawn insult.

"I am sorry. Forgive me. There is a chill in the air and I was worried you might catch a cold," he says quickly.

What irked him most when she switched to this gloomy form of dress was that he was suddenly denied the chance to observe her facial expressions. Now he tries to visualize her reaction to his injurious remark. He needs to know if his apology has been well received. But behind her barrier, she remains an enigma, impossible to figure out. It has become exhausting even to have a discussion with her. In fact, he finds himself in a position of weakness in her presence. In the past he had had the upper hand, because of her inability to seduce him with those rounded thighs of hers. She turns around and starts to walk away without so much as a word to him.

He is about to hurry after her, to apologize again if necessary, but she returns with an empty soda-bottle crate, which she rests just outside his door. Suddenly, she pounces on a cockroach trying to escape from the crate. After stepping on it, she starts to crush the dead insect. While still in the act of pulverizing the roach's carcass, she stares at the Cerebellum. Rage radiates from her, like a neutron bomb.

"Don't look at me that way, please. Ever since I was twelve, I've been crushed like this cockroach, every day of my life . . . or even worse."

Skillfully, she positions her buttocks on the crate's narrow edge, while at the same time maintaining the crate's balance in this vertical position. This is not the first time she has done this, but he still cannot overcome the feeling that she will lose her balance any moment now, and roll onto the floor. A comic scene, no doubt, except that her inflexible worldview would inevitably endow it with a serious twist.

"You're a true gentleman, Mister Poet, the first man to ever treat me right," she adds calmly, after gaining control over her emotions. She compliments him, but, in the same breath, curses his sex. He likes it when she addresses him as 'poet,' the identity he assumed when he moved into this place. He figured this was the vocation that could justify—in the eyes of these simple folk—that he held no regular job and spent most of his time cooped up in his room. It also had the advantage of diverting attention away from his scientific background.

But there was another dimension to this metamorphosis from scientist to poet that transcended such pragmatic considerations. This was a more romantic streak, deeply rooted in his early years, that he became gradually aware of over time. He liked to compare himself to Guy de Maupassant, who had himself lived in a brothel in nineteenth-century Paris, and who managed to turn that experience—a largely disreputable one—into the apogee of creativity and excellence. He managed to transform promiscuity into a modernistic symbol of heroism, and this had inflamed the Cerebellum's youthful imagination. The Cerebellum's adolescent infatuation with de Maupassant was never, however, based on a desire to emulate his sexual exploits. He never thought it possible to find a meaningful sexual experience in a brothel. It was rather out of lust for experience, out of a need to challenge traditions, a thirst for adventure . . .

This was a thirst that fate would later will him to quench, but to the extent of intoxication.

"You still have some tea left?" She does not wait for him to offer his hospitality.

"One extra-strong tea coming up for the princess." His joviality hides his embarrassment at not being a good host. He heads for the kettle.

It occurs to him that they both pretend to be friends, while in reality, neither of them really trusts the other. This sums up their relationship perfectly.

"Let's get serious for a moment. There's something important I need to talk to you about." She trembles ever so slightly on top of the soda-bottle crate.

He has never felt comfortable talking to her across the open doorway, but now he is particularly ill at ease, as he senses that the subject she is about to raise could be of a confidential nature. Then he remembers Didi's predicament, and how he got himself entangled in her messy affair to start with. He cannot believe that something this serious could have slipped his mind for even one moment. But in the final analysis, Didi is not that close to him. She is no more than a chance acquaintance. Theirs is a superficial relationship that in no way justifies involving himself in her dangerous and absurd story.

"I hope everything is okay," he says absentmindedly as he pours the tea.

"One of my customers, Sheikh Abdel Muhsin—the Cub—says there's something in God's shari'a called pleasure marriage . . . could this be true, my dear poet?"

He stirs the sugar in her tea glass, then unhurriedly does the same for himself. After handing her the glass, he pulls his chair to the open doorway. Sitting down, he rests his own glass on the floor.

"The Cub?" The nickname catches his attention.

She sips her tea in her funny way beneath the veil, impervious to the hot steam it must be channeling toward her face. She makes an extended gargling sound as she cools the hot liquid inside her mouth. Although the distance between them cannot be more than a meter—Condoleezza balanced precariously on her crate on the roof across from the open door, and he on the cane chair just inside the room—they are divided by an impenetrable barrier. Closed doors are the key to privacy.

"He's a bearded student. But you haven't answered my question. For the love of your father . . . this is really important to me," she says, resting her glass on the floor.

The Cerebellum finds it hard to take her seriously. There is an anger brewing in him toward this whore, who will fornicate with every paying stranger but refuses to be alone with him in the same room, who is now exposing him to the January chill while she is warm and snug in her movable tent.

"We do not allow pleasure marriages. Only the Shi'a condone them," he replies impatiently. What is important, right now, is how to save Didi. Here he goes again; his mind has wandered back to Didi's troubling affair.

The Cerebellum is suddenly under attack from a barrage of noise: a mother shouting at her son; the buzz of a train rolling on the rails that separate their slum from the main street; an Umm Kulthum song; a cat mewing in sexual fervor; the never-ending buzz of traffic on Sudan Street; a man bursting into laughter. . . . The sounds have crystallized after being submerged in his subconscious. Just thinking about Didi's predicament has pulled him out of his stupor, aroused his senses.

"So aren't the Shi'a Muslims, after all?" He can tell she has knotted her eyebrows in concentration. His success in—even partially—penetrating the veil's defenses feels good.

"Of course they are Muslim, but they also have set restrictions on pleasure marriages." He is starting to see exactly where this is leading to. It is easy enough to deal with a boldfaced whore, but a religious one is quite a different matter. Why will people not accept their lot in life?

This is quite absurd. But what is even more absurd is that he, the genius scientist, has no one left in the world to talk to other than Condoleezza the whore, not counting candygirl, of course.

"Thanks, knowledgeable poet." Her eyes seem content. With feminine simplicity, she ignores his warning. Then she adds, "So . . . did you pull a lion or a hyena?"

"Why is everybody suddenly so fond of lions and hyenas? I ended up capturing a zebra, my dear, a gorilla, a rhino . . . happy?"

"Then you've come back empty-handed." She sets loose a volley of promiscuous laughter, completely at odds with her attire.

"Would you defer the pleasure of making fun of me to another time? I am in a real fix right now."

"No need to worry yourself at all. Consider your account with the Good Lady settled, dear. We wouldn't want a small thing like that to spoil your mood."

He almost gave himself away with a slip of the tongue. Luckily, she interpreted what he said according to the information available to her. Yet he cannot help but view her generous offer with suspicion. He should be grateful, but he has never trusted her. The Cerebellum takes off his glasses and wipes the lenses with his shirttail. He is not even sure if today's events have actually transpired. Perhaps the shock of his re-exposure to everyday life in Egypt, after his long seclusion, has allowed his imagination to get the best of him.

But what exactly is Condoleezza up to?

chapter 4

Charlotte, North Carolina
Monday, January 8, 2007
2100 EST

"I hope you have good news for me tonight," Alpha says as he hangs up his worn bomber jacket. He doesn't even bother to say hello.

"Good evening, Alpha. Actually, there's good news and there's bad news . . . shall I start with the good?" It's Martin's turn to be caustic. The man's insolent stare really pisses him off. It's as though he's blaming him in advance for any possible failure.

Alpha doesn't reply. He's carrying a carton of doughnuts and a paper bag—probably full of sodas. He leaves his stuff in the kitchenette and reappears with a can of Pepsi. He leans his heavy body against the wall next to the entrance. Right above his head is a red-alert lamp in case intruders get into the outer apartment. Since he started working here, Martin has never seen it flash automatically, although they do test it every three months to make sure it's operational. The man's round face is a radiant crimson, as if he, too, were sounding a red alert.

"Actually, I'd rather hear the bad news first." He sips his drink, then stares Martin in the eyes as though trying to read his thoughts even before he articulates them.

"Mickey Mouse has escaped. A highly professional job, really," Martin admits.

"The subject has escaped. How?" His face is the color of a tomato.

"He went down into a subway station. Simply disappeared in the crowd." Martin tries to hide his discomfiture.

"So, the subject has escaped." The fat man produces a Mars bar from his pocket, unwraps it, and angrily bites off a chunk.

"And the good news?" he asks with his mouth full of chocolate.

"We managed to locate the hideout of the guys who arranged the escape . . . a farm on the outskirts of Cairo." He points to the middle screen, which shows the farm in black and white, caught by satellite.

As he speaks, Martin evokes the importance of this achievement, at least in his mind. He won't allow the fat man to paint today's operation as a total failure. He must understand that the game is still on.

"So, the subject has escaped. But he was within our grasp," Alpha mutters as if talking to himself. He clutches a fistful of air.

Martin gives him a challenging stare. He won't allow Alpha to put him down this time. Still, he's exhausted.

"Do they suspect that they're under surveillance?" Alpha rests his hand on the gray steel safe where they keep their crisis management plan and some automatic weapons.

"That's highly improbable. We tracked them down by satellite. There was no involvement from our agents on the ground." Martin gets up. It's time to leave.

"Did we at least manage to identify these guys?" Alpha's ponytail shakes when he talks.

"The address is not in our database. It could take a few days." Martin puts on his tweed jacket.

"Any news on recruiting for Agent Beta's replacement?" Martin lobs a question Alpha's way before leaving. He tries to act as though this is not vital to him. But who is he fooling? The fat man knows better than anyone that ever since their third colleague stopped coming to work, they had gone from eight-hour shifts to twelve.

"They'll let us know in due course." Alpha's expression shifts from blame to awkwardness. He sinks into his chair and turns to face the screens. Martin has noticed that Alpha's conversations—ambiguous to start with—become even more enigmatic whenever this subject is mentioned. Ever since Agent Beta disappeared, the two men have avoided mentioning him, like an aristocratic family burdened with the shortcomings of a prodigal son, or a daughter who has eloped with a stranger.

"My daughter's only four . . . I hardly get to spend time with her any more because of the new working hours," Martin retorts sharply. Over and above the long working hours and total absence of holidays, there's the extra hour lost on the train commute each way. If he goes on like this, he can kiss his family life goodbye.

"I'll pretend I didn't hear that. By now you should know, Agent Gamma, that disclosing your personal information may have possible repercussions on national security. You simply don't have the right to mention these things." He avoids looking at him, pretending to read the reports on the computer screen.

"You can't even begin to imagine how I feel. My daughter's birthday is tomorrow. She'll miss her father . . . she's starting to feel like an orphan," Martin shouts.

He can no longer control his emotions. Nevertheless, he's ashamed of this sudden show of weakness. It's no big deal, really, and he should never have brought it up. His seclusion from the rest of the world, for hours on end, must have affected him. The long shift's effort has drained him, diminished his capacity to control his anger. But what infuriates him most of all is the sight of this man's chubby, cherubic face, which so efficiently masks his total lack of human compassion.

"You haven't been listening. This is the Ghost Center. When you walk through that door, you leave your problems outside. Your family, your life . . . you park all that next to your bike. Here, you're a ghost. No past. No future. Your real name does not appear on any records. In short, nobody would give a shit if you were to fall off the face of the planet. That's because you don't exist to start with." This time, Alpha turns and looks him in the eye as he speaks.

Martin shudders as he faces Alpha. He realizes that what he just said goes against the grain of everything he's acquired from years of training. Shit always happens when an intelligence officer starts to think of himself as just another employee, and then tries to lead the life of an ordinary guy. At that point, he starts making mistakes. He falls into the "What if?" trap. But the words of the fat man with the ponytail ring in his ears. He said that if he were to disappear from the face of the earth, no one would notice.

Could this explain Agent Beta's vanishing act?

"So the subject has escaped. But he was within our grasp," Alpha mutters as Martin heads for the exit.

In spite of the anti-chemical-warfare air-filtering system that has cost millions of taxpayer dollars, the air is stale. Martin can barely breathe. The ceiling and walls are caving in on him. He desperately needs to get out into the night. To walk under the dome of the sky. Just to stroll in open space. It doesn't matter if it's clear or raining. How he longs for a lungful of fresh air.

Martin steps into the passage that leads to the external apartment. He's forced to spend a few seconds in this confined space, drowned in a flood of fluorescent blue light. The feeling that he's about to suffocate becomes overwhelming. He's on the brink of losing control and acting like a madman. Shuddering uncontrollably, he listens for the click of the center's door going into the lock position, in order for the exit into the outer apartment's bathroom to open up. It crosses his mind that, just before he disappeared, Agent Beta had started to question the morality of their operation. One day, he went so far as to wonder whether the assassinations of scientists, in particular, were legal. He never really objected or dissented or anything of the sort. It was just that he asked some questions, strictly private thoughts that he happened to say out loud, no more. So, could it be . . . ?

He moves toward his bicycle, which he parks inside the outer apartment, right next to the door. As he reaches for the handlebar, a framed photo on a side table catches his eye. It's a college football team in full gear, with helmets and shoulder pads. He's smack in the middle.

Martin smiles to himself. The photograph is, of course, phony. He's never played the game in his life. It was Photoshopped and placed here, part of an elaborate cover. A fake picture that holds no memories. Worthless, really.

In his mind's eye, he can visualize another photograph of himself—a true one. It was taken a few years ago, in the foyer of the NSA in Crypto City. He's standing in front of a polished wall of black granite in a good suit and a striped tie. Carved into the wall, right above his head, is a triangle containing an eagle clutching a silver key in its talons, the NSA seal. Above, inlaid in gold, are the words "They Served in Silence."

They'd allowed him to display the picture inside his office at the agency, on condition it would never leave the building. So, when he was forced to resign, they wouldn't allow him to keep it. Such is life: one photo over there, another here. The truth merges with the lies. Honesty shies away in the face of deceit. The only truth will always be that the strong are in control. This is the unbearable truth that has weighed on his chest for years, without his ever realizing it. He remembers he can be seen on the monitors in the operations room. Alpha may be watching him at this very instant. Scrutinizing his every expression. Surveillance goes on incessantly. At all times. Everywhere. And who knows what goes on in the minds of the fat, bald men sitting behind the screens, as they munch their junk food?

He throws the door wide open and welcomes the pang of fresh air, like a long-missed lover. A much-needed breeze that restores—at least partly—his confidence in the constancy of things.

Giza, Egypt
Tuesday, January 9, 2007
Evening

There is an unfamiliar knock on his door. These are not Condoleezza's decisive taps, joined with the penetrating scent of her cheap perfume mixed with Dettol. Nor are they the Good Lady's thumps, invariably accompanied by her incomprehensible bellowing—which have become rare, in any case, as she finds it more and more exhausting to climb the stairs. These are polite knocks. Like a government clerk asking permission to enter the undersecretary's office, or a regular guy standing in awe in front of the police inspector's door.

The knocker is, no doubt, a stranger. Could it be a trap? The Cerebellum hesitates for a second. Then he concludes that if his pursuers have indeed succeeded in reaching the other side of his door, it would be all but futile to try and resist. Slowly he turns the handle.

"Sorry to barge in like this. I hope I haven't come at an inconvenient time."

It is a tall, skinny youth. His features are dark and delicate beneath a fresh haircut, obviously the fruit of more expert scissors than those of the local barber. He wears jeans and a brown sweater of soft wool— cashmere, probably. His eyes radiate intelligence under small round spectacles, like those of a telegraph operator in a Western.

"You must have the wrong apartment." He does not need distractions right now. He has enough on his mind as it is.

The young man looks familiar, though. The Cerebellum now recalls having bumped into him once or twice on the stairs. But he remembers him with a wild Afro. He is not sure whether the boy is a customer or a tenant. Why cannot people just leave him alone? Leave him to deal with the catastrophe that has fallen out of the sky and landed on his head.

"I'm your neighbor from the first floor. I've been thinking of paying you a visit for some time now. But I hesitated." The young man speaks in calm, confident tones, in contrast with the prevailing norms in this neighborhood of rough buildings and even rougher manners.

"How can I help you?" replies the Cerebellum with reserve. He intends to get rid of the lad as soon as he can.

"I just wondered if you would take a look at some of my work. I'd really like to learn from the experience of an important poet like yourself. If you can spare the time, that is."

The Cerebellum notices he is holding a folder.

"You said you lived on the first floor . . . but that is the Good Lady's apartment. Do you work for her?"

"I'm a student. I don't have a full-time job. The Good Lady happens to be my mother." He lowers his gaze.

"Come in, please." The Cerebellum points to the only chair in the room, in front of the computer. He cannot afford to offend the Good Lady's son. He has enough problems as it is. He heads for the kettle and fills it from the barrel, taking care to evade some floating insects. He is embarrassed by the absence of running water in his room, as opposed to the other apartments in this house. Funnily enough, he has never felt ill at ease when preparing tea for Condoleezza.

"My name is Tahir," the young man says. "I expected your room to be full of books . . . and sheets of paper all over the place." Then he stops in front of the laptop and nods, as though the machine holds the answer to all the secrets of the universe.

"Where do you go to school, Tahir?" The Cerebellum tries to hide his discomfiture, which has multiplied with the realization that the room must surely stink of urine. In the absence of sanitation, he has had no choice but to rely on the covered bucket, which he has not yet taken out to its usual location at the far end of the roof. He has gotten used to the smell, but others must find it unbearable.

"I'm in my final year at the Faculty of Sciences . . . pure mathematics," the young man says calmly, then, with a hint of shyness, quickly adds, "So far, I've passed with honors."

The Faculty of Sciences . . . mathematics . . . passed with honors. Quite implausible. This guy is not serious, just a kid talking big . . . or perhaps worse. Could he be part of a wider conspiracy against the Cerebellum?

He puts the kettle on the stove and returns to Tahir. He produces the dice from his pocket and throws them on the metal table in front of the young man.

"Tell me, Tahir . . . what is the probability that I will get two sixes?" He intentionally confronts the kid with a question that only a few people can answer. Now he will be exposed. Or at least he will get distracted enough not to notice the Cerebellum's bleak, smelly living conditions.

He refuses to believe that a young man who has grown up in this environment can possibly end up a worshiper at the altar of mathematics, a connoisseur of its aesthetics. His question will, no doubt, embarrass the youth. The sea, as the saying goes, shall test the diver. And the dramatic manner in which he threw the dice will further unnerve the kid. Guilt starts to creep into his heart. He never thought he could be so cruel. And what if it turns out the young man is not lying, after all? A youth like this deserves encouragement, and here he is trying to break his oars.

"Master Pascal has taught us that you'd need to throw the dice 24.555 times on average to get two sixes," the son of the clairvoyant—who also runs her house as a brothel—replies without hesitation.

A flush spreads from the Cerebellum's cheeks to his ears. The mere existence of this young man, in this place, is against all the rules. A child who is born and bred in a brothel, in a house with no number, on a street without a name, in the middle of a slum that does not even exist on the records, should grow up to be a pimp or a drug dealer. And if he were to choose the righteous path, he would turn into a terrorist. But for this environment to nurture a poet and a mathematician . . . that is a phenomenon that simply conflicts with the laws of nature. Nevertheless, it revives hope for someone in the direst of circumstances, obliges a wise man to review his postulates, to rethink his entire existence.

The kettle's whistle calls him to prepare tea. Tahir observes his every move with curiosity. Perhaps the Cerebellum's confusion upon meeting this young man is all too apparent. Maybe the mathematics student thinks he is insane. It takes an effort for the Cerebellum to control his emotions. His feelings of guilt for trying to embarrass the young man have metamorphosed into much more positive sentiments. He is overwhelmed with joy, like a beggar who finds a diamond in the dirt. He feels elevated by the sense that the world is good at heart, and that all this ugliness surrounding him is only surface rust covering its true metal, which, as it turns out, is pure gold. With the possible exception of beautiful Didi, whom he first met a few years ago, he has never encountered a living person who has instilled in him so much hope.

But there he goes again. No matter how far his mind wanders, it always comes back to Didi's predicament.

"Okay. So what comes first to you, Tahir, poetry or mathematics?" the Cerebellum asks as he relaxes on the edge of his bed, still holding his tea glass.

"That's precisely the question that's baffling me. Can't they go together?"

"They can," he replies, laughing.

He needs to exorcise Didi's image from his mind, to overcome this feeling of impotence that she arouses. He extends a hand to the young man, pointing to his folder of poems. He cannot help noticing the shiver in the kid's hand as he passes him the juice of his dreams, hand-written on a thin pile of copy paper. The Cerebellum rests his glass on the floor tiles, then slides his finger down the first page, starting from the top. He repeats the same procedure on the next page, then the one after that. In under a minute, he has read the entire collection. He returns the folder to the young man.

"You have genuine talent, Tahir . . . but you must understand that poetry is a long journey."

"What do you mean? You must be joking. Or are you just making fun of me?" The skinny kid shakes in anger.

"Please listen to what I have to say first." The Cerebellum knows only too well how hard it will be to convince the kid that he can actually read and absorb information at this extraordinary speed. The only way is to give a practical demonstration. So he goes on, without giving him the chance to reply:

"Take, for example, line nine in 'A Diet for Lonely Hearts' on page twenty-six—"

"But the pages aren't numbered!" Tahir interrupts sharply.

"True . . . but go ahead and count," he says calmly.

Tahir starts to count the pages out loud. He stops at page twenty-six to find the poem that the Cerebellum has alluded to. He says nothing.

"Line nine says—and correct me if I am wrong—'when I shut my eyes, I can still see you, standing there in front of me.' Well, that is a cliché, Tahir. It was a beautiful image when we heard it for the first time. But now, after about a zillion repeats, it is worn out."

The young man cups his chin in concentration, then nods.

"As literary criticism goes, that's acceptable," he says. "But I still don't buy your hocus-pocus. Come on, man . . . the son of a duck is a floater, don't forget."

"Did you not just say you had nothing to do with all the hocus-pocus going on around here?" The Cerebellum raises his glass and blows to cool the tea before taking a sip.

"Sure, but you still can't take me for a ride."

"As for me . . . I am the easiest guy in the world to take for a ride," the Cerebellum laughs. He tries to steady his hand to avoid spilling the hot tea into his lap.

If Tahir only knew how many times the Cerebellum has been fooled, he would never have taken offense at what he just said. But how can he explain his sudden transformation from suspicion to trust? Why has he come to trust this overconfident youth?

"I live with my mother, that's true. But I pay my own way," the boy says in earnest. "Perfectly legitimate activities, of course. . . ."

His olive complexion turns ashen.

It occurs to the Cerebellum that his mother's line of work must surely have ingrained in Tahir's soul a lifetime complex. Perhaps he feels the need to refute any potential allegation that the very flesh on his shoulders was bred from the proceeds of sin. The Cerebellum is developing a profound sympathy for the boy. If the mere sight of his own father, going out onto his balcony in his underwear, still produces shivers down his spine, then what about this boy, who grew up in an environment the Cerebellum cannot even imagine?

"Do not try to convince me that you can earn a living off poetry these days." The Cerebellum is regaining the curiosity he thought he had lost years ago.

The youth ventures a smile for the first time.

"I tutor high school kids in math." The boy talks with the confidence of an old man with a lifetime's experience behind him.

So he is not content with being a good student and a poet, but he also has to pay his own way. The Cerebellum fails to understand how this environment could produce such a conscientious human being. Then again, could this simply be the case of a young man trying to promote himself in the eyes of others? Could the boy be expressing a deep-seated need to overcompensate for an ugly reality and an even uglier upbringing? Or does he have yet another objective? Is he part of a well-conceived scam, a sophisticated con job? His suspicions start to plague him again, yet the Cerebellum's gut feeling refuses to give way. This young man's heart is as pure as surgical cotton. After all, what could he possibly gain from a penniless man like himself—especially after the gang grabbed his life savings?

He suddenly remembers the gold coins the old man dropped into his pocket. At the time, he was too surprised to take a good look at them, and the subsequent chain of events never gave him the chance to get them out of his pocket and examine them. By the time he got back to his hideout, the whole thing had simply slipped his mind. How could he possibly forget all about the ten gold coins for a whole day, when they are probably the only available lifeline for little Didi? But whoever said they were gold coins to start with? They are probably worthless trinkets, the kind they use to dupe kids and fools. The whole thing could even be one big illusion, just another rosy daydream. Can Tahir have picked up the scent of the gold coins? But how could he, if the Cerebellum had never mentioned a word to a living soul?

"I'm always cooped up in my room. No friends come, and I visit no one. Reading, writing, and the Net . . . that's the story of my life," the young man says calmly.

He probably thinks it is necessary to explain why he knows so much in such different fields, despite his tender age. As though knowledge needed an excuse.

Or perhaps he just needs to set himself apart from the rest of this house's inhabitants and their visitors.

"I can see you are conscious of your appearance. That is rare among young people these days." The Cerebellum decides to pay him a compliment. But the young man responds with a suspicious stare.

64

"I meant . . . that is quite a haircut. I have been looking for a good barber," the Cerebellum adds quickly.

Who knows what suspicious thoughts might go through the mind of a youth who has grown up in a place like this?

"It's Condoleezza. She does it better than any hairdresser," the young man replies after some hesitation.

It strikes the Cerebellum that the boy has just called the young whore Condoleezza. Now he knows what she meant when she said he was not the only one with an education around here. He also noticed the blush on the boy's face when he mentioned her name. How can he make Tahir understand that his relationship with the young prostitute is no concern of his? He is in no position to judge Tahir. In fact, he feels a genuine empathy toward him. In a sense, he has so much in common with the boy. His life can certainly be summed up in writing, reading, and the Net.

He decides to change the subject.

"Do you know, Tahir, what the golden number is?" Before all else, he must establish whether the boy is telling the truth. He needs to be certain that he is not a member of a criminal gang or part of a new plot—to add to the conspiracies that are being spun against him in every corner.

"You mean the golden ratio?"

"Actually, they are one and the same." Why does he feel his heart speed up? You would think he was being tested himself, or that the fate of the universe depended on the kid's response.

"We get the golden ratio by selecting a point on a straight line that divides it so that the ratio of the long segment to that of the line as a whole is equal to the ratio of the short segment to the long one."

The Cerebellum can see that the young man loves showing off his knowledge just as much as he does.

"And what would that ratio be, precisely?"

"1.618," the kid says, as though he were stating a fact that any school kid should know.

"Okay. So give me examples of this ratio as it occurs in nature."

The Cerebellum's jubilation that the kid is giving the right answers goes beyond reassuring himself that he harbors no ill will toward him. When all is said and done, this youth may well provide the assistance he needs to deal with Didi's situation.

"Well, for example, it's the ratio that determines the pattern of a pineapple's scales."

"And what else?"

"And the spiral structures in a nautilus's shell."

"Okay. What else?"

"And the screw-like displacement of leaves in the branches of a pear tree."

"And a rose's petals," the Cerebellum joins in enthusiastically. The language of numbers offers a profound pleasure enjoyed only by a select few.

"And the distribution of bars in Mozart's Sonata no. 1 in C Major," the boy adds without hesitation.

"As for the pyramids of Giza . . . well, we could go on and on." Finally, the Cerebellum breaks out in laughter.

Just looking at the stars sparkling on the screen's clear night sky steadily dispels the Cerebellum's anxiety, like the waves eroding a child's sand castle on the beach. The strain in his neck and shoulder muscles eases with each soundless electronic step. Biceps glides smoothly over the square's marble floor. To the left, a public transport bus is at its stop. To the right, there are shops, some of which specialize in virtual body parts—sexual organs and all. Other stores sell the clothes to cover them with. He has not found candygirl at her usual spot by the swimming pool, so he is looking for her in some of their favorite places: the book and music store, the benches in the park nearest the house, the shopping mall. And now he is heading for the Latin Club.

But what if he cannot find her? What would he do if she were to suddenly disappear from his life?

This happens to be the only fear that, from time to time, throws its shadows on the Cerebellum's parallel universe. In the material world, everyone has an address, a job, family connections through which you can trace them. Over there, we are all shackled by a combination of fear, love, sex, money, tradition, and the illusion of stability. But here in virtual life, an individual is no more than an electronic signal, free as a ray of sunshine. Like an electron, you can potentially exist in more than one place at the same instant. You would not even give Newtonian physics the time of day. On an impulse, you may disappear without warning, or switch identities. A man can turn into a woman, a child into an old person. You can substitute your fat body with a skinny one, without needing to explain yourself to anyone.

In the parallel universe, these kinds of escapades are routine. They start off as an adventure, but they can quickly turn into a gamble. The Cerebellum reminds himself that this is no different from the risks people take in their corporal existence. The potential for betrayal is inherent in life's every aspect. If not for the maternal instinct, a newborn would have no guarantee of a continuous supply of care and nutrition. A husband's trust is his only assurance of his wife's fidelity. The relationship that binds Biceps and candygirl is also built on confidence. His emotional bond with her is no less real than a man's relationship with a lifelong friend. And the trust they share dwarfs the trust that exists between spouses.

He stops in front of the new florist. After quickly scanning the alluring colors and shapes, he steps inside. He buys a bouquet of red roses—to symbolize feverish love—and takes advantage of its beauty to expel the fears of both the material and virtual worlds from his heart. Then he hurries toward their favorite dance club.

As usual, he is welcomed to the Latin Club by its spicy rhythms. As he makes his way inside, he absentmindedly reads snippets from the conversations of clubbers who are dancing or just hanging out. But the words slide out of reach before he can make sense of them. Whatever it is they are saying, it does not matter anyway. The place is packed, yet there is no sign of his lover. Then he notices her friend, Wendy90, dancing with a cool dude.

You said: Hi, Wendy. I am looking for candygirl. Have you seen her?

Wendy90 said: hi biceps haven't seen her today. sorry

The only place left to look is their favorite hideout: a quiet enclave on the mezzanine with a view of the dance floor below.

Before he reaches the top of the stairs, his heart is already leaping with joy. But then he sees that candygirl is having a conversation with a guy called Mad Max, whom Biceps has never met.

candygirl said: dya know max one of these days i may just give u a hot french kiss

Mad Max turns to Biceps.

Mad Max said: if you don't mind Biceps this is a private conversation.

You said: No kidding.

candygirl said: hi biceps dya mind if we meet later . . . the park next 2 my place n about half an hour

You said: But . . . I have missed you . . . and . . .

Biceps holds the bouquet as a piece of material evidence that would, without a doubt, convict him on the charge of stupidity. The Cerebellum does not succeed in putting together a coherent sentence on the keyboard.

candygirl said: its only half an hour honey

Biceps turns his back on them. He needs to get the hell out of here, to go back to wherever he came from. The Cerebellum's head is about to explode. The words will not come to his rescue. He just does not know how to deal with this situation. The problem is, he is unable to grasp what is going on. Candygirl made no attempt to hide whatever she was doing, which, in a way, was worse than denial. But all this does not make any sense at all. In virtual reality, there is just no excuse for cheating. And then, if she did not love him, why ask him to meet her in half an hour? There must be a reasonable explanation for all this.

He discovers he is moving Biceps haphazardly and that he is now trawling the riverbed. He has made him walk underwater, like a lunatic. He feels his soul being drawn from his body, as if he were actually drowning, or freefalling in space. He struggles to catch his breath. Uneasily, he pulls the inhaler from his pocket and pumps a double dose down his throat. He needs to control his emotions for the next thirty minutes. He must pull himself together until all becomes clear. But what if his suspicions turn out to be true?

"All right," the Cerebellum says out loud in Arabic, in reply to the parting remark of the electronic girl, who is no longer on his screen.

Now, of all times, he remembers the gangster who calls himself a doctor. What have they done to you, Didi?

Instead of sympathizing with the kidnapped girl, he finds himself pouring out his anger on her. That reckless woman who seems to think that her good looks place her on a higher plane than mere mortals, that they even afford her a certain immunity. Time and again, she gets herself into trouble, then puts the burden of her rescue on a guy like him, who cannot even save his own skin. What business does he have with gangsters and criminals and movie producers and their debts? Is it not bad enough that he is being targeted by some of the world's mightiest and most feared agencies? Never mind that he is up to his ears in debt, that he has just lost his life savings, or that he has been reduced to receiving handouts from whores?

What really irks him is that, all of a sudden, he is expected to turn dust into gold in order to ransom the reckless beauty. He leaves his chair and heads for his jacket, which is hanging on the door hook. He pulls out the piece of paper that the Doctor had torn out of his notebook, and returns to his decrepit chair. With quick taps he creates a new email account that he will use exclusively to communicate with the gang. It is essential to apply extra caution when using the Internet, so that neither the gang nor his original pursuers can discover his hideout.

"Damn children and the heartache they bring," he says to himself as he starts to type his message. But Didi is not his daughter, nor even a relative. He smiles as he realizes that he has just repeated his mother's favorite maxim. He stops typing for a second. What is required, right now, is to establish a channel of communication with the gang. It may not be such a good idea to try and bargain with them. He quickly revises his message:

```
Dear Doctor,
This is to let you know that every conceivable effort
is being made to put together the required sum.
Unfortunately, it may take a little longer than
expected. How is our pretty friend?

Sincerely yours
```

He smiles again as he dispatches his message. "Every conceivable effort is being made." He likes that. He marvels at how he can find humor in such a crisis. On the screen, Biceps has lost his way and is now pushing helplessly against a rocky hillside. He is surrounded by tropical palm trees whose colors have faded away with nightfall. He decides to fly back to the park, in order to get there in time for his meeting with candygirl. He presses the "fly" icon and Biceps starts to levitate. As he gains altitude, the city lights spread out as far as the eye can see. The Cerebellum starts to feel better as he smoothly drifts toward the largest concentration of light. This will remain his chosen world, even if candygirl abandons him. He can feel the vigor of life pulsate in Biceps's veins in a way that surpasses any sensation the Cerebellum has known.

His destiny is being drawn here, on the magic screen, not out there in the alleys packed with prostitutes, pickpockets, and trash; not even in the designs of sophisticated criminal gangs and intelligence agencies.

Biceps parks himself on a bench in the park and waits for his beloved to appear. He discovers he is still holding his bouquet of red roses. This amplifies his shame. He rushes to the closest trash bin to get rid of it. Then he gets back to his bench. Her wild, delicious form comes into view, exactly on time.

```
candygirl said: missed u honey
```

The Cerebellum's heart throbs as if pounded by a drunken drummer in a rock band. He can hardly get a grip on himself.

```
You said: Oh, really.
```

Luckily, the dialogue takes place by typing on the keyboard. Otherwise he would never have managed to keep his emotions in check.

```
candygirl said: if i didnt know better i d think
maybe u r jealous
```

```
You said: Actually, I am more bewildered than jealous.
```

```
candygirl said: i admire u so much but not 4 ur mus-
cles. u know u can buy them from the shops. it s ur
mind I love ur deep understanding of life. ur spirit
ur genuine desire 2 understand others and connect
with them
```

```
You said: And can a great mind protect its owner
from pain . . . particularly when he has been
betrayed?
```

No sooner does the word 'betrayed' appear on the screen than its echoes start to reverberate in the Cerebellum's consciousness. Whatever gives him the right—he, who has never been married or even had a real relationship with anyone else—to claim he has been betrayed? He was born different. A fact that has been impossible to deny since the third grade, when he discovered he was better at arithmetic than his teacher. Since then, the course of his life cannot possibly be described as normal. But now, as he faces the computer screen, he does not feel the slightest regret. Being a loner has always suited him most. His particular disposition has protected him from the emotional disturbances that usually impede the intellectual development of the young, and has afforded him a crystal-clear vision of the world around him. One of the fruits of his isolation has been to spare him the very betrayal he now laments to his dumb screen. So how could he—after all these years—put himself at the mercy of an electronic doll, who would vanish without a trace if the power were switched off?

candygirl said: betrayal? wht r u talking about?

You said: Can you deny that I caught you in the middle of a romantic situation with another guy? Would you not consider that a betrayal?

candygirl said: the traditions u r talking about r not absolute. they only made sense in a certain historical context. 2 maintain social order 4 example. 2 protect the family unit and raise the kids in a better way. 2 avoid unwanted pregnancies when the mother s economic situation didn t allow her 2 care for the child. For men 2 feel confident they r actually supporting their own chldren. 2 avoid the spread of stds like aids. all these considerations jst don t exist here. this is the world of genuine freedom. there s no place here for jealousy and chauvinism.

we live without food but never feel hungry. we both
have the right 2 have as many relationships as we
want with no boundaries or guilt. there s no religion
here. no blessing and sin. no heaven and hell. don t u
realize tht even the gods don t exist in ths dimension

The Cerebellum taps the rusting table with nervous fingers. He
grasps candygirl's logic but cannot work out all its implications. She,
too, possesses a clear mind, which is probably why he was attracted to
her in the first place. But her words bring all the rules tumbling down.
He needs to mull over what she is saying, but he fails to control his
growing anger.

You said: Then you are not denying you are having
an affair.

He needs to get to the truth in order to free himself of this mur-
derous suspicion. No matter how painful it may be, the truth is better
than losing his mind altogether.

candygirl said: how do u know i m not married in the
material world

You said: I had always thought of our relationship
as unique.

candygirl said: and u r rght wht we hve is unique
but that doesn t mean we can t both hve other
relationships

You said: I may be able to live with other relationships in the material world . . . on the basis that we
are dealing with two different dimensions of existence and that you have physical needs in that other

dimension that cannot be satisfied here. But what is really driving me crazy is that you feel the need for another relationship in virtual reality. Am I incapable of satisfying your needs, here at least?

The Cerebellum hits the keyboard so hard that the laptop shakes on the metal table.

candygirl said: u r immensely knowledgeable biceps ur conversation never fails to impress me yet u still hold on 2 the material world s traditions n way of thinking. u r trying to import them over here 2 this new universe. this can only limit ur takeoff. can t u see we r witnessing the birth of an unprecedented way of life here. one that the world has never seen the likes of before

You said: On the contrary, this parallel universe has come to represent the essence of my existence. That is why I need to maintain my bearings here, too. As for you, I can see you perceive it as a place to have fun . . . a new kind of videogame.

The Cerebellum can feel the rumblings of an earthquake starting to shatter his world. The Good Lady's building is about to collapse on top of him, together with its two prostitutes and their clients.

candygirl said: reality has indeed merged wth videogame 2 the extent that it s no longer possible to tell when one starts and the other ends. take a second 2 imagine the degree of freedom that the virtual world affords us. all our shackles disappear. here freedom is absolute and ppl s capabilities r infinite.

Reality has merged with videogame. Precisely. The Cerebellum cannot deny that. It would probably have been possible to deal with the conundrum posed by candygirl's behavior if only the two worlds had remained distinct from one another. He might have been able to accept her premise and even to experiment with her . . . except that— thanks to the innocent beauty, Didi—reality has intruded on his life, polluted the virtual world with its mist of greed and insecurity, to say nothing of the sense of responsibility that, overnight, crept into his soul: that feeling of guilt that now haunts him.

> You said: You are killing me with your words . . . do you not realize that you have just signed my death warrant?

He feels one warm tear roll down his cheek. Hiding in the virtual universe in order to escape the evils of reality was a delicious dream. But, like all dreams, it has evaporated under the scrutiny of daylight's first merciless ray.

> candygirl said: I m actually throwing you a life vest. opening the door 4 u 2 a new life a life without restrictions or limits. anyway why don t u think it over till we meet tomoro ok

Like a lazy student shutting a book that's too demanding, the Cerebellum folds his laptop with a thud. Adopting the tone of a gang boss who wears U.S. Marines sunglasses and talks like a New Age businessman, he mumbles, "All right."

chapter 5

Giza, Egypt
Wednesday, January 10, 2007
Evening

The Cerebellum throws his ivory dice on the table. With the lust of a professional gambler, he listens to their tinkle as they tumble on the metal surface. He bets that he will roll a seven. This can happen if he gets one and six, or two and five, or four and three. One of the dice bumps into the laptop's edge and comes to rest at two. He holds his breath. If the other one stops at five, he will have won. The second die bounces on the uneven surface and finally comes to a standstill at the very edge of the table. It gives him a six.

"Shish du," he mutters in disappointment in Turkish, the lingua franca of backgammon.

Little do people who enjoy a game of chance realize that a die is one of the fruits of human ingenuity. He holds up one of the dice to the light and examines it. He knows only too well that its center of gravity coincides with its geometric center. A fair die is one that has an equal chance of landing on any one of its faces, otherwise it would be loaded. That is why dice are designed so that the sum of each two parallel surfaces is always seven. He turns it between his finger and thumb. You barely notice the tiny depressions that indicate the number on each surface. Yet their number does make a difference. The miniscule mass gouged from them does have an effect on a die's center of gravity. It crosses his mind that his own fate is determined by one throw of these dice. Then he remembers the poor elephant who had to lose his life so they could make these fancy dice out of its tusks. It too tumbled in the twirls of life's lottery, whose complexity defies our comprehension.

A familiar knock pulls him out of his contemplations. He goes to the door. For the first time, he welcomes the pulsating black tent with a curiosity that borders on affection. She holds the soda case, indicating that her visit tonight will not be a fleeting one.

"What's wrong, Mister Poet? For once you come to the door right away. Is anything the matter?"

"I have missed you, Condoleezza. What is wrong with that?"

He has not felt the need for another person's company in a long time. But right now, he needs to hear a friendly voice, even if they are going to talk a lot of nonsense.

She lets loose a volley of laughter, totally incongruous with her attire. She balances her African behind on the case's thin edge and looks him straight in the eye. The Cerebellum realizes that the expression on his face must speak more eloquently to her than the warm words he just said on the spur of the moment. He is getting a little confused. It dawns on him that he has never treated her like a flesh-and-blood human being, with her own feelings, thoughts, and ambitions. He only saw her as a faint image in a bleak world. An agent of a dimension of existence he rejected. He had migrated to the parallel world precisely to escape from that dimension. He cannot recall a single time when he had listened to her chitchat with interest, or shared with her an opinion on a subject he considered important. True, he has never looked down on her for being—let us face it—a fallen woman. Of that, at least, he is innocent. Yet his attitude toward her was much worse. From the very start, he flattened her existence, which is what he did to everybody else . . . great men and scoundrels alike, murderers and saints alike. He stripped them all of their humanity, but on an equal basis.

He can see clearly now, as he confronts a woman who hides her overwhelming sexuality behind a curtain of black cloth. At last he realizes that by choosing candygirl as his lifelong partner, he elevated her virtual existence to the level of reality, and thus flattened the external world, reducing it to background decoration on the stage of life. Yet today, as he stumbles under the burden of electronic betrayal, he starts to feel that his alternate life, which he had assumed to be purer and safer, has not turned out to be that perfect, after all. He is not at all confident of his ability to deal with Condoleezza from this recently acquired perspective, now that she has attained a new status, shouting with color, pulsating with vitality . . . so he heads for the kettle to prepare tea.

He can feel her gaze burning into the back of his neck. To make him feel vulnerable, the young whore only needs to stare at him from behind her invincible barrier. There is no denying that. He curses the veil and everything it represents. In the West, they see this form of dress as humiliating to women, a sign of their inferior status. On the symbolic level, they may be right. But the Salafis are also right when they stress its protective value, bunkering women away from hungry eyes, elevating them to a position of strength in their day-to-day dealings. By hiding her face, a veil saves a woman from having to expose her emotions. It plugs the leak of her human weakness. The Cerebellum has finally put his finger on the reason for his intuitive anger at veiled women everywhere.

"Will you play backgammon with me?" she asks coyly. She has noticed the dice on the table.

"I never play backgammon."

It's true, he has never played the game. Yet in his subconscious, it has come to symbolize an idealized state of existence, free from all worries. A few moments ago, the ring of the dice took him back to his college years, to merry gatherings at cafés and rowdy parties in a furnished apartment nicknamed "the Blimp," in which they soared in the stratosphere, over clouds of blue smoke. In all these affairs, the Cerebellum was only a spectator, never a participant. He followed the comings and goings from the corner of his eye, while most of his concentration was focused on devouring a book. He read at a speed that left the others dumbfounded. With time, they got used to it, and came to take his mental superiority for granted.

Now, as he waits for the water inside the kettle to boil, he is surrounded by the roars of laughter that thinly coated the sexual energies of others, their blind rush to unknown destinations. The rowdiness of youth has become entangled in a warp bubble that stubbornly refuses to follow Time's other phases, into oblivion. Instead, it has chosen to linger on in his room's darkest corners, waiting for a magical word that may enable it to reimpose its presence among the living, like a confused ghost who cannot accept the finality of his annihilation.

He hands her the tea and turns to fetch his loose-legged cane chair. Before pulling up the chair, though, he picks up the dice from the tabletop with uncharacteristic sleight of hand and pockets them. He is not sure if she has caught his move, or if she was too absorbed in trying to sip the boiling liquid from beneath her veil, in that funny way of hers. He sits inside his room's perimeter, facing her across the open door.

"You're looking good, Holy Sheikh."

"'Mister Poet' is fine, but 'Holy Sheikh' is taking it a bit too far." He starts to laugh.

His desperate situation has released the laughter that has been frozen in his heart for years.

"Mister Poet, well, of course . . . but now I'll also call you Holy Sheikh."

She is starting to sound weird. He cannot quite explain the change in her attitude. He has never heard her tell a joke with religious connotations before. Is this some kind of test?

"Why don't you keep your religious titles for your young bearded visitors?" He decides not to take her seriously.

"It is precisely for my sake and theirs that you must agree to be called Holy Sheikh," she says in earnest. He can detect a pleading note in her voice.

He softly rolls the dice inside his pocket. Their tinkle can hardly be heard, drowned by a baby's wail, a man's coarse laughter, the barking of an angry dog . . . their sound simply dissolves in the clamor of the surrounding slum. Why does Einstein's contention that God does not play dice with the universe come to mind? The genius physicist was expressing his rejection of Heisenberg's uncertainty principle. But genius, no matter how exceptional, has its limits. In the end, the principle was proven right and Einstein wrong.

"All right . . . you can call me Holy Sheikh, if it makes you happy."

"I owe you one, good sir. Please don't get me wrong . . . but you scratch my back, I scratch yours. I always pay my dues."

Finally, she is about to show her cards. She would not have paid his debts to the Good Lady if she did not expect something in return.

"I hope you do not expect me to take up fortune-telling. Even if I were crazy enough to try, the Good Lady would turn my life into a living hell . . . and yours too." His past experience with the hocus-pocus business is still vivid in his mind. Those days when he used a haunted apartment in a fancy tower as his hideout: apartment 1301.

"You take that back . . . and keep your voice down. She could be listening," Condoleezza whispers, her eyes shifting nervously toward the staircase. She quickly changes the subject: "You know what I like most about you? You're always dressed up, like you're ready to go out. Even your shoes, you never take them off . . . even though you never leave your room. At first, I'd think Mister Poet was expecting guests . . . but no one ever showed up. Being well dressed must come naturally to you."

Where is this leading to? He is not sure. But one thing is for certain: he must never underestimate the young whore. How come he had never really noticed her before? Simple people are anything but simple-minded. On the contrary, someone like himself, a so-called genius, has proved to be the world's most naive man. Stupid, even. He really must be careful about what he says to her. But, right now, the problem is him, not her. The confused state he has been in ever since he bumped into the world's most beautiful girl in a side street close to Dokki Intersection. Yes, Didi, who keeps nagging mercilessly at him, nearly driving him crazy. It was her predicament, after all, that cast him out of his virtual paradise, and landed him in this world teeming with danger, cruelty, and injustice.

"Tell me, Holy Sheikh, would you by any chance have a fancy cloak in your closet? I mean, it would look so good over your shirt and trousers."

"I certainly have no cloak . . . I do not even have a closet."

Can the idiot not see the clothes hanging from the three hooks on the wall? And why would she expect him to wear a traditional cloak, anyway? The way she said "Holy Sheikh" is still ringing in his ears. She was not joking or even trying to be sarcastic . . . she sounded as though this was how people normally addressed him. She must be seriously trying to lure him into the fortune-telling business.

"Don't you worry about that. Leave it up to me."

"Hold on for a second . . . and listen carefully . . . I am not a sheikh. I have never worn a cloak and I never will. What's more, after all these years, I do not have the slightest intention of conning people out of their money!" he bursts out.

He has never really trusted her. The moment he started treating her as an equal, she tried to implicate him in some criminal act. He finds himself pouring out the disappointment and anger that have built up over the years, by rejecting her silly proposal that, to begin with, he does not even understand.

"You misunderstand me, Mister Poet. I have nothing to do with con jobs and hocus pocus, or any such stuff. God forbid! I only trust you to do the right thing. That's all."

Her loud perfume hits him without warning. It smells of violets with a trace of sweat. Yet an even more potent scent assails his senses: that of hormones gone wild, the secret perfumes of physical inter-course. The smell of a thousand men clings to her body like a radioactive halo that no veil will ever hide, that no perfume can erase, that soap is powerless to wash off.

The Cerebellum is overcome by sympathy. It washes away all the fear and anger that, only a moment ago, had poisoned his blood. He no longer feels exposed before this woman, who hides behind her protective costume and promiscuous laughter. It is she who is now bare before him, naked as the day she was born. He can no longer ignore her tragic history, her paradoxical present and overcast future. She has no cover left to conceal her scars, no bandage to protect her raw wounds. Her hideous reality has materialized in an unprecedented way. Yet he wants to take her in his arms, to shield her from the world's callousness, if only she would not feel offended by that. Yes, he has come to respect her religious feelings, no matter how confused they may be. Only now does he grasp the importance of that straw of superficial religiosity that she so stubbornly clings to.

"You're no different from other men . . . always unfair to me," she says, as though responding to his thoughts.

"Zakzuka, where are you hiding, you good-for-nothing?" The stairwell rings with the Good Lady's voice.

"What do you want from me? Level with me, Condoleezza," the Cerebellum says quickly, ignoring the call of the she-ghoul.

"All I ever wanted was to make an honest living . . . and you're the only one who can help me." She presses her hands against her ears over the veil, as though she wants to wipe the Good Lady out of existence.

"Well said. We will find you a new line of work," he replies with enthusiasm.

"Zakzuka, you bitch!" The bully's voice hits them like unbridled fate, instantly dissipating all the world's rosy dreams.

"I've tried that . . . last time I even applied at the hairdresser's in Sudan Street. But still no luck, although I'm the best at cutting and blow drying. Let's face it, who'd hire someone like me?"

"We can try again," he says.

"But I've gotten used to what I do. There's another solution, though. That's where you can help."

The Cerebellum feels embarrassed by what he has just offered. He actually promised to find her an honest job. Spoken like a successful industrialist who can simply hire her in one of his plants, or a high-level bureaucrat giving instructions to his chief of personnel to create a job for her. He forgot—or chose to forget—that he is no more than a lonely fugitive who is too scared to be seen on a Cairo street, a man who spends most of his life in virtual reality. The best someone like him can hope for is to pay off his debts and find a source of revenue to cover his meager expenses. She could see that he was incapable of helping her secure a job, but was considerate enough not to put him on the spot.

"And just what would that magic solution be?" he asks softly, as the thoughts race inside his weary mind.

"The magic solution is marriage. I mean *pleasure* marriage. But we need a respectable sheikh to officiate at the wedding in accordance with the rules of God and His Prophet. If it has to be done the Shi'a way, I can live with that. I just need it to be Islamic." Condoleezza speaks slowly, with resolve.

He hears her out, nodding slowly. He can see she has everything figured out. Well, of course. Her words are perfectly in tune with the logic of things. In the final analysis, she is a professional interacting with the market in its current state. If she has managed to survive thus far, it is because of her understanding of the law of supply and demand, her ability to navigate society's currents. He, on the other hand, is doing his best to seclude himself from the new Egyptian society, to convince himself that things have not really changed, that the Egypt he has known and loved is still a towering island in the stream of time . . . that everything happening around him is no more than a layer of rust, and that the metal's quality remains as pure as ever. So was his reclusion then compulsory, forced upon him by fear of his pursuers? Or was his a migration of choice, an act of escape from a country he has lost touch with, in which he can no longer lead a normal life?

It could well turn out that, through electronic migration, he has unintentionally set a new trend, a reverse migration in reaction to the takfiris' success in imposing their belief system on society.

"Come here right this moment, you damn bitch! There's a customer on his way. You need to get ready. You should thank your lucky stars that men show interest in you, even though you look like that horrible American woman."

The Cerebellum bursts into laughter, for the nth time in the past few days.

"All you have to do is nod . . . and tomorrow the best cloak in the country will be yours." The whore stands up and takes the soda case with her. In a second she is gone. Yet her erotic scent lingers, hovers like a mystical spotlight, exposing the world's lies, bringing out into the open all that is hidden.

Charlotte, North Carolina
Wednesday, January 10, 2007
1130 EST

Martin starts a new game of FreeCell. He moves the display from the laptop to the central screen on the wall. It relaxes him to see the gigantic playing cards spread out before him. This game is not just a pastime. It's a school of philosophy, in every sense of the word. That's why it requires a clear mind and crystal vision. But where is he supposed to get a clear mind after spending the night tossing in bed, conjuring sleep but never finding it? In front of him on the counter is his coffee mug, next to two cans of Red Bull, all empty. His eyes are wide open, thanks to the triple dose of caffeine, but his thought process is erratic.

Today is little Amy's fifth birthday. But he's stuck with the morning shift all month, and never gets home before eleven. He won't be able to share his little girl's special moment, and all because of Command's incompetence. Until now, they have failed to find a replacement for the agent who vanished without warning. But he doesn't know who to blame or where to lodge a complaint. Who is this Command that is responsible for recruiting staff for the Ghost Center, anyway? Martin tries to control his anger and relegates the whole thing to the back of his mind. He tries to focus on FreeCell.

The game starts with the cards scattered randomly. The objective is to build them up in four columns, one in each cell, from ace to king. To free the required card, the player is allowed to move them around, provided they're arranged in columns alternating between black and red. Martin reminds himself that FreeCell is a miniature model of life. It sums up the struggle waged by humanity from time immemorial to extricate order from chaos.

"Civilization is defined by the capacity to impose your will on everyone and everything around you," he says out loud, then starts to move the playing cards. "To impose your will on everything . . . people, animals, plants, even inanimate objects." He spreads his arms to demonstrate the extent of the mission.

The first lesson he's learned from FreeCell is that the difference between success and failure depends on arranging the cards in the right order. Your life or death hangs on whether or not you make the right decision at the right time. And, of course, Lady Luck must smile upon you. That's because luck and planning are mutually dependent; it's impossible to determine when one starts and the other ends. The second lesson is that the more successful the player, the better he's cushioned against failure. Simply put, the player's gains allow him to withstand the consequences of his mistakes and still stay in the game.

"Staying in the game is the secret to success," he tells the screens in front of him, then continues in a more oratorical tone, "The rich get richer while the poor get more and more mired in debt, and the same applies to nations. Empires can make tactical mistakes and still come out victorious in the end . . . and the biggest proof for that is —"

He stops in mid-sentence.

He was about to cite the United States as a case in point. Despite its many mistakes, it continues to be top dog. But he can't completely rule out the possibility that Command is recording everything that goes on in the Center. He certainly can't risk someone wondering about his loyalty.

"This is COBRA 1 speaking. Have reached the theater of operations. Will proceed to install equipment." The voice comes to him across the loudspeakers from thousands of miles away, as though to demonstrate that, despite all its mistakes, America continues to rule the world.

In a matter of minutes, the left-hand screen shows the image from the camera that Unit 1 has just installed. It's a frontal image of the headquarters of the guys who facilitated Mickey Mouse's escape. Because it is taken by infrared camera, its colors shift to green. Though it's a bright day in North Carolina, it's already night in the Middle East. As for the satellite image that has remained on the right-hand screen for the past thirty-six hours, it shows a number of scattered buildings surrounded by vegetation. There are rows of trees surrounding both the outer perimeter and the main building.

The new image only shows the entrance to the farm. It is protected by an enormous gate adorned with sculptures of horses in different positions. On both sides of the gate there are fortress-like rooms with small openings, whose obvious function is to facilitate the farm's defense with firearms. This is an important piece of information. Nothing to worry about, though. His guys—three units made up of seven well-trained agents, who have just arrived at the theater of operations—are capable of handling almost anything. The image shifts to one side, then the other. The agent tries zooming in and out, but the camera must be fixed to a tree or a light pole. Their guy is probably just testing the equipment by remote control from inside the vehicle.

"COBRA 2 speaking. Will leave the vehicle and proceed on foot."

The image immediately shifts and focuses on Unit 2 as they cautiously move to the right, just outside the farm's perimeter. Its three members are dressed like farm laborers. Martin catches his breath. This is an extremely dangerous stage. The camera that Unit 1 has just fixed stops following the agents' progress. Instead, it scans the farm's interior to ensure that Unit 2 hasn't been detected. Martin concentrates on the satellite picture. Despite the absence of color, he can see clearly. He doesn't notice any unusual movement inside the fence. Since the start of their satellite surveillance, Martin has detected six individuals inside the farm. Two guards with automatic weapons are permanently based on the roof of the main building. Right now, they're chatting in the corner farthest from Unit 2. Martin can also make out that they are smoking.

In the movies, the bad guys always smoke. And the good guys too—especially in the oldies. It was the silver screen, after all, that inflamed his imagination, catapulting him into a career in intelligence. His dream had always been to be sent to Casablanca on a mission, to put on Bogart's smoking jacket and frequent the hottest nightspots, hoping for an Ingrid Bergman to show up. To match wits against unforgettable characters . . . but certainly not to spend his life in front of a computer screen.

"COBRA 3, start distraction maneuver. COBRA 2, remain at the base of the tree until COBRA 3 has taken up position." Dangling a ball-point pen from the corner of his mouth, he whispers into the mike in a husky Bogie imitation.

Unit 3, on the motorbike, is evidently struggling against the field's uneven terrain just outside the left-hand fence—the one closest to the two armed guards on the roof. Martin follows their progress on the satellite image because they're out of range of the ground-based camera. Finally the bike comes to a standstill at the point closest to the guards. The objective is to divert their attention from Unit 2. The bike's headlight is on. The two agents will pretend they're having engine trouble.

"COBRA 3 speaking . . . distraction maneuver in progress."

After a few tense moments, Martin gives Unit 2 the all-clear. With lightning speed, one of its members starts to climb a tall tree just outside the perimeter. The frontal camera quickly scans the garden inside the fence. It reveals no enemy personnel in the area. The picture goes back to the agent on the tree. He has reached a high point and is starting to attach his equipment. Darkness provides an element of protection, yet climbing trees in the dark is no stroll in the park. Once he has secured the camera, he'll fix the microwave gun that is used to bounce waves off the windows and thus enable their computer to eavesdrop on voices inside the building. Then he'll install a heat-sensitive infrared sensor that will locate the positions of all personnel. Everything is going according to plan. Martin's heart beats like a drum. His eyes are glued to the satellite image. It is vital to ensure that the two guards remain on the far side of the building. Even in the seclusion of the Ghost Center, he's finally getting his share of suspense. All he needs now is for Ingrid Bergman to show up.

Suddenly, the door of the main building is thrown open, casting a long triangle of light upon the garden. Three armed men come out. Martin's heart misses a beat.

Could the farm be equipped with surveillance cameras? The satellite image doesn't provide an answer. The agents would have sounded the alert if they'd spotted any cameras. But he knows, only too well, how easy it is to hide a camera. The agents' lives may be at risk. The success of the entire operation is now in the balance.

"All units, Code Red. Repeat, Code Red. COBRA 2, take a protected position and freeze. COBRA 3, intensify diversionary action and keep me posted!" Martin shouts into the microphone, allowing the pen to fall from his mouth.

A timeless, charged moment follows.

Martin can't tell exactly what's going on. The technology simply won't come to his rescue. The satellite image shows people reduced to symbols: a circle for the head embedded inside the shoulders' rectangle. Rifles and machine guns are thick black lines. The members of Unit 2 have disappeared among the vegetation and are indiscernible in either the satellite image or the frontal camera's picture. Whatever happens, they're trained to defend themselves. However, the man hanging from the branch is in danger, there's no denying that. Moreover, the operation's value depends on its secrecy. If word got out, the whole thing would be deemed a half-failure, even if its objective were met. The three armed men turn right. They're moving toward the distraction team. A sigh of relief escapes Martin.

"COBRA 3 speaking . . . distraction operation is going according to plan so far." The voice reconfirms what Martin has just seen on the satellite image.

"COBRA 2, you may proceed," he whispers into the mike.

The farm's main building suddenly appears on the center screen, replacing his game of FreeCell. The tree climber has succeeded in placing the camera in a perfect position, exposing the larger part of the farm.

"COBRA 3 speaking . . . distraction operation approaching Code Red . . . request permission to abort before armed elements can surround us . . . I repeat, request permission to abort."

"Permission to abort granted, COBRA 3. I repeat, withdraw immediately," Martin orders through the mike.

"COBRA 2 speaking . . . mission complete, we're ready to withdraw." The voice of the agent, whom he doesn't even know, sounds sweeter than a Diana Ross ballad. On the screen he can see the members of that team rushing to their car.

"All units return to base immediately. Thanks, guys, for a successful operation." Martin smiles at the three screens in front of him. What d'ya say to that, Bogie?

At last the farm is under surveillance, which, of course, includes eavesdropping on all communications and conversations between group members in and around the building. It's only a matter of time before they identify the organization's leaders. However, chances are it's only a gang that doesn't answer to any government.

Martin is overcome by a sense of relief. But his euphoria quickly dissipates when he remembers his beautiful Amy. What's the use of success if a father can't be around to celebrate his little girl's birthday? What good is a job that doesn't provide the most basic working conditions? Is he making all these sacrifices out of sheer patriotism . . . or because of a deep-seated desire to control the lives of others? Who makes the decisions to assassinate foreign scientists without a trial or even credible evidence of wrongdoing, anyway? Is there really a legal or moral basis for their operations? Who will take the blame when all is said and done?

Would Bogart tolerate any of this?

How could he ever face Amy if all this were to become public knowledge? What would he say to her if his photo appeared on the front page, next to the serial killers and dirty businessmen? But he knows, only too well, that that would never happen. He's a ghost among ghosts, nameless, faceless. If he makes one slip, he's more likely to become another missing person, or an unexplained drowning victim. He's not just another employee, he keeps reminding himself. He's not allowed to complain or even to quit. Hesitation and doubt are a luxury he can't afford. He willfully entered into a Catholic marriage with the kind of agency that neither recognizes morality nor respects the law. He's a liar among liars, a thief among thieves, a killer among killers . . . so he'd better stop whining like a baby. After a moment's contemplation, Martin returns to his postponed game of FreeCell.

chapter 6

Giza, Egypt
Thursday, January 11, 2007
Evening

The Cerebellum stands in the middle of the room with both arms crossed over his chest, like an Egyptian mummy. Before him, on the bed, is a traditional brown cloak embroidered in gold thread. He has spread it out over the blanket to take a better look at it. The contrast between its fine soft wool and the coarse, worn-out blanket could not be more pronounced. It must have cost Zakzuka an arm and a leg. But if he decides to wear it, where will that take him? This whole story stinks from the start. He smiles; at least she did not get him a traditional wedding sheikh's costume, the ones they wear in old movies.

He carefully picks up the gown and slips it on over his only suit. The gray suit that, he remembers with chagrin, had been so elegant in its day. He squeezes his slim body between the table and the window in order to see his reflection in the half of the window frame that contains a glass pane — the other half is blocked by a sheet of plywood. He buttons the jacket. His shirt, beneath it, is crumpled but clean. In a neighborhood populated by panel beaters, pickpockets, and whores, he must look pretty respectable. If Condoleezza and her customers are looking for someone to bestow a modicum of legitimacy upon their illicit activities, they have found themselves the right man. And he really has no choice but to go along with their devious plan, if he wants to stay in his hideout, pay the rent and Internet bill, and be able to afford his bare survival needs. To say nothing of the new burden placed on his shoulders: the responsibility to save innocent, beautiful Didi.

Well, there is no such thing as a free lunch. At least it is going to be interesting. He stumbles from one interesting experience to another, while all he ever wished for was peace and quiet. That is the story of his life. He is the kind of person who climbs out of a hole only to fall into a well, as his mother, God rest her soul, would say. Luckily, by now, he has liberated himself from all ambition, and even from hope, and has shrugged off regret. What use are any of them, anyway? He has learned to take the blows life throws in his direction in stride, even with serenity.

In the end, the Cerebellum decides to remain bareheaded. He will never claim a religious role. After all these years, he simply refuses to turn into a charlatan. He is a businessman, no more. His role is to provide a product; a service that, unfortunately, is in demand these days. He is an existentialist philosopher at heart, a secular Sufi floating on life's ocean, as he likes to describe himself.

As he contemplates his reflection in the windowpane, he remembers his father's sinewy figure, in his preferred form of dress for the summer: white underwear. He was the exact opposite of his mother, who would never allow a soul to set eyes on her unless she was fully dressed, makeup and all. The Cerebellum recalls the expression on Umm Suad's face, the day she came from her village to visit her daughter, the little housemaid. His father opened the door in his underwear— not a farmer's modest undershirt and long johns, but a foreigner's sleeveless undershirt and briefs. Although he welcomed her and asked her in, the good woman's face adopted an expression of amazement, quite funny really, which did not leave her until she had gathered her daughter's belongings and pulled her away by the hand, never to return.

His mother loved to cook. He can see her now, standing right there, in her navy-blue dress with the white spots, protected by her pink, delicately embroidered apron. "I'm on fire, my love, I'm on fire," she sings softly. What a chic way to fry onions! The best perfume can never compete with the aroma of his mother's frying onions. Even her housekeeping chores she fulfilled with ease, when it was necessary. She reminded him of Zaynat Sidki playing the maid—or 'camarera,' as they say in old movies—humming and barely touching the fancy furniture with her duster, like it was the world's most enjoyable pastime. What his mother hated most, though, was to hang up the laundry to dry in the balcony. She thought it was beneath her; it made her look bad in the eyes of the world. Soon, hanging the clothes to dry became the maid's primary duty.

That is why his father's insistence on donning nothing but his underwear all summer nearly brought down the family. Not that the lady of the house objected to her husband making himself comfortable in his own home, but this habit led to the disappearance of a succession of little maids. His mother, of course, was a mild woman. But if she got angry, she got angry. If, for instance, the adolescent Cerebellum failed to promptly comply with her instruction to go to the market on an urgent errand, she would sulk for months on end, ignoring him as though he were not even in the room. Consequently, had his father not managed to contain the crisis—with uncharacteristic wisdom—by volunteering to take care of the laundry himself, things would have inevitably gone from bad to worse.

After all these years, whenever the Cerebellum remembers his father, he can only visualize him on the balcony with the laundry basket and a serious frown . . . and nothing to cover his bony figure—and his implausibly large sexual organ—but a sleeveless cotton undershirt and briefs.

But why must he revisit his childhood anxieties, right now?

As he presses the laptop's power button, it crosses his mind that he never asked any of his friends over to their home in Lazughli Street, not until his father had passed away just after he graduated from university. To be precise, he has spent most of his life imprisoned in a capsule. Maybe it was all to prepare him for this final stage that—however long it lasts—he will have to spend on the run, escaping from nameless satanic forces. He makes an effort to control his emotions. This is no time for memories. He needs to force himself to concentrate. At the very least, he must find a way to save Didi. Her nagging tragedy has brought to light a sense of impotence that has been building up in his soul, for years.

Perhaps there will be a reply from the "Doctor" in his inbox. As he waits for the Internet connection to load, he reviews his previous message to the gang boss. He has not received a delivery failure notification, so it must have reached its destination. Its wording leaves no doubt that every effort is being made to put together the required sum. All he asks is reassurance that Didi is okay. He is happy with his cautious draftsmanship, which does not give away his identity. He signed off with no name, just "sincerely yours," because he knows that all Internet messages are closely monitored. Giant bots are constantly trawling the Net in search of their targets. After all, the World Wide Web is controlled by electronic intersections. All of these are managed by servers produced by U.S. companies. This makes it easier for U.S. intelligence agencies to monitor all the information that passes through them. The Cerebellum has no doubt that if he ever makes the mistake of posting personal information online, the hounds will quickly pick up his scent. Then it will be only a matter of time until they figure out his physical location. That is why he has taken care to create a new Internet address, exclusively for communications with the gang. But what is the use of all these precautions if he cannot establish contact with the gang to start with?

He feels lonely. His head starts to throb. A hammering headache is around the corner. He resists the desire to search for candygirl. Without her, his life is colorless. He might just as well admit it. His pulse pounds like inner drumbeats. He feels the dice in his pocket. Why does he insist on transferring the complexes of the material world onto virtual life? Is it not time for him to join the millions of others who are exploring new forms of relationships? But he is right to consider her liaisons a betrayal. Cheating is cheating, whether it happens in Egypt or Indochina. Betrayal is betrayal, whether it manifests itself physically or transpires across the ether. To be betrayed by those closest to you has been humankind's worst nightmare since it first walked the earth. Such fears can be erased neither by modernistic arguments nor by technological feats.

He has always thought of himself as a liberated man. Nonsense! He is trapped like everyone else. Caught in the octopus grip of the zeitgeist. What can be expected of a weary wanderer like himself, traveling the roads of modern Egypt—a country that has itself lost its way—when even outer space is full of potholes? He is a murky character from a Baselitz painting, a man turned upside down. He is a prisoner of the frame, driven by history. A faithful follower of the spirit of the age . . . and the age happens to be one that will leave a bitter aftertaste.

His heart's pounding intensifies. He has just received a message from an unknown sender. His finger trembles on the mouse as he clicks it open. Then he starts to read the very short message, all the time gulping for breath.

> Dear sincere friend,
> Your delay has led to a transfer of ownership. If
> you need to inspect the merchandise, I am attaching
> a video. Current price 200 grand.
> The New Owner

The words slap him in the face. "The New Owner," short and sweet, like poison. Decisive as a sword. There is one lingering hope: perhaps there has been a misunderstanding. After all, he could have received this message by mistake. It could be a bone fide commercial transaction . . . but the devil will just not leave him alone. Could beautiful Didi be this merchandise that the New Owner is referring to? Even worse, could the ransom have been raised to two hundred grand? How many scams would he need to pull, how much pimping, to make that kind of money?

He double-clicks on the attachment as nausea creeps up his throat.

He gasps at the sight of Didi at the center of the screen. Eyes glued to the image, he pulls out the inhaler. The girl's wrists are tied to the arms of her chair. Her eyes are blindfolded like an al-Qaeda hostage.

But she is holding her head up. She does not shudder in fear. She does not appeal for mercy. Captivity has not broken her. Every hair of his body stands on edge. Such recordings bring to mind bloody outcomes. He must prepare himself for the worst.

A fat man's back appears in the picture. His body eclipses most of Didi. This is definitely not one of the guys from the Pajero. He starts to talk to the girl, but the Cerebellum cannot make out what he is saying. His head is perfectly bald. He probably shaves it every day. He bends over her. With a sudden motion, he rips off her red sweater—the one she had on the last time he saw her. Then he walks out of the frame, leaving the girl exposed to the camera, sheltered by nothing but her bra. Her delicate breasts tremble. He can see she is hyperventilating. Her skin is soft and pale like a baby's. A tortured moment passes. He is not sure if she will collapse. Cry out, Didi! Perhaps some noble soul will come to your rescue. Plead, my girl. Beg your captors. Maybe their hearts will soften. Instead, with a violent movement of her head, she spits straight into the camera. The laughter rolls off-camera, like a villain has escaped from an old Arabic movie and been reincarnated in this nightmare. This nightmare that has become part of the Cerebellum's new reality.

The recording stops.

The Cerebellum presses the replay icon but as soon as Didi's shackled image reappears, he stops the video. He just cannot bear to look any more. He never thought the gangster Doctor would be this ruthless. And he was actually pleased with himself for a cleverly drafted message. Every effort is being made to put together the required sum. How blind could he be? These people do not understand mere words . . . it is either the money or, as the bodyguard had said in the Pajero, "We'll sell the princess to one of those networks."

And now, all depends on him.

The Cerebellum's head is about to explode. A constant hammering sinks into his consciousness. Could it be the ring of his father's wooden pegs falling out of their cloth bag onto the balcony's dusty tiles? Or is this the rhythm of Latin music, filling up his world with joy, as he swirls in a liberated dance with candygirl? It takes him a few moments to regain his composure, then he turns toward the door. But he realizes the knocking is not coming from there, but rather from the floor. Then he remembers the deal. It must be his friend, the U.S. Secretary of State's lookalike, knocking on her ceiling—probably with a broomstick. She is giving him the signal to put on his new cloak and come over to her room to perform his new duties.

Giza, Egypt
Saturday, January 13, 2007
Evening

The atoms that make up our bodies were formed in the crucible of the stars.

The Cerebellum purses his thin lips in a semi-successful attempt at whistling. From the glassed side of his window, he contemplates the night sky. A triangular patch of clear sky is visible from his vantage point, underlined by the dark, ugly buildings that watch over the alley like weary ghouls and the interweaving wires that carry the electricity, telephones, and of course the Internet, thus bestowing a grudging legitimacy upon the slum. The stars, however, have been blurred by the smog that has gripped Cairo by the eyes and lungs. It occurs to him that the farther out he looks into space, the deeper he is diving into the distant past. The echoes of the Big Bang that has brought our universe into existence still reverberate out there, among the farthest galaxies that we can now observe with our state-of-the-art equipment. But we are not sure they are still out there by the time we receive the light emitted by them. For all we know, they may have ceased to exist before Adam walked the earth. Even without advanced telescopes, we can still detect the echoes of the Big Bang in the static that disturbs us from time to time when switching radio and TV channels. The Universal Background Noise, they call it. The noise with which the world persistently bombards his tired old mind.

His body feels heavy, as though his blood has turned into molten lead. The sight of little Didi being abused has poisoned every cell in his body. The Cerebellum feels surrounded by noise from every direction. But it has become impossible to distinguish whether it originates from the external world or from within, from nearby or far away, if its source lies in the material world or in virtual reality. It is even beyond his reach, now, to tell if these echoes come to him from the hostile present or from the past that refuses to be stowed away.

He welcomes Tahir's polite knock and heads to the door. He needs the young man's reassuring smile today.

"What's up?" The young man greets him in his generation's language.

"You come at just the right moment. I was pondering an important question. Would you be willing to lend me your thoughts?" The Cerebellum goes to prepare tea.

Tahir half-reclines on the bed, supported on his elbows, and waits.

"Would you be so kind as to point out the three most important theories the twentieth century has contributed to science?" The Cerebellum leans forward against the barrel to fill up the kettle. The water level is low and dozens of dead insects are floating on the surface. He fills and empties the kettle a few times, till the water is clear enough to use.

He has been sloppy these past few days. He neglected cleaning and ventilating the room, filling up the water barrel, and emptying the bucket. Until recently, he considered these daily chores to be sacrosanct. The disruption of his rituals has helped to amplify his anxiety.

He takes Tahir's silence to mean he expects further elaboration.

"The twentieth century surpasses all preceding ones in two accomplishments: the scale of its wars and carnage, and its significant contribution to science. Now, what are its three most important theories in mathematics and physics, the ones that will ultimately affect the progress of civilization?"

"The theory of relativity," Tahir says.

"Precisely. In other words, time itself is no longer constant. If one person stays still, while another travels at high velocity, the traveler will age more slowly. What else?"

"Quantum mechanics." The young man is starting to get bored.

"Excellent. In other words, tomorrow, you could wake up on Mars. One more . . . you still need to come up with one more theory."

The young man is not making an effort. There is something on his mind. Or several things. Anxiety, fear, and stress: the afflictions of modern man. A sense of insecurity. This is what humanity has been left with, after the twentieth century succeeded in shattering—with hard scientific evidence—every possible form of certainty.

"Chaos, you wunderkind . . . chaos theory!" the Cerebellum shouts. He starts to laugh nervously.

Three theories, each, on its own, capable of shattering the static world-view that has for thousands of years provided people with a sense of security, in the face of the unknown. All three have now combined forces to bring humanity's towering temples to ruin . . . and the last of the three theories, in his view, is by far the most eloquent in describing the march of life.

"The brain itself functions according to chaos theory. Even the human heart beats chaotically." He hands the glass filled with tea to the young man, then sits in his unsteady chair.

He studies the kid's face, hoping for a reaction to his evocative statement. But he looks completely glum. No wonder. Here he is talking his head off about chaos theory from a purely theoretical perspective, while, ever since he was born, Tahir's life story has been nothing but chaos.

Chaos is the one fundamental truth. Everything else is a mirage. Science has proved that for us. It has mercilessly chased away our illusions. Then why does it come as a surprise when the twenty-first century kicks off with the total rejection of scientific method? The revolt of certainty against doubt. Take us back to the days of witch doctors. Whatever you do, do not just leave us out there to face oblivion, on our own. Osama bin Laden, Pat Robertson, Jean-Marie Le Pen . . . these are the men of our times. Modernism has run its course and now we are back to square one, to prehistory, to the time before certainty, before humanity developed a sense of security. Now, people have no choice but to regain control, withhold their trust in reason, abandon science, ever confused and confusing.

Science is a boat, and every boat is destined to sink. Right, Tahir? But no. Not you. You are innocent . . . free of such thoughts. We are all sinking except you, Tahir . . . except you and Didi.

"Do not worry about all that, Tahir. With all your intelligence and sincerity, you will not be staying here for long. Soon you will be crossing Sudan Street to Mohandiseen . . . or maybe you will get yourself a villa in one of those new gated communities, in the suburbs."

The kid turns to him, as though hearing him for the first time today. He takes a moment to reflect, then replies in his calm, confident voice: "And what good would it do me to move to any of those places, Mister Poetic Genius? So long as there's one single slum in the country, then the whole of Egypt is living in it. Anyone who thinks a locked door can protect him, or that a high fence will make his kids safe, is living in a dream. One of these days it will all blow up in his face."

The boy's words shake him like an earthquake. Here he is, talking theories while Didi is eyeball to eyeball with the most unscrupulous of criminals. No, animals. And while he is doing his best to escape this painful reality, burying his head, like an ostrich, in the sands of mathematics, Tahir confronts life's lances and arrows with his bare chest.

The Cerebellum takes two steps toward his jacket, on a hanger suspended from a nail in the wall. He quickly dips two fingers into the breast pocket. He is perfectly aware of the risk he will be taking by revealing his secret to the boy. But his instincts tell him the kid is to be trusted. In any case, he stands no chance of freeing Didi without Tahir's help. He picks up one of the gold guineas, but it slips between his fingers. The coin hits the dusty floor tiles with a ring. The kid picks it up and takes a good look at it before returning it to the Cerebellum.

"What do we have here?" Tahir knits his brows.

"Do you know anything about coins, Tahir?"

The Cerebellum studies the coin for the first time. It has the luster of pure gold. It is not a guinea, as he had assumed, but an Islamic coin. It is inscribed in three concentric rows of Kufic script.

"To be honest, not really. But I know someone who does."

"An expert?" the Cerebellum asks, still contemplating the coin. He can barely make out the inscription: "There is no God but God and Muhammad is his prophet."

"He owns a shop in Zamalek that sells stamps and rare coins . . . they call him the Señor."

"I bet this is gold," says the Cerebellum slowly. "If it wasn't for the shine, I would have even said an antique."

Tahir takes the coin back. He bites it between his molars, then looks at its rim.

"Exactly . . . gold. But you didn't say where you got it from."

"Well, it is a long story. But what matters is, it could get us some real money."

The plan is starting to come together. For the first time since he was forced inside the Pajero, he is starting to see some light at the end of the tunnel. Finally, he stands a chance of ending this crisis that Didi has gotten him into. Then he can put his life back together again. Perhaps even find a way to resolve his problems with candygirl.

"If it turns out to be ancient, it could be worth a fortune," the young man says with a sudden burst of enthusiasm.

The Cerebellum feels like hugging the kid. But he must control his emotions. He needs to be wary of this hope that is creeping into his heart. Danger is still lurking out there, and this boy could turn out to be a crook, after all. Besides, even if he does manage to put together the required money, there is no guarantee that he will be able to free Didi. He must get a grip on his emotions, right now. For Didi's sake. He must handle the entire situation with his customary calm.

"Listen, sir. Since the moment I came in, you've been subjecting me to an avalanche of questions. Now it's my turn. Can I ask you just one?" the kid says after reverting to his previous gloom.

"Of course, Tahir." The Cerebellum braces himself for a mathematical brainteaser that will allow him to show off his genius yet another time.

"Is it true that you and Condoleezza are now working together?"

chapter 7

Charlotte, North Carolina
Sunday, January 14, 2007
0900 EST

Working on Sundays is a curse. Not just occasionally to catch up on work, but every Sunday of every week. And not just Sundays, but Saturdays, Mondays, and every other day. With no holidays and not a single day off, with no end in sight. Even when you have the flu and are running a fever. It's merciless, really. Knowing everyone else is relaxing. The pious go to church. Regular guys just wake up late. Laze around with their kids. Cuddle the family dog. Go outside to mow the lawn if the weather is fine. Make love with their wives on a rainy day. That's the American dream that Martin misses so much. And to make things worse, he no longer receives fair compensation. No decent salary, not even opportunities for promotion. He's simply a cog in a giant machine that couldn't care less about what happens to people's lives. He does his job because it's necessary. Someone has to do it for life to go on. Like making sausages, sweeping the streets, or cleaning sewers. The kinds of jobs you know someone has to do, but you never imagined that one day, that someone would be you.

With heavy steps, Martin makes his way into the Ghost Center. He's getting more rebellious by the week. There are no signs of a third agent joining them anytime soon. His life is zipping away like an untied balloon, but he no longer dares to raise the matter with Alpha. His reaction is hard to predict, not to mention Command's response if they start to suspect he has doubts about the whole operation. Getting into this line of work is not easy. But getting out is even harder. It's akin to a Catholic marriage, or, to be more precise, it's like joining the Mafia or al-Qaeda. If he goes on pressing Alpha, he may get himself into very deep water. In fact, he's starting to wonder if his fat coworker can do anything to speed up the recruitment process in the first place. Who makes the decisions, then? And where the hell is Command physically located?

"Morning, Alpha." Martin hangs his coat next to his coworker's. Every day there are new stains on its brown leather. The jacket is starting to disgust him. He actually thinks he can discern a thin film of filth covering its surface: beer stains, ketchup, oil from French fries, grease from his Harley, and, to top it all, a blend of dirt, sweat, excrement, and stuff he'd rather not think about. He moves his blazer to another hook.

"An intriguing discovery . . . there are definitely lessons to be learned here," Agent Alpha replies with his mouth full. He's holding a big bag of fries. He doesn't even bother to look at him.

He waits for the man to elaborate. He may have detected a hint of blame in his tone. But Agent Alpha keeps quiet. His eyes are glued to the central screen. Martin approaches cautiously. It shows a plan of the farm. The buildings are yellow, the adjoining gardens pistachio green. Martin himself had designed this composite plan. The computer superimposes the information it receives from the surveillance cameras and infrared sensors on the satellite picture. Enemy agents appear as red dots. Right now, there are no green dots, which means that their own agents have returned to their safe houses. Alpha is wearing a knit cap like a rapper. His ponytail flows beneath it onto his back like a sparse red waterfall.

"Do you notice anything unusual, Agent Gamma?" he says without looking at him.

"Like what?" Martin wants to give himself some time to study the picture properly.

"Like the number of individuals inside the building, Einstein." The man's sarcastic tone is really getting on his nerves.

"There are only three individuals left. Yesterday there were six." Martin doesn't understand what his problem is. What's Alpha blaming him for?

He notices that Alpha has restored Mickey Mouse's photo on the left-hand screen. It's the same fuzzy profile, shot while the subject was in motion, that he's grown familiar with over the years. Beneath the photo, they've listed all the basic information available about him:

Name: Mustafa Mahmud Korany (believed)
Aliases: The Cerebellum
Nationality: Egyptian
DOB: March 7, 1955 (believed)
Academic qualifications:
-    BSc in civil engineering, specializing in reinforced concrete—Cairo University, 1977—highest honors
-    Masters of material engineering, Cairo University, 1979
-    PhD in reinforced structures, University of Cambridge, 1982
Professional activities:
-    Faculty member, Cairo University, 1982–87 (believed)
-    Professor, then head of construction engineering department, Baghdad University, 1987–99
-    Team director responsible for reinforced structures, Iraqi nuclear program, 1989–92
Current address: unavailable
Living family connections: unavailable
Friends: unavailable
Female/other sexual relationships: unavailable
Hobbies/activities: unavailable
Real estate/investments: account in Arab Bank, Dokki Branch—current balance: 0

There's nothing new there. Why did the darned Alpha want to put it up on the screen again? Is he trying to remind Martin that the subject they're trying to nail is smart enough to be nicknamed "the Cerebellum"? Or is this Alpha's convoluted way of saying they're back to square one, that all the progress of the past few days has gone down the drain?

"That's a good observation . . . there are indeed fewer individuals. But the problem is, no one left the farm, all night," Alpha replies sharply.

"Are you sure?" Martin stops short of suggesting that he may have dozed off during the night.

"I've gone over the DVR images a hundred times. Our equipment has not registered anyone leaving the farm, yet the number has decreased from six to three. It's confirmed." The fat man crunches his last chip, then crumples the empty pack and throws it on the counter next to his keyboard.

"So there must be a tunnel leading out of the farm. They must have used it to avoid surveillance." Martin talks slowly. He's just starting to grasp the magnitude of the problem.

"A clever remark. Maybe three or four days too late, though." A yellow smile flashes across Alpha's lips and quickly disappears. "Take a look at this."

Alpha points to the right-hand screen, which shows the satellite image in black and white. He clicks the mouse to zoom out so that the area surrounding the farm becomes visible. Then he moves the cursor until the arrow points to a small square next to a dirt road that runs parallel to the main road. He zooms in, and Martin can see it's a bamboo hut. The tunnel exit must be hidden in there.

"We're dealing with one hell of a criminal outfit," Martin says, after a long silence.

"Correct. Government agencies don't resort to such measures when operating inside their own territories."

"The gang's operations are none of our business, anyway. We're only interested in the Mickey Mouse link." Martin tries to downplay the setback.

"The bottom line is: we have no record of who came in and out of the farm in the past few days. Mickey Mouse will almost certainly have taken advantage of this period to cover up his tracks and go into deep hiding." Alpha grinds his teeth, ending the conversation.

The fat man gets up and heads for his worn-out jacket. Without a word, he disappears into the passageway leading to the outer apartment. Martin starts to pick up the crumpled plastic bags and empty coffee and soda cups. He throws all the trash into the bin in the kitchenette and comes back to wipe the counter with a moist sponge. He really can't bear to work in such a pigsty. He sits for a long time staring at the three giant screens. Nothing much is happening. All is quiet over there. Out of the left-hand screen, the Cerebellum sneaks a peek at him from the corner of his eye. The nickname 'the Cerebellum' reminds him of an old comedy called *The Brain*, starring David Niven. In the movie, the British actor played the role of a highly intelligent gang boss. Eventually, he became known as the Brain. The police even tried to calculate the size of the brain of someone this smart, and they concluded that he must have an oversized head and must therefore suffer from constant neck aches. They even suggested that he probably walked with his head tilted sideways. In his childhood, that movie gave him a million laughs in front of the TV. But today, he sees himself as one of those clumsy investigators whom David Niven made fools of.

He should have noticed that no one was coming in and out of the farm. It was his duty to organize better reconnaissance of the surrounding area. He should never have let the fat man catch him with his pants down. He bangs the table, shaking with rage. The entire operation is in jeopardy now. He doesn't really care if Mickey Mouse escapes assassination. The man no longer poses a direct threat to the United States or to Israel. Probably he never did. But what really irks him is that it was the son of a bitch who discovered the secret tunnel. Now, in his usual insolence, he has the opportunity to put the blame for their common mistake squarely on him.

But what's the link between Mickey Mouse and this criminal gang anyway? He's never been known to have links with organized crime, so it's unlikely that he's directly involved with them. There must be a missing link, then. If he looks hard enough, he'll find a go-between. And that person is the key to the success of the whole operation. It is that individual who allowed Mickey Mouse to escape, just when they were about to get him. If they fail to figure out who that person is, they'll never manage to locate and eliminate the subject. Would it be the old man with the funny hat . . . or someone else, even shrewder, who has managed to keep in the shadows all these years? How did all these people succeed in evading the watchful eyes and ears of Echelon, the spy network that can listen to an ant's footsteps in the farthest desert and the flapping of a butterfly's wings in the most impenetrable forest?

Martin plays the recording of the day they chased the subject and notices the girl who got into the Pajero with him. He freezes the frame and focuses the picture on her face. Then he runs it through the face-recognition software linked to their database. The amount of information in their database exceeds what is stored in all the world's libraries put together. Moreover, their network has access to all the world's known databases. In a matter of seconds, the girl's basic information is on the screen in front of him:

```
Name: Didi Shawarby
Aliases: unavailable
Nationality: Egyptian
DOB: November 21, 1983
Profession: actress—has played minor roles
Additional information: sister of Ahlam Shawarby, a
movie star murdered in 1999. Despite intense media
coverage, the case remains unresolved.
```

"No . . . she's not the brains behind all of this," Martin says audibly. Then he brings to the screen all the available shots of the old man with the hat.

Martin is surprised to discover that, despite having caught the man on tape more than once, he can't get a clear picture of his face beneath his Turkish hat. In place of his face, he only gets a blur. Some technical error must have occurred in the filming. Or does the man deploy top-notch technologies that can prevent the most advanced lenses from capturing his face? Who on earth possesses technologies more advanced than their own?

He repeats the attempt . . . same result.

Now he's completely perplexed. He can't find a logical explanation for all this. One thing's for sure: the American Empire's sense of uncertainty has not diminished after its victory in the Cold War. In fact, the feeling of impending danger surges with every increase in their financial and technical resources. In his mind, he compares the security agencies with a person obsessed with cleanliness who is, nevertheless, the first to fall sick. It's as if there were a law of nature that protects the weak from being completely wiped out. Or as if the planet were attached to an invisible but highly sophisticated gyroscope that always manages to maintain the balance of things. With brutal irony, fate plays with people's feelings. No matter how important they may think they are, no one gets any peace of mind.

Martin smiles and, without thinking, starts a new game of FreeCell.

Giza, Egypt
Monday, January 15, 2007
Evening

"God gave me one child who's brainless and the other with two brains," his mother shouted when her kids had given her all the aggravation she could take. She had just entered the kitchen and gotten the shock of her life. Akeel—his brother, two years his junior—had taken a raw chicken out of the fridge and started to take bites out of its leg. The Cerebellum, who was twelve at the time, just stood in the corner, smiling slyly. She snatched the chicken from Akeel and started to scold the Cerebellum, shaking the chicken as irrefutable evidence of his crime. The boy genius only replied that it had been scientifically proven that cooking food makes it lose much of its nutritional value. At this point, Akeel—who had Down syndrome—started cackling with innocent laughter. It was thus the Cerebellum's insolence that had prompted the mother to shout out her verdict, whose echoes would continue to surround him for the next forty years or so.

The Cerebellum smiles, shuddering on his loose-legged chair, in front of the laptop. He has lost touch with the world around him. He has never succeeded in defining the explosive charge that the simplest word can carry, its capacity to shake the most powerful of men to his core. By repeating her lamentation on more than one occasion, his mother had transformed it into another law of nature, giving it a place in the lexicon of mathematics, next to the dodecahedron, the fourth Platonic solid, the golden number Φ, and Pascal's conundrum: is $^{-1}/_1$ equal to $^1/_{-1}$?

His mother never mentioned her curse to anyone outside the family. From early childhood, the Cerebellum understood that Akeel was their most tightly kept secret. This, however, did not prevent his mother's curse from opening up a window in his overactive mind, through which a torrent of doubts found their way into his forming soul. He could not quite figure out if she was expressing relief that God had made up for the lack of intelligence of her younger son with the superior intelligence of the elder, or if her complaint was, in fact, a double one: that fate had burdened her with two kids, each flawed in his own way.

Whatever she had meant, what counted was that he, at least, was the official son, the one his parents were proud to show off. That status alone was more precious than all the world's tenderness. He existed, was a known and recognized entity, not one of life's ghosts who fill up people's homes, seldom to walk the streets, and when they do, remain unnoticed, condemned to live their lives voiceless, entering life's stage and exiting without leaving a trace. What exactly was the use of all the tenderness that both parents piled on poor Akeel, if they felt too embarrassed to admit that he even existed on the face of the earth?

The Cerebellum hesitates to press the computer's power switch. He has no doubt that candygirl is the only source of happiness he has ever known. But what she is asking is hard to accept. Not—to be honest with himself—because of her insistence on a new form of relationship, more liberated than anything his parents—God rest their souls—could have fathomed. But because, through that very insistence, she marks out the parallel world as fundamentally divergent from reality. She thus denies virtual reality the status of a comprehensive form of existence, reducing it to no more than another way to have fun. A new videogame, with the novel feature of allowing social relationships to develop among the players. In other words, the exact opposite of what the Cerebellum has been looking for: a dimension no less real than the world to which Saddam Hussein, George Bush, beautiful Didi, Akeel the idiot, and his fashion-conscious mother all belong to. One as tangible as the Mossad, the CIA, this house of prostitution and chicanery that he has adopted as his haven, the slum in whose folds he and millions of other souls have taken refuge.

Mechanically, he produces his two dice and throws them on the table . . . he anticipates, he hopes for . . . no. To be precise, he wagers — let us call a spade a spade — that he will get a 'dabbash' this time, meaning two fives.

Damn . . . a 'du yak,' the most miserable of combinations.

He recalls the disgust that would form on his father's face whenever he got a 'du yak' in the café. Wavering between life and death, suspended, as he is, in this surrealist place between an unbearable reality and a virtual world that refuses to materialize, the Cerebellum realizes, for the first time, how much he has loved that man. In spite of the emotional gulf that separated them until the end of his days, he adored his father. The Cerebellum attributes that gulf to the bitterness that filled the man's soul to the brim. The rage that put a distance between him and the rest of humanity, including his firstborn son — perhaps with the sole exception of Akeel, whose idiocy earned him a dose of tenderness that the man bestowed on no one else. The Cerebellum racks his brains, trying to remember if his father had ever put into words his perceived grievance, or if he had ever pointed a finger at the person responsible for it. But, in the attic of his memory, he cannot uncover a single instance of a grave injustice he had fallen victim to.

The man was always complaining, but the source of his angst never went beyond trivialities. He was a bureaucrat at the Egyptian Survey. Just another clerk, obsessed with some minor slight or other. Trivial matters, like the undersecretary commenting on his memo in red ink rather than blue, or one of his subordinates remaining seated when he came into the room, or the office boy delaying his tea in the morning. But the major elements of his life seemed to be—at least in the young Cerebellum's eyes—generally positive. The man who had started his life as a surveyor in Munufiya eventually found his way to Cairo, received consecutive promotions, and ended up claiming he was more qualified than a thousand engineers. In a matter of a few years, he had replaced his daily slog in the mud with a job delineating the boundaries of agricultural plots, spending a few hours behind a desk every day, signing documents. But rather than thank his lucky stars, he still kept repeating, day after day, "People with brains who can get things done can't get any respect in this country. They only value useless academic degrees."

True, the Cerebellum could never sympathize with his dad's grudge against the world . . . but how could he not hold the man in the highest possible esteem?

Through sheer intelligence and resolve, he had succeeded in breaking the vicious cycle perpetuated by generations of landless serfs, whose existence, for thousands of years, was defined by mud, bilharzia, and indigo gallabiyas. He managed to take his family many steps up the social ladder, to the class of clerks and clerics. The man spent a lifetime challenging the whole world, in a million different ways. There is no denying that. Not least of which was his unfortunate tendency to expose himself in his underwear to the public. But at the critical moment, he did grasp his wife's phobia and did not hesitate to relieve her of the chore that weighed heaviest on her heart.

The world shakes violently around the Cerebellum. He comes out of his reverie in stages. It takes him some time to realize that the source of the noise is a violent knocking on his door. Could the cops have come to arrest him, now that he has joined the long queue of con men that has filled the country? Or have enemy agents at last uncovered his hideout? Then he hears the feminine voice that he is starting to grow comfortable with, despite all his reservations about its owner.

"Holy Sheikh . . . Mister Poet . . . open up, good sir . . . I'm almost out of breath." Condoleezza's voice is uncharacteristically perturbed.

As soon as he opens the door she rushes inside. In unmistakable exhaustion, she throws herself on the bed. The Cerebellum freezes. Her decision to enter the room points to some catastrophe that must have happened. He dare not shut the door and offend her religious sensibilities. Yet he is worried that someone may be following her. What if their safety requires the protection of a closed door?

She starts to sob loudly. As she shakes, the bed's loose springs squeal intermittently. She gestures to him to close the door.

After sliding the bar across, he instinctively takes a step toward her. He wants to take her in his arms, to comfort her. But at the last moment he hesitates. He would not want her to misinterpret his intentions. By allowing herself to be with him in the same room, she is seriously compromising her principles. She would not have done this unless it was absolutely necessary. Besides, he is so perturbed by her behavior that he has lost the capacity to comfort anyone. Dark thoughts race through his mind unchecked. Will his end come at the hands of pimps and charlatans, in a part of the city whose existence the state does not even recognize to begin with? And what about Didi? What will become of her? After all, he is now her only hope of survival.

More importantly, what about candygirl? The mere thought that he may never see her again is unbearable.

The Cerebellum admits to himself that he is more upset by the loss of the quiet existence he managed to achieve after years of suffering than by any direct threat to his life. Chaos always wins. Entropy will ultimately drown the universe. Loudness has successfully invaded his solitude. Everything has been suddenly thrown into question.

He controls himself with some difficulty. Then he heads for the teapot. The tea ritual has become his main channel of communication with Condoleezza. Despite their relationship, which is growing by the day, he is still denied the opportunity to identify her moods from her facial expressions. For the thousandth time, he curses the damn veil.

He hands her the steaming glass. She stops sniffling. Tea always has a magical effect on her. She rests the glass on the floor. The taste of tea is more eloquent than any possible words of comfort. Its tang on his tongue calms him down, too. Then, he notices brilliant red spots on the floor tiles, tracing her footsteps to the bed. Drops of blood. Condoleezza was bleeding when she came in. She is probably still bleeding as she sits in front of him. The glitter of blood merges with her usual smell of hormones. Today it has gained a new note. The scent of fear and anger floats on the waves of her cheap sensual perfume.

"What did that brute do to you?" he whispers.

He is shivering all over. A little while ago, he married her to a stocky, middle-aged customer, a steel merchant from Bulaq. He conducted the ceremony according to the rituals he has, by now, perfected. First of all, he held Condoleezza's hand in his left and the customer's thick hand in his right. The man's palm felt rough, like the steel rods he handles every day. He asked the customer, in the classical language, how long he wanted the marriage to last. The man chose a whole hour rather than the usual thirty minutes. Then he turned to his partner and asked her to name her dowry and postnuptial settlement. She insisted on a hundred pounds and not a piaster less. When the customer nodded—with a face that displayed the sexual fervor of an aroused bull—the Cerebellum asked him to look at his watch and indicate the time to the minute and second. Then he announced that they were married until precisely 22:33:40 on Monday, January 15. The Cerebellum had derived some comfort from avoiding the use of Qur'anic verses in the ritual. In his descent, he has not quite hit rock bottom.

"Thank God my face is covered and no one can see the bruises. He said, 'Aren't we married? Well, this is what married men do to their wives,'" She talks calmly, then, in her funny way, takes a sip of tea from behind the veil.

"The bastard," he mumbles.

"Is it true, Mister Poet?" She holds the glass with both hands, as though she is searching for some warmth in this universe, whose every corner emits cold.

Did you not know, sanctimonious Condoleezza, that the average temperature of the universe approaches absolute zero?

"I have never been married," he replies absentmindedly. He resists the impulse to visualize the horrific scene she alluded to in her matter-of-fact way. The problem is, he has become an accessory to the crime. He can no longer apportion blame here and there. He has been denied the refuge that comes with the condemnation of others. He cannot even claim that the whole thing is none of his business.

"By God, this is *too much* to bear." She rubs her hips with both palms, like a peasant girl.

A fleeting smile crosses his lips. Her use of the English words "too much" has a comic effect. Master Shakespeare must be turning in his grave. Then the misery of the situation reimposes itself on his mood.

"Why don't you get yourself a God-fearing job and save yourself all this humiliation?" he says impatiently.

"After all the trouble we've taken, are you saying I don't fear God?"

Is it blame he detects in her tone, or is she just pleading for mercy? He is no longer sure whether Condoleezza is totally naive or if she is a mistress of deceit. Sure, they have agreed to call their operation "pleasure marriage," but everyone knows it is prostitution in disguise.

"You know only too well that this is fornication, a million times over." He preaches as if he were innocent, as if he bears no responsibility whatsoever for her activities.

"Half of Egypt is getting married this way, Mister Poet," she shouts into his face.

"That still does not make it right," he replies, decisively.

"Being half-blind beats being completely eyeless." She avoids looking him in the face.

"Why don't you get yourself an honest job, my girl? You gave Tahir a great haircut. You have talent. You would save yourself the humiliation. Nobody would do these terrible things to you. You would be much better off . . . rather than the costume you are wearing that makes you look like a witch." At last, the Cerebellum has put into words what he has wanted to say for years.

"I hope, good sir, you won't turn out to be one of those secular extremists the sheikh condemns to hell every Friday in his sermon."

The Cerebellum explodes with laughter. He wants to say he is a secular Sufi, not a secular extremist, but her silence brings home the terror of the situation. He chooses to keep quiet.

She goes on: "So, you'd have me turn into one of those girls parading down the street in tight jeans with their hair exposed for everyone to see? Do you realize that each time a man looks at them, a sin is counted on both their slates? How many sins would that make per minute, good sir? Or per hour? How many sins would add up in a whole day, or a month, or a year? What about a lifetime?"

The Cerebellum does not know how to react to this way of thinking. Her ability to resort to arithmetic in order to reduce the weight of her sins compared to ordinary women simply blows him away. According to her calculations, she is much less of a sinner than a perfectly chaste woman who bares her head. So Condoleezza, too, is attracted to the language of numbers. He knows only too well that whatever he says, she will not budge an inch. The magic of numbers will always captivate the human mind. He is surprised how profoundly mathematics has penetrated the human soul, even when it comes to the way common folks understand religion. She has reduced religion to an accounting system that she employs to maximize her gains and reduce her losses.

After a while, Condoleezza breaks the silence.

"The veil you're asking me to give up provides me with a sense of security that I need more than anything else," she says. "You just don't get it. What happened today is perfectly routine for someone like me, who's been abused by men since the age of twelve. It's not just the humiliation, the feeling that even your own body doesn't belong to you. What's worse is that there's no one there to protect you . . . there's no security. I want to feel secure just once in my life, Mister Poet."

The Cerebellum is dumbfounded. The truth is, he knows next to nothing about sex, or the horrible things people can do under the influence of their desire. His physiology has spared him this terrible blessing. Hormonal imbalance, the doctors call it. He can remember the parties his friends used to throw in his youth, usually in the rented apartment they nicknamed "the Blimp." Amid the roar of laughter, beneath an aromatic cloud of blue smoke, he used to contemplate this overwhelming sexual energy that motivated his friends. The extent to which their sexuality controlled both their conversations and their actions never failed to astonish him. It sometimes possessed them to the point of making them seem totally blind to reality. Even the extremist religious movement that was coalescing in those days was no less motivated by sheer animal instinct . . . the power of sexual deprivation. But he was spared all of this absurdity. He was free of its clutches, and thus capable of seeing things clearly. Is this genius or a lifelong curse? He has no idea.

"Do you need a doctor?" Now he is ashamed of himself. Instead of providing help, he has been blaming her.

She ignores the question. Her eyes are fixed on a dent in the wall, a superficial dimple where the paint has peeled off, exposing the ugly cement. He is not sure that she has even heard him. After a while, she speaks:

"My cousin raped me when I was twelve. I didn't dare say a word . . . what could I have possibly told my parents, or anyone else? Can you blame me for not bringing scandal to myself and shame to my family? Anyway, Father would have put the blame on me. I'm the one who'd have been thrown down the waterwheel well. I lived in fear. I felt totally ruined. When I turned fourteen, I ran away."

Condoleezza leans forward to pick up her glass for her last sip of tea. She talks in a matter-of-fact way, as though she was telling a funny anecdote or a piece of news she read in the paper, something concerning strangers. The Cerebellum's left foot is getting numb. He never takes off his shoes except when going to bed. The words will not come to his rescue. How dare he pass moral judgment on Condoleezza and her ilk, when he does not even belong to their world?

A violent quarrel erupts between two men in a neighboring building. The walls of these overcrowded dwellings are as thin as cigarette paper. There are no secrets here. Privacy is an impossible dream. A woman cries out, "Don't do it, Mursi. It's your father." Profanities are thrown in the air like a sprinkler irrigating a golf course. A child's wailing attacks him from more than one direction. A cocktail of sound from a thousand television sets surrounds the Cerebellum, penetrating everything and everyone like cosmic rays, putting into question the constancy of facts, and giving people a pretext to deny the scandals that their neighbors have overheard: perhaps the listener has made a mistake . . . was it not a rowdy scene from a sitcom?

"I cannot understand anything any more. Why do Egyptians behave this way?" The Cerebellum shakes his head.

"You'll never understand why Egyptians do the things they do, till you realize that we're a people who flog the victim and idolize the oppressor." She is a child, really, but she speaks with the wisdom of a sage.

Where did she get this penetrating vision that most intellectuals lack? His admiration for this poor girl has just grown a thousandfold.

"Would you like to rest here for a while?" he asks without thinking, then quickly explains, "I know I will not be getting any sleep tonight."

She says nothing. But suddenly she rises and throws the door open. Was she offended by his suggestion? Once outside, rather than turn right, toward the stairs, she heads in the opposite direction, to the bucket that he uses for a toilet and mostly leaves in the open air. He is a little embarrassed. It is not as clean as it should be. He suddenly becomes more keenly aware of the state of his room. The originally sky-blue walls have now faded. Time and abuse have left them stained and pitted with dents the size of golf balls. The light from the pitiful bulb that hangs by a wire from the ceiling barely scratches the darkness, turning the room into a playground for ghosts and shadows. A frosty jet of air, gushing through the crevices of the window's faulty sealant, stings the Cerebellum in the back of the neck. This volume, defined by walls, ceiling, and faded floor tiles, is quietly imploding. The whole world is caving in on him. From safe haven, his room has suddenly metamorphosed into a prison cell from which there can be no escape, except for his final procession to the grave.

After a while, she reappears in the doorway.

"Don't you have stuff to do on your computer?"

He is surprised by her question.

"Just so I can make myself comfortable," she explains.

The Cerebellum regains his seat, facing away from her. The screech from the rusty bedsprings confirms her decision to spend the night here. Almost immediately, he regrets having asked her to stay. He starts to curse his gullibility, but under his breath. Her story, her very existence, is an enigma. She is becoming too much of a psychological burden for him to bear.

Suffocation . . . the world is starting to run out of air. Coming from afar, a coarse voice approaches him. Sound bites from the doomed ferry's last moments, immortalized by the black box recording. Al-Salam '98. Words that reach him from the depths of the Red Sea.

"The boat is sinking, Captain."

The Cerebellum taps his keyboard and the world opens up before him, in the form of the clear blue screen. He throws the dice on the table three times as he waits for her delicious form to appear. Then he takes a deep breath and his pulse slows to normal.

All worries suddenly evaporate. His fears, failures, and aching conscience, his cumulative personal humiliations and his sense of national defeats are all washed away by the first electronic look from candy-girl's eyes.

chapter 8

Giza, Egypt
Tuesday, January 16, 2007
Dawn

> candygirl said: hi biceps i can t even start t tell u
> how much i missd u all week. d u realize this is the
> first time we ve been separated 4 more than a few
> hours since we met a couple of years ago

As usual, she is relaxing in her lounge chair. Her orange hair cascades over her breasts, intensifying their seduction. Her electronic figure is perfectly shaped, and, more importantly, eternal. She will never grow old or get sick. People know no fear here. They experience no stress, hunger, overeating, or stomachache. This place is anchored in stability. Everything is constant. What does it matter if its very existence is an illusion?

> You said: I have been thinking about you, every
> second. The external world's ugliness grows by the
> day. What is important is not to allow such trivial
> matters to come between us again.

The Cerebellum is surprised by his last sentence. He typed it without thinking. He did not say, "I forgive you for having brazenly betrayed me." He did not pretend to have misunderstood the whole thing, and that betrayal had never occurred in the first place. Instead, he accepted that betrayal is, in itself, only a trivial matter. His transformation was both radical and instantaneous. It came as a surprise, even to him. Burnt by life's brutality, he has suddenly become more liberated than the libertines. Which is just what happened to his neighbors and associates, all those who live here in these Cairo slums.

candygirl said: i was sure u d understand. wanna dance

You said: Dancing sounds good. But on the way to the club I would like to stop by the kids' slides.

The two avatars rise and leave the house. Side by side, they stroll down the square. Other couples are promenading by the fountain in the middle of the square. He can read snippets of their conversations before they wander off, outside the screen's boundaries. A man sweeps the marble floor, which was squeaky clean to begin with. On top of his head, the number of currency units he has earned so far is indicated in small letters. He does not talk to anyone.

You said: 1 on its own approaches zero, but 1+1 approaches infinity.

candygirl said: i love it when u use arithmetic 2 describe day 2 day stuff. u know how much I admire a smrt guy

You said: We are a perfect match, intellectually . . . not to mention our physical compatibility, of course.

candygirl said: i loved it when ya told me about the secrets of the pyramids. if I didnt know u r a professional boxer I d have thought u were maybe a math teacher or a physicist

The Cerebellum presses the chuckle icon. Biceps's electronic body issues a gurgling sound and shakes strongly.

You said: A physicist . . . how funny. You know, I got into a brawl last night. I gave the first guy three broken ribs, the second lost all of his front teeth . . . as for the third one . . . well, the poor guy got a concussion and was taken to the hospital in a coma.

candygirl said: wow u r so exciting. i ll let u in on a secret biceps. the one thing that arouses me more than ur math talk are the stories of ur fights with the bad guys. but what started the whole thing last night

You said: Well, I was on my way home after a wild night at the Black Cat. It was about 4:00 a.m. I decided to take a shortcut to where my Lamborghini was parked. As I was passing through a dark alley, I came across these three thugs trying to take advantage of a girl who was walking alone. I do not know what would have become of her if I had not appeared at the right moment. What is important is that I gave those three bad boys a lesson they will never forget.

The Cerebellum presses the laugh icon to emphasize his self-confidence.

candygirl said: wow u r my hero. wanna start a private chat

You said: Great idea. But as agreed, let us stick to
typing.

What scares the Cerebellum most of all is that she will want to
exchange pictures or videochat. So far, she has never asked for anything like that.

She opens a chat window and their electronic forms freeze. The
Cerebellum does not feel comfortable with this mode, despite the
privacy it affords. It partially removes him from the virtual world. He
resolves to get this conversation over with as soon as possible.

candygirl said: ya know i was just tryin out the stuff
i ll be wearing on the catwalk. that s why i m in my
baby dolls with nothing underneath

Her last sentence takes him by surprise. This is no longer an electronic
entity speaking. She is actually referring to her physical body, located at
a precise spot somewhere on the face of the planet. She is taking their
relationship to a new level, a step they have never even discussed before.
He shuts his eyes briefly, trying to imagine what she looks like.

You said: I can almost see you right there, in front
of me.

candygirl said: i want u to touch my skin. just slide
your fingertips over my leg. see. doesn t it feel like
warm butter

You said: I know you are a model and that you specialize in lingerie . . . but your beauty, as I imagine it, exceeds what is humanly plausible.

candygirl said: let me feel ur muscles. wow ur arm
feels like steeeel

Candygirl's laughter reverberates in the Cerebellum's ear. He is not quite sure where all this is leading. He has never before experienced sexual desire. Not once. However, he now feels a strange current flowing through his body. He is living a delicious adventure, albeit a risky one. He allows himself to be carried away by the current.

You said: You know, I spend at least three hours a day at the gym.

Feminine laughter materializes in a sensuous cascade all around him. Can this virtual girl succeed in waking up his instincts, despite the physiological dearth of male hormones?

"What are you doing, Mister Poet?"

A sudden headache grips the back of the Cerebellum's head. His skull will surely split apart any moment now.

"What are you doing, good sir?"

Like a merciless steel fist, the whore's voice draws him back to the ugly reality he has been trying so hard to escape.

Giza, Egypt
Tuesday, January 16, 2007
Morning

"Don't you have a radio somewhere around here? I like to listen to a song by Halim or Shadia or Fayza Ahmad before breakfast." Condoleezza's eyes are still sleepy.

She sits cross-legged on his bed in her flowing black gown, with both her face and hair exposed. Her features are delicate. There is an innocent air about her, despite the bruise that covers almost her entire left cheek, just beneath the eye. Her hair is erect like sticks of spaghetti, due to too much hair straightener. She rubs her eyes with her hand, still clad in a black woolen glove.

The Cerebellum smiles and shakes his head in apology.

"I guess it's better that way . . . Sheikh Abdel Muhsin—the Cub—says that singing is Satan's Qur'an."

Now she is wide awake. Furrows form on her young forehead. Her plucked eyebrows are knit together in concentration. Apparently she was not joking about what her young sheikh had said, so he decides to keep quiet.

Actually, a few moments ago, Condoleezza had caught him unawares, trying to flex his nonexistent muscles in front of the laptop. Despite his immediate confusion, he wondered if she had accidentally uncovered herself in his presence. She may not have been fully awake, and would hit the ceiling when she realized what she had done. He was about to warn her, but he was enjoying watching her facial expressions too much. It was a long-awaited pleasure just to observe her mood swings, as though she was influenced by weather patterns whose mysteries science had not yet uncovered. The truth is he had missed talking to her the way people talk to one another. So he chose to risk her anger rather than prompt her to re-erect the barrier that separates them.

But now that she is fully awake, he realizes she knows exactly what she is doing. He tries to explain her sudden reversal: first coming into his room, then spending the night on his bed, and now exposing her face and hair. He can only be suspicious of her intentions. Is she positioning herself for a renewed attempt at sexual seduction?

"Would you like some tea?" His question of last resort whenever he does not know what to say.

In any case, he is invulnerable to seduction. The low testosterone levels in his bloodstream have immunized him from all physical desire. Or perhaps this whole testosterone story is one big bluff, a crust of scientific terms that only describe the phenomenon superficially. Maybe his suffering is merely a symptom of an ailment of the soul, whose grip is more powerful than a deficiency in this hormone or that. Could his father's overblown masculinity—to the point of aggressiveness—be at the root of his problem? Maybe his disgust at the sight of the man, standing in his underwear in the balcony, went beyond his discomfort with what people would say. Perhaps his child's mind grew suspicious of the muted sounds seeping through the closed door of his parents' bedroom, sensing danger in what was going on in private, a frightening, repulsive activity he did not even want to imagine. For the rest of his life, he has chosen to burrow into the safety of virginity. Who knows what goes on inside people's souls, particularly in those early formative stages? Who can say which minor detail imprinted in a child's subconscious will forge his personality for the rest of his life?

As he rests the kettle on the flame, it occurs to him that people's fates have always been determined by the law of probability, like rolls of the dice he carries in his pocket. Had his father been more modest, he might well have grown up, like ninety-nine percent of young men, wasting ninety-nine percent of his thoughts on sex. Had the hormonal imbalance hit him in a different way—if he had suffered from a defective pituitary gland, for example—he would have become a giant. He smiles. Thank God for allotting him the lesser evil. If testosterone had flooded his brain, it would have flushed away any sign of genius, and had he grown up a giant, he would have found it all but impossible to successfully elude his pursuers.

The instant he hands her the hot glass, he is overcome by an urge to throw his dice. But as soon as he lets them loose on the metal table, he quickly pulls them away. He returns them to his pocket without finding out the result that Lady Luck has chosen for him.

"Have you ever been to Helvetia?" Again, Condoleezza's question catches him by surprise. He understands that she is referring to Switzerland. But why use the ancient name?

"Unfortunately, I have never been there."

"Which countries have you been to?"

"England." Why this sudden interest? he wonders.

"Fantastic!" Her features light up with a childish smile. "Then you must've met Queen Bess."

"Queen Bess?" he laughs.

"The pretty lady with the crown who's on all the English stamps."

"Do you get many letters from England?"

"I wish . . . but who am I to get letters from England, anyway?" She looks embarrassed. "Friends sometimes bring me stamps . . . I don't know how to say this . . . I'm really into stamps. I'm cooped up here in this tight place, yet they make me feel like I've traveled all over the world."

So Condoleezza is a stamp collector. Incredible.

He wonders what the cub sheikh would have to say about collecting stamps. Would he blast it as an ungodly innovation? After all, is the devil not the source of all innovations?

The Cerebellum says nothing.

She too must be desperate for human company. Apart from cheap sex with her customers—her husbands, as she frantically tries to call them—and her relationship of mutual exploitation with the Good Lady, she must need someone to spill her guts to, or simply to chat with like normal people do.

"What does it feel like to talk to me from behind the veil?"

In the past, he has been fixated on his own point of view regarding her veil. But what about her own angle? How does it feel to deal with others from behind such an impenetrable barrier?

Who knows, she may have shared his awkwardness all along.

"From my side, it's okay. The block is on your side. You were so distant. I felt you couldn't bear to look me in the face."

The Cerebellum feels like a cold shower has been suddenly let loose over his head. He does not know what to say, now that he realizes how much she has sacrificed today, just for his friendship. It is a favor he never asked for, does not deserve, cannot even repay.

Morally, Condoleezza has stripped herself bare for him. She never renounced her beliefs, but she made the decision to bear the consequences of breaking the rules, just for his sake. He knew her before she put on the veil. Seeing her face now is nothing new to him. In fact, she exposed much more than her face to him in the past, and offered even more. But all this was purely physical. Today she is exposing herself emotionally. He knows next to nothing about sex. Only generalities. He is quickly discovering that a sexual act is, at heart, the act of mutually exposing oneself. Revealing the most deeply concealed pains and desires. So the whore had, in fact, wanted to seduce him.

"It is true that God has denied women many of their rights. But they'll be more than adequately compensated in the afterlife," Condoleezza says after a long silence.

Then she takes a cautious sip of her tea.

He is not quite sure what she means. And what has all this to do with her decision to take her veil off today? It is as though she is trying to read his thoughts and then respond to them. Perhaps her line of work has taught her to uncover men's deepest secrets. But does she not realize that he is not like other men?

In the past, he has deprived her of her humanity. There is no doubt about it. He never once tried to see her side of things, or to sympathize with her unwavering struggle against a society that has grown accustomed to devouring her flesh. He had not even bothered to listen properly to what she was saying. Today he looks at her, sitting cross-legged on his bed, sipping her tea the way normal people do, without the need to slip the glass behind her veil. And he realizes that she is a true hero. She had to fight every step of the way. Even donning the veil in the first place must have taken enormous courage. The same is true now for removing it in his presence. In both cases, she stands accused. No matter what she does, she will always remain in the dock.

But realizing all this does not bring him any closer to her. It only redoubles his discomfort and shame. He is unable to build bridges right now. First, he needs to look inward, to understand what has happened to him. For the first time in his life, he has had erotic experiences: one a little while ago with candygirl, and now another with Condoleezza.

"God would never deny women any of their rights. That is why there is no question of some kind of blanket compensation for women in the afterlife. They shall be judged according to their deeds, just like men," he says with finality.

His embarrassment has quickly mutated into aggression.

The sharpness of his reply, in turn, intensifies his sense of guilt. She says nothing. Her eyes are distraught. The paint on the wall behind her is peeling off from the humidity. Its upper corner is discolored a disgusting algae green. Her silence is a dagger butchering his guts.

There is someone knocking at the door. For once, he welcomes an infringement of his privacy.

This erotic magic has worn him out.

Condoleezza rises with a burst of energy. She smoothes her gown with experienced fingers, and in a matter of seconds she has transformed herself back into a black unfathomable mass. She opens the door as if she were at home. For a split second she freezes, facing Tahir's tall, slightly bent form. Their glances collide. The Cerebellum thinks her body is shuddering slightly.

"May peace be upon you," she mumbles before disappearing.

"Sorry. I didn't mean to intrude." In spite of his faint smile, the young man seems perturbed today.

"Not at all. We were just chatting." The Cerebellum observes the mathematics student's face, trying to make out if he believes him.

The boy takes a quick look at the unmade bed. He knows only too well how strict the Cerebellum is about making his bed as soon as he wakes up, and how he keeps the black blanket he uses as a cover geometrically trim all day long, despite the pitiful state of its fabric.

"You could have fooled me," Tahir says with unmitigated sarcasm.

He remains standing there, obviously uncomfortable with the idea of sitting on the bed in its current state.

The Cerebellum recognizes the futility of trying to explain. In a brothel, it is absurd to waste time on such matters anyway. He offers him the chair and sits on the bed himself.

"So did you pull a lion or a hyena?" The Cerebellum finds himself echoing the expression he has been hearing over and over again in the past few days.

Didi's predicament remains in the back of his mind, buzzing in his subconscious, like an electrical drill applied mercilessly by an Iraqi militia member to his skull. The mess that girl has got herself into is terrifying and he certainly is no Superman, nor even Batman. The only remaining card he has up his sleeve is the gold coins, left him by an old man whom he is not even sure whether to count as human or jinn. But whoever made him responsible for the girl and her own folly? Where did this overwhelming sense of responsibility come from . . . especially to a man like him, who cannot even afford the luxury of walking squarely down the street, having to slither, instead, among the shadows? This is a complex problem. It has taken the shape of an Archimedean polyhedron. Perhaps the mathematics student has come up with a solution today. Who knows?

"You can package sunlight in bottles and sell it to gullible people if you please, but what I don't understand is why they keep on buying them? It's driving me crazy," the boy says, ignoring his question.

Despite everything, the Cerebellum still enjoys a good debate with Tahir. His intelligent and knowledgeable arguments are a rare treat in this decrepit neighborhood. In any case, he will go along with this conversation for a few more minutes. Soon the boy will be ready to reveal the results of his search for a buyer, and how much the gold coins will fetch. But whom exactly is he accusing of bottling sunlight?

"There is always a market for illusions," the Cerebellum laughs. Does he really need to remind the fortune-teller's son of that? "The universe is a cold and barren place. People are lonely and vulnerable. Most of the time they have no alternative but to seek refuge in myth and illusion."

Has no one taught him in college that the average temperature of the universe is minus 270° Celsius, barely three degrees above absolute zero?

"What about science?" Tahir is at that stage of his life when it seems that science can provide answers to all questions. He reminds the Cerebellum of himself in days long gone.

"Science is great. But it is not worth that much on the market." The Cerebellum reminds himself that he is a scientist after all, a genius. Had he been born in another country, he would be competing for a Nobel Prize. Imagine . . .

In the rush to escape his powerful pursuers, he almost forgot all that.

"And the truth? What about the truth?" The boy is either plain stupid or playing dumb.

"The shop that deals in the truth is full of empty shelves. Its display window looks fine, but it just does not have any goods to sell. So would its owner stand a chance of making a profit? The store that sells illusions, on the other hand, is packed with products, goodies that come in different shapes and colors, ready to wear and custom made. Everyone will find their size there. Its merchandise is marketable because it accommodates all our needs."

"Don't intellectuals bear a special responsibility?" Tahir must be intentionally trying to embarrass the Cerebellum. Or could he perhaps be expressing genuine concerns? The Cerebellum's remarks cannot possibly come as news to him.

"Let us stick to selling the coins, shall we? What is it going to be . . . a lion or a hyena?" The Cerebellum grinds his teeth.

"A lion, of course. And a really big one. But first, tell me this . . . is it true that you're playing the wedding sheikh these days?" The boy speaks quietly, but his voice carries a dangerous undertone.

Finally, the Cerebellum realizes that, ever since he entered the room, Tahir has not been talking about philosophical matters at all. He has been making specific accusations toward him. But what does he stand accused of? The kid's emotions must run deep. Could he be angry because he discovered Condoleezza in his room? What does that say about Tahir's relationship with the dark-skinned girl, who by now is the only prostitute left in this crumbling house? The Cerebellum is curious about Tahir's attitude toward the whores who practice their profession in his mother's house. Did he grow up demanding his right to "freebies," as Condoleezza likes to call them? Or did he shrug off the whole matter, considering them regular people performing regular jobs? Has he managed to compartmentalize the thorny issues of his life? Did he succeed in separating these women's professional lives — at least mentally — from his relationships with them?

"Some people speak loudly about principles, but when the time is right, they don't hesitate to prey upon these poor girls."

The Cerebellum does not know how to respond to this. He is fed up with human relationships and their inevitable complications. He misses virtual life, with its simplicity and clarity. Everyone lives on their own terms. Others can either accept him as he is or leave him alone. The whole game is being played out in the open, even betrayal. No one needs to make the mental effort to explain.

"By the way, I've moved into Samia's room. God blessed her and she moved away from this place."

The boy is referring to the room facing Condoleezza's. At the very least, he would be able to hear the comings and goings of the girl, her customers, and, of course, the Cerebellum. It would be futile to deny his involvement in the young whore's activities . . . as if denial ever solved anything.

"Like you said, God blessed Samia and she has left . . . but we are still here, and we need to survive," the Cerebellum replies after some thought.

After living in this place for so many years, it dawns upon him that an urban slum is fundamentally different from the village in a Yusuf Idris story or the alley in a Naguib Mahfouz novel. In fact, it is the exact opposite. Here, people are constantly on the lookout for an opportunity to escape. Their lives are transient, their relationships provisional. They have no roots in this earth. It is not just poverty and deprivation. There is no loyalty here whatsoever. Neither loyalty nor a sense of belonging. The millions who live in these slums are suspended in midair, with no future in sight. Escape is the ultimate definition of success. Just continuing to live in these places means you are condemned to a slow death. This makes the Cerebellum the perfect slum dweller. The only true existence he leads is inside his private, imaginary world. There is no future for him here, and no real relationships with those around him . . . and here he is now, letting go of his principles, losing his humanity inch by inch.

"I hope you don't think this is about jealousy or anything of the kind," the boy says, confirming the Cerebellum's suspicions.

He was mistaken to think that Tahir would never fall for one of his mother's whores. This inexplicable repulsion that places the world's oldest profession lower on the ethical ladder than a corrupt official or an incompetent bureaucrat who may wreck peoples' lives with a flick of his pen, this profound bias that remains at the heart of the Cerebellum's middle-class values, simply does not apply here. He was wrong to judge Condoleezza so harshly. She is a more credible human being than anyone he has ever known. Tahir must have seen this all along, to say nothing of her overwhelming feminine attraction.

"Jealousy would be completely out of place, because nothing has happened between me and Condoleezza." The Cerebellum rests the pillow against the wall to make himself comfortable.

"I've never blamed her for what she does. When all is said and done, she's a victim. At least she's trying to find God. But a distinguished poet like yourself . . . why would you want to take part in such a scam? That's what really bothers me." The boy shakes in the chair, whose creaking makes the Cerebellum wonder whether the rotting cane will hold, even though the kid is skinny.

"Condoleezza gives a great haircut. Did you know that? She stands a chance, after all, of quitting what she's doing and leading a decent life," the boy adds.

The kid's words hit him where it hurts. Now he stands accused of encouraging the girl to go on with her life of prostitution. Suddenly he is responsible for both Didi's and Condoleezza's fates, even though there is nothing he can really do for either of them. His predicament is no less severe than theirs.

"Are you insinuating that educated people cannot become victims, too?" the Cerebellum says.

He becomes aware of Condoleezza's earthy scent surrounding him. It will linger around his bed for days. After years in this house, can he mistake this overpowering perfume that envelops a faint mixture of sweat and female hormones?

"Listen, I don't know who you really are. But you're no poet. I'm not stupid. You're a world-class scientist. Still, you just don't get it. . . . I've struggled all my life to be like you someday. And I'm not alone. There are millions of young people like me out there. We consider education to be our road to salvation. Then you let us down this way. . . . What is it with you, exactly? Can't a genius like you tell that shattering people's dreams is worse than breaking their bones?"

The Cerebellum's body is covered with a cold sweat. He pulls the inhaler out of his pocket, but does not use it.

"I cannot begin to tell you how much hope you have given me, Tahir. I just could not believe that this environment was capable of producing someone like you. That is why I want you to never lose hope. If I made a mistake, it is because I had no choice. Time will reveal all. Just as I trusted you with the coin, you must now trust me. You must tell me the results of your inquiries . . . it is a matter of life and death. Not for my sake, but for a beautiful young woman. She is innocent, ambitious, and full of life, just like you." The Cerebellum's voice is choked with the emotions accumulated over his years of despair. He has been worn down by this responsibility that has been put squarely on his shoulders. Yes, Didi's fate has become an unbearable burden.

The boy stares at him with suspicion.

"The Señor wants to know what you did to the coin to make it shine this way," he says slowly.

"By God, this is how I found it."

"The Señor is quite sure it's genuine. He checked it under the microscope. How many more do you have?" Tahir is still scrutinizing his face, as though it may unwittingly reveal his secret.

The Cerebellum heads for his jacket without hesitation. He slips his fingers into the breast pocket and draws out the remaining coins. He piles them up in three rows on the table, next to Tahir's hand.

"They are ten, counting the one you have. I need a certain sum. Whatever you can get above that is yours." Now he has taken the risk and put it all in the boy's hands.

"And the money goes to the beautiful girl you've been talking about?"

"She owed someone a debt. Now they are holding her until they get their money back. A human trafficking gang. She has no one but me in the world. Now her life depends on you."

Tahir nods. He does not see anything unusual in this story. The Cerebellum starts to feel a little more confident. The boy has decided to trust him.

"I don't want any money for myself, but I, too, hope to save a certain girl. Although she may not feel the same way about me, I still consider her to be innocent, despite everything she's done." The young man's eyes flare up with unmistakable emotion.

The Cerebellum is not quite sure whether he is talking about Condoleezza or whether he has another lover who is also in danger of being swept away. This mighty river, whose torrents are getting more voracious by the day, is fed by multiple tributaries. It does not matter anyway. What counts is that love continues to resist. It pulsates in the heart of every living creature, no matter how cruelly fate has treated him, no matter how deep his despair. Only love can stand up to oppression. It elevates Tahir above the heaps of garbage, muddy alleys, and collapsing buildings. Yes, love . . . our last refuge.

Charlotte, North Carolina
Tuesday, January 16, 2007
0900 EST

The mess that welcomes Martin this morning is worse than usual. The fat man is rocking nervously in his chair. There is popcorn scattered all around him. A few of the flakes have actually stuck to the counter in a small pool of spilled Coke that, by now, has mostly dried up. Pizza crusts top the piles of empty cardboard boxes and Styrofoam cups. Agent Alpha acknowledges his arrival with a shake of his ponytail and a glance from his bloodshot eyes. Splashes of mustard stain his white shirt. The man is getting crazier by the day.

"Operation Mickey Mouse has reached Code Red," he calmly informs him.

"What happened?" With his eyes fixed on the screens, Martin sinks into his chair.

"Command is uneasy, particularly in light of the sophistication of the group that has facilitated Mickey Mouse's escape." Alpha points to the farm's satellite image. Now the picture is wide enough to include the cottage that houses the exit of the escape tunnel.

"Frankly, I've never really understood the importance of this Mickey Mouse guy. He's only a structural engineer, not even a nuclear scientist," Martin says as he starts to type on his keyboard.

He needs to review all the messages that have arrived throughout Alpha's shift, to get ready for the next step. It doesn't look like it's going to be easy.

"This guy is the world's foremost expert on reinforced structures. He's capable of designing bunkers hidden deep underground or inside mountains that can withstand our state-of-the-art bunker-buster weapons. If a certain country manages to take advantage of his skills, it could reverse the balance of power in the Middle East, particularly in the Persian Gulf area. We'd risk killing the goose that lays the golden egg. That's the nightmare scenario Command is starting to worry about, especially with this highly professional group on the scene. And we don't have the slightest idea who they're working for," the man says in earnest, as he picks up popcorn from the counter and puts it into his mouth.

Martin detaches his gaze from the laptop screen for a second. He nods slowly as he absorbs what the fat man is saying. The situation is critical. Yet he's overcome by a delicious sensation. The Ghost Center is in the limelight at last. Now he knows that there's a Command out there somewhere, following what they're doing, even depending on them to achieve its goals. There's no room for complaints about working hours any more. No room for trivial matters. Action will be swift and decisive.

"In that case, why not go to the local authorities? Surely *they'd* be capable of locating Mickey," Martin says, after perusing some top-secret documents on his laptop. They're classified GAMMA, as they've been collected through eavesdropping on a foreign intelligence service after breaking its code. There's nothing there to indicate an organized effort to smuggle a scientist out of Egypt.

"The objective is to eliminate Mickey Mouse, not to alert the Egyptians to the treasure they have at their disposal," the fat man says with a full mouth. He's starting to devour the crusts of cold pizza.

"But the Egyptian authorities can at least make sure he never leaves the country."

Martin starts looking at the remaining messages. They're classified ZARF, meaning they're the fruit of satellite eavesdropping on communications. But again, he finds nothing useful in them.

"Never forget that Israel is our one true ally in the Middle East. The increase in the power of any Arab state will, in the final analysis, come at the expense of Israeli hegemony." Alpha wipes his mouth with his shirt sleeve.

"So what's the next step?" Martin asks the question that has been nagging at him since Alpha said the operation had entered Code Red. The man's reply has magnified his apprehension. He's only too aware of the horrible measures they may resort to.

The fat man rises and heads for the restroom. After a long time, he returns, accompanied by the sound of the toilet tank filling up. He stands facing the central screen with his hands in his pockets. His back is bent slightly backward to balance his enormous belly. Then he whispers, "The thread begins at the farm."

chapter 9

Giza, Egypt
Wednesday, January 17, 2007
Evening

"I think I'm a Qur'anist." Tahir nods to make his point.

"What is a Qur'anist?" the Cerebellum asks absentmindedly. The kid's odd statement has taken him by surprise.

"I'm not sure. But if the government throws them in jail, they must be doing something right." The youth's smile is tentative. His body is relaxed on the Cerebellum's bed, which, today, he has carefully made. His expression, though, is anything but relaxed.

They met about ten minutes ago. The Cerebellum was leaving Condoleezza's room, and he found Tahir standing silently on the landing. He brought him over to his place on the roof. Perhaps the kid was eavesdropping on what was going on inside the whore's room. Maybe the silly ritual that takes place with the arrival of each new customer piqued his curiosity.

Condoleezza had knocked on her ceiling with a broomstick to call in the Cerebellum. Dutifully, he rushed down to perform his functions, play the role from which he now earned a living. By now, the Cerebellum was used to all this nonsense, but perhaps Tahir still found it hard to understand, and even harder to deal with.

"I mean, in what way are these Qur'anists different from other Muslims?" the Cerebellum asks in earnest.

"It seems they have a modern interpretation of Islam. Anything would be better than the rigid fatwas one hears these days." Tahir speaks absentmindedly, as though he were gossiping about a movie star's divorce or a team's acquisition of some soccer player. "I wish young people would stop taking such matters at face value," he says. "Otherwise, we may end up like America, where every day someone invents a new religion. And then it all turns into big business."

The Cerebellum is getting angrier by the minute. He has reluctantly come to accept poor Condoleezza's attempts to repackage prostitution with a religious coating. After all, she is an ignorant woman looking for salvation. But when someone like Tahir starts to confuse these delicate matters, it is time to take a stand. "An objective stand with your friend," to quote Sadat. The Cerebellum has become increasingly attached to this young man, who has resisted corruption all his life. He has pinned so much hope on the young intellectual. Of course, the Cerebellum has no problem with Qur'anists, or anyone else. Tahir has the right to believe in whatever he wants to. Only it should come after due consideration. Faith should be based on awareness. Why do young people take matters so lightly?

When did we collectively fall into this mental vacuum? How did it manage to infest our new generations, without us even noticing? When did these profound transformations take place in our society to start with? The Cerebellum no longer knows whom to blame for all this. He throws the dice on the rusty table. Who knows what the Fates have in store for this country?

Then it crosses his mind that perhaps the kid is intentionally making fun of him, even trying to provoke him to anger. He remembers what he has just said to Tahir. He blurted it out without giving it serious thought. Now he feels doubly embarrassed. How dare he complain about turning religion into big business, when it has become the world's most lucrative enterprise? When he himself has become a top practitioner?

He has taken particular care to avoid including religious references in his ritual with Condoleezza and her clients, consistently refusing to comply with their unspoken plea to lend spiritual legitimacy to their activities. How can he convince Tahir of all that? But has the kid not heard with his own ears what was going on behind closed doors? Did he not recognize that the Cerebellum was intentionally adopting the tone of a clerk in a government registry, or the legalistic jargon of a lawyer's assistant, rather than a wedding sheikh's sanctimonious ramble? He has not even put on the cloak Condoleezza got him. Not once. Is all that not enough?

He is a charlatan. There is no denying that. A pimp, even. But he has never traded in religion. He firmly opposes involving religion in anything beyond the spiritual relationship between a man and his Maker. Does the kid not know that? Has he forgotten that he is dealing here with a secular Sufi, as he so often describes himself?

He is only a clerk, explaining to the customer the terms of the contract. He goes over the oral agreement with them: the duration of the marriage—it is usually half an hour—and the sum of the dowry and end-of-marriage compensation. This varies from one customer to another, according to Condoleezza's assessment of his financial situation, how much she likes him . . . and, perhaps, other factors that he tries not to dwell upon. But the Cerebellum never once claimed that this was a religious wedding. He is just another clerk explaining the terms of the contract. Has Tahir not listened to all this when he was eavesdropping behind closed doors?

His body shakes so hard his cane chair nearly falls apart. He realizes he has lost the boy's respect. While the young man, despite growing up in this sewer, has succeeded in preserving a modicum of dignity, he, the venerable scientist, the outstanding genius, has tripped into the first pothole along the road. He has failed his first test.

"Don't take it so seriously. I was only joking." The kid tries to defuse the situation. Then he changes the subject. "Do you know, Mister Poet, what a googol is?"

A googol. Just hearing the word relieves his tension, revives his soul. It brings him back to his preferred world of abstract ideas. Can mathematics exist independently of the human mind that created it? And why not? Are mathematical equations, after all, not the most eloquent expression of the nature of the universe? He remembers Sir James Jeans's famous question: Is God a mathematician?

What would his father—God rest his soul—have said if asked what a googol was? Most probably he would have referred the whole matter to his genius son, whom he considered his life's primary achievement. This explains why the man—whose vitality had been sapped away by hypertension and diabetes since he was a young man—stubbornly hung on to life until he saw his son an engineer and a member of the college faculty. He endured liver fibrosis, the shrinking of his sole functioning kidney, and hemorrhages of the esophagus, until at last he witnessed his life's project bear fruit before him. Then he was ready to meet his God, a satisfied man. The Cerebellum tries to convince himself that had the man lived a little longer after his son's graduation, he would have made his peace with the world. Perhaps he would have even given up his habit of going out on the balcony in his underwear.

But what would the iron-willed man's reaction have been had he lived to see his son in his current shame, on this lonely shore where the game of numbers has tossed him? His defeat goes beyond personal failure. Such a waste of hope. The struggle of consecutive generations of Egyptians has gone down the drain. Such is his tragedy. And such is the tragedy of his entire generation.

"One followed by a hundred zeros," the Cerebellum replies to Tahir's question, his eyes still fixed on the dice. "To help visualize this number, mathematicians calculated the number of raindrops that fall on New York City in a period of twenty-four hours, then in a month, then in a whole year. And the figure turned out to be much less than one googol."

"Okay . . . and who discovered it?" A genuine smile illuminates the young man's face, for the first time today. Then he, too, has discovered that the alternate world of numbers can provide the best escape from the depressing one we live in.

"A kid in an American kindergarten. On the spur of the moment, he just wrote it on the blackboard," the Cerebellum says, laughing.

Could a kid in an Egyptian kindergarten ever discover a new number? More important, if this genius kid existed, was there a teacher in this whole country who would take him seriously? And how would this discovery reach the mathematician who would calculate its value and put it into a scientific format? The background din—this essential component of the life of all Cairenes, especially those of them who dwell in the city's slums—has been rising for the last few minutes. A man growling in anger. A child's hysterical shrieks. Perhaps some intra-family theft has been uncovered, or a marital infidelity that can no longer be ignored. But he need not concern himself too much with these matters.

"Why not move on a little, graduate from kindergarten and maybe go to college? So tell me, smart guy, what is the largest number that modern science has ever formulated?" he continues.

The Cerebellum's question sounds easy enough, yet its answer may be beyond the level of this student, who, let's face it, is still an under-graduate. In any case, there is no harm in teaching him something that may prove useful to him in the future.

Condoleezza's voice suddenly materializes in his ears. She is a good-tempered girl who rarely gets into fights with her customers or the neighbors. But it is her voice, no doubt about it, and it sounds shrill and angry.

"A gigaplex, meaning one followed by a billion zeros," the youth replies immediately.

His answer indicates a high level of knowledge, but, as he had expected, it is not the right one. Part of him wants to give the boy the correct answer. But his conscious mind insists that Condoleezza may be in danger.

"Is that Condoleezza shouting?" the Cerebellum asks. He tries to distinguish her words as they reach him in intermittent waves. It is a brawl of some kind. Someone else must be talking back to her, but in a lower voice.

Tahir listens for a split second, then, without a word, he rushes to the door. The Cerebellum follows suit, but more deliberately. He has an urge to shout to him that Graham's number is the largest number known to humanity. So large that mere figures are insufficient to write it down. He struggles to pull himself away from the perfect world of mathematics, to return to a world that is uglier than ugliness. Yet he is inundated by feelings of guilt. If Condoleezza is really in trouble, he must rush to her rescue. But Tahir is far ahead of him, in both chivalry and common sense.

She is standing in her open doorway, yelling at her latest customer, who is on the landing, trembling. It is a young, pale-skinned guy, who replies to her in whispers. In spite of his light-red beard, his features are childish. If you saw him walking down the street, you would describe him as a pious, well-mannered youth. As it happens, this is the very same cub sheikh who owns the international patent for the devilish theory that sugarcoats prostitution as pleasure marriage.

"The duration is over . . . to continue would be fornication," Condoleezza snaps. She has already slipped on her gown and is trying to fix her veil as she speaks.

"But I'm not done yet . . . please, put yourself in my shoes," he mumbles in shame, while trying to smooth out the wrinkles in his gallabiya. He seems to have put it on in a hurry.

"The dowry you paid barely covers a half-hour marriage." She disappears inside her room for a second and reappears with his skullcap and sandals.

The Cerebellum cannot hold back his laughter and bursts out in a loud cackle. You have been hoist by your own petard, idiot cub. He turns to Tahir, who is frozen at the very same spot where he had found him half an hour ago. Rather than sharing the Cerebellum's reaction to this farce that borders on absurd drama, his face is pale, as though he has seen a ghost.

Condoleezza locks herself in, leaving the Cerebellum and the two young men on the narrow landing. One is a believer in pleasure marriage, the other a Qur'anist. The Cerebellum wants to shout, "What the hell has happened to young people these days?" But he chooses to keep his mouth shut. He is no better than any of them.

The kid sheikh fixes his skullcap on his head and quietly slips away down the stairs.

"Ramsey's equation," the Cerebellum says to Tahir, after an extended silence.

His words succeed in drawing the kid out of the dark tunnel of his emotions.

"What?" he says distractedly.

"Graham's number is the largest known number. It is impossible to write it down in mere figures. The only way to describe it is through a mathematical equation known as Ramsey's equation," the Cerebellum explains.

Tahir says nothing. Anger collects in his eyes, as though the Cerebellum had insulted him gravely. He turns to go back to his room and, without a word, shuts the door behind him.

Charlotte, North Carolina
Wednesday, January 17, 2007
1100 EST

"We must win at any cost. Survival of the fittest, remember?" Martin keeps repeating to himself.

At these critical moments, he cannot allow his mind to wander. When he first joined the NSA, they taught him that thorny questions—whether ethical or legal—will most probably distract you. "You need to decide from the very start: are you a Hamlet or an Alexander the Great?" they said. "Then you must understand that there's no place here for Hamlet and his fellow ditherers." History is a struggle for existence. If our ancestors had hesitated, the Indians would have killed them off one by one, then scalped them, and used their scalps as decoration for their chiefs' tents. If his forefathers had allowed ethics to tie their hands, he wouldn't be here today and the greatest empire in history would never have existed. This is how his consciousness was formed. Now he needs to draw upon everything he's learned.

Alpha did not leave when his shift ended. The decision to raid the farm has put the mission into high gear. Their delay in discovering the tunnel must have raised doubts about the effectiveness of their entire surveillance operation. They can no longer ignore the possibility that they are about to lose Mickey Mouse's trail forever. The moment the subject cleaned out his bank account, he was poised to elude the spotlight of their electronic surveillance. Now he can easily disappear into the foggy area that only Third World slums can provide.

It is true that technology has permanently transformed intelligence operations. Rather than complain about the dearth of information—the so-called "fog of war"—they are now confronted with the challenge of reaching swift conclusions amid the flood of information at their disposal—appropriately dubbed "the thick cloud of electrons." Since every living creature produces some kind of signal that can potentially be traced electronically, the interaction of billions of signals every second makes tracking a given subject impossible, unless he happens to leave a distinctive track to differentiate himself from all the others. That's why it's imperative for a surveillance operation to keep its target within the range that it can easily monitor. Otherwise he'd simply dissolve into the sea of backwardness that still covers most of the planet. The subject would thus go out of the bounds of history that the empire has created to guard its own interests, as Fukuyama likes to think.

Right now, the only hope left is for the agents to find a clue inside the farm that would enable them to pick up Mickey Mouse's scent. Whether the required information is contained in physical evidence or in individual memories, their agents on the ground are trained to harvest it.

The adrenaline is flowing through his veins. Anticipation fills him, coupled with a delicious numbness. Only his fat boss's continued presence after the end of his shift spoils the moment. He can see that the detestable Alpha is not going to risk leaving him alone today, so he's going to enjoy running the show himself, implicitly putting the blame on him for their previous failure.

Units 2 and 3 are about to launch their assault on the farm. Unit 1 has already started a diversionary tactic from the main road. The white rental Peugeot has stopped right in front of the main gate, completely blocking it. One of the agents has raised the hood to indicate engine trouble, while the second—a woman wearing a blonde wig—is ringing the bell.

Agent Alpha picks up a movie-theater-style popcorn bucket, filled to the brim, from the counter and rests it on his lap. He doesn't touch its contents.

Martin follows the screens with interest. The middle screen shows a composite plan of the farm. Data from the ground-based cameras and infrared sensors has been superimposed by computer on the satellite image. There are only three red dots inside the farm, while they have six green lights surrounding it from three sides. The three guards are all located on the side facing the road, obviously watching the blonde from behind their windows.

Martin is satisfied. The distraction tactic has worked. Just put a Middle Eastern guy within sight of a blonde, and he'll forget the world. More significantly, these guards are anything but professionals. Had they been well-trained, they'd have reacted with caution and monitored the farm's back and sides.

Alpha siphons Coke into his mouth like an elephant dipping his trunk into a lake. The popcorn bucket shakes on his lap. As usual, he stays silent.

There's movement on the left screen, the one showing the building's main entrance. The front door is thrown open and there's a fat man in the doorway. He scans the garden before ambling toward the outer gate. He leaves the door open. The image doesn't show a firearm, but he could always have a pistol concealed under his coat. Martin's heart pounds violently. He anticipates Alpha's instructions to the agents. In their black ninja fatigues, Units 2 and 3 have taken up offensive positions next to the fences on both sides of the farm.

The fat guard strolls leisurely to the outer gate.

"COBRA 2, COBRA 3 . . . proceed," Alpha suddenly shouts into the mike. His hand delves into the popcorn bucket on his lap, as though he'd just given the start signal on some TV show for a competition on how fast you can munch popcorn.

Like hooded black spiders, the four agents climb the two fences with alarming ease. Then they rush toward the farmhouse.

At that moment, the fat guard reaches the main gate. He opens the peephole and checks out the agent. Inside the building, the two red lights haven't budged. Excellent. None of the guards has realized what's happening.

Through the open door, the agents rush into the building. The fat guard's negligence has made their job easier. For a few seconds, he's unable to visually monitor the agents on the left screen. He can locate them, though, as moving green lights on the middle screen. Each pair of green lights heads for one of the red. Alpha crunches popcorn like a tireless concrete mixer. Martin checks the images from the cameras that are built into the eyeglasses of the attacking teams, but they're shaking too hard to be of any use. The agents are moving too fast. There's a lot of violence going on. But he doesn't have the slightest doubt about the outcome.

Before the fat guard can open the outer gate, one of their agents' voices comes across the loudspeakers.

"The situation is under control. Have encountered light resistance. One subject down. The second is still alive. We've kept him in good shape, as per instructions. No casualties in our ranks. Will proceed to comb the building."

Just then, the fat guard unlocks the gate and sticks his head out to take a closer look at the agent with the blonde wig.

"COBRA 1 . . . take out remaining target . . . don't take unnecessary risks," says Alpha with his mouth full of popcorn.

Martin wonders if the agents who are now risking their lives in this operation, in one of the most dangerous parts of the world, realize that their leadership is following their travails as they would an entertaining movie. They probably take the inexplicable crunching in their earphones for quirks in the encryption equipment.

Martin cannot see the agent's face on the screen. But through the lens in her eyeglasses, he scrutinizes the fat guard's face with a curiosity bordering on pleasure. How will the eyes of a man on the brink of death appear to the outside observer, even though the subject doesn't have an inkling of what he's in for? Shouldn't a special mist linger in his look . . . some metaphysical announcement that the end—or the beginning—is at hand?

But the man's eyes simply display a natural stupidity, like a cow chewing grass: the mental lethargy that afflicts security guards after years of tedium, with a trace of animal desire aroused by the proximity of a female.

The guard doesn't need much persuasion to let the pretty agent in. Once inside, she wastes no time. She doesn't give him a chance to ask how he can help, offer the hospitality that is customary in this part of the world, make a pass at her, or even try his hand at sexual harassment. She simply grabs his head from behind with both her arms. It's all over before the man can absorb what's happening. The lights are out, as the martial arts instructor used to say in the academy. With a quick twist of the neck, the lights go out of someone's life, with all the love and hate that have filled it to overflowing, with its unique experiences and trivial aspirations. The smile of a baby girl he loved, the touch of a woman he desired, the taste of a meal his mother used to prepare in his childhood . . . they all vanish with a quick twist of the neck.

"The subject is out of the game," the agent says calmly. In different circumstances, her voice might have been described as sexy.

The subject is out of the game. Because of her years of training, the agent utters the words mechanically. Yet every word is based on detailed studies. It is imperative to dehumanize the victim, to glorify the kill. But this doesn't bother Martin much. Human history, after all, is a continuous chain of wars, a never-ending procession of organized killing. Dehumanizing the other is an essential component of all cultures. It is necessary to distinguish between killing outside the group— by deeming it a noble act of heroism—and committing the same act in its midst—by calling it the basest of crimes. The only innovation the modern nation-state has introduced is to employ technology to sugar-coat some of these contradictions. This has become particularly useful now that the media's concentrated coverage brings these horrific acts of killing to every family's living room. Some legal contraptions and fancy terminology have come in handy . . . the most salient of which, in our age, is the "War on Terror."

Martin recalls a casual remark Agent Beta made just before he vanished. He said that the War on Terror had never been geographically defined. The battleground had suddenly been expanded to encompass the universe. The laws of war—as they had both learned—do not prohibit killing, so long as it takes place on the battleground. At the time, Martin had thought that his colleague's remark—if true—implied that issuing a death sentence had now become contingent on the whims of guys like themselves, people who have neither names nor identities. The authority to take a life had been moved away from the courts and their laws . . . and miles away from accountability.

Luckily, that day he'd said nothing.

Today the picture is much clearer to him. People will never change. In their hearts, they haven't evolved since Cain and Abel walked the earth. We all know that, but we still need to uphold a lie called 'civilized behavior.' The double standards of human values must never be exposed. The myth of civilized behavior must be preserved at all costs so that democratic states may continue to commit mass murder on an unprecedented scale and maintain a serene mind and a clear conscience.

Still, he's not going to lose any sleep over this. What does worry him, despite the fancy legal terminology, is whether his current actions are legal. This concern has especially haunted him since he left the NSA and joined this ghost organization, unshielded by any political or legal umbrella. Its only protection is its cover of complete secrecy. In other words, his organization is not much different, in the eyes of the law, from organized crime.

"The subject is out of the game," Martin repeats out loud in an attempt to regain his focus, which is getting more scattered with each crunch of Alpha's popcorn.

"The building is completely under control," the commander of the attacking team confidently responds to the agent in the blonde wig.

"COBRA 1, continue to keep watch from inside the vehicle, but move away from the gate to avoid arousing suspicion," Alpha says, taking a long sip of Coke.

Why the hell does the fatso think that the mundane instructions he's barking into the mike are so brilliant that he can justify staying on after his shift? Or has he remained just to heighten Martin's sense of injury? He feels a strong urge to slap him as he gulps his Coke. He visualizes the expression of surprise on the man's face as popcorn flies in every direction.

Martin gets a grip on himself, then moves the image of the only guard who's still alive — the only one left in the game, to quote the agent in the blonde wig — to the right-hand screen. The poor guy is now the center of attention.

Their guys have already undressed him. He stands there shivering from the cold and humiliation, trying to shield his genitals with both hands. After gagging the guard with a tennis ball shoved between his teeth, one of the agents places noise-canceling headphones over his ears. Another agent completes the setup by hooding him. Now he's completely isolated, floating in his inner space. There's nothing to keep him company except fear, humiliation, and his bruised dignity.

This is only the beginning.

The theory of sensory deprivation, developed by Canadian scientist Donald Hebb in 1951, has become the bible for everyone involved in their line of work. It has provided the scientific solution to the problem that has baffled investigators for thousands of years: how do you torture your subject without even touching him?

Martin quickly corrects himself: "Never ever mention the word 'torture.' Don't even allow the thought to pass through your mind," he quotes one of his teachers at the academy, under his breath.

Martin has studied, in minute detail, the findings of Operation Bluebird, the research program that the CIA conducted in the fifties and early sixties at a cost of billions of taxpayer dollars. Then he learned how U.S. agencies collaborated with the Brazilian army to develop these findings in the field. A comprehensive program was developed to soften up targets prior to interrogation. Yes, soften up—'torture' is a word that can never be pronounced or even thought.

The next step will be to force the subject to stand in a stressful position for a long period. With time, his pains will multiply. Soon they'll exceed the worst forms of torture. Scientists were quick to establish that just feeling that you're causing yourself this terrible pain can do more than anything else to shatter a person's resistance. Rather than torture the subject, the interrogator forces him to torture himself.

The two members of Unit 2 are responsible for softening up the subject. Unit 3's agents have already started the search for any material clues that may lead to Mickey Mouse. One of the two agents has searched the clothing of the first guard to be terminated, but found nothing of value. No ID, no personal notes, not even a cell phone. The other guy went searching for computers throughout the building, but found none. Too bad! Computers are usually a treasure trove of information. This is one of the drawbacks of working in the Third World. The agent is now going through the papers on tables and inside drawers. Martin thinks it highly improbable that he'll find anything of significance. He was taught in the academy that these people belong to a culture that depends primarily on oral communication. That's why TV and cell phones have spread so quickly there, whereas books remain marginal. If they manage to find a cell phone, that would be really good news.

The two agents belonging to Unit 2 have made the naked guard stand on top of a chair. They've forced him to spread both arms in the air in the position the whole world has become familiar with from the pictures from Abu Ghraib that, naturally, the U.S. government attributed to a few bad apples. Martin, however, knows only too well that the practice is a standard page from the interrogation manual used by all the world's intelligence agencies—American and non-American alike. One of the two agents is preparing the wires that he'll plug into the electrical supply through a small converter to reduce the voltage so that the electrical current won't kill the subject. This particular agent is a certified nurse. U.S. agencies are not allowed to use these modified interrogation techniques except in the presence of qualified medical personnel. Just like individuals, states sometimes need a fig leaf to hide their sensitive areas.

Simply put, the idea is to force the subject to stand with both arms spread horizontally for an extended period. If he allows them to relax, a sensor he holds in his palm closes an electrical circuit, whose shock forces him to raise them again. They taught them all this at the academy, under the pretext of training them to withstand enemy torture. This was perfectly justified in light of the experiences of U.S. POWs in Korea and Vietnam. In taped interviews, they were forced to confess to anything their interrogators wanted them to. But nobody ever told Martin that he himself would one day be required to implement these very techniques on his subjects . . . to soften up, not torture, of course. He smiles.

A man has not really reached maturity until all his principles have been shattered against the rock of reality. Martin pinches himself in the leg to regain his concentration. He can't figure out what's wrong with him today. This level of distraction is quite unusual for him. Alpha gives him a quick look. Has he given himself away, somehow exposing the dangerous thoughts passing through his mind? After placing the subject in the required position, the two agents relax into armchairs. Like chefs at a three-star restaurant, they wait for their subject to simmer. Meanwhile, the other screens show the members of Unit 3 trashing the place, as they search for anything useful. One of the two agents exits the building and crosses the garden to the fat guard's body, next to the outer gate. He searches it with professional efficiency and comes up with a cell phone, which he pockets, then calmly walks back to the building.

Alpha stands up and, with steps that make each part of his enormous body bounce, heads for the coat hanger. He puts on his worn-out brown jacket. Martin can't believe he's actually leaving without so much as a word to him. Not even a "See ya." As though he didn't exist, as if he were just another inanimate object, no better than the chairs, counters, and computer screens. He doesn't really need instructions from the fat guy, but the man is always putting him down. He can feel his anger rising. He wants to go for the man's throat, to get that son of a bitch.

"But isn't the man innocent . . . I mean Mickey Mouse? Do we have evidence he's committed a crime in anyone's book?" Martin's voice is coarse. He has no idea why he said such a dangerous thing. But he no longer gives a damn. Now he's going to force the fat man to respond.

The man, who was about to step out, turns around slowly. He studies Martin with an odd expression of concentration. When he finally speaks, his voice is calm, but the threatening undertone is unmistakable:

"When such poisonous thoughts cross your mind, I want you to close your eyes and think of your little girl—don't tell me her name— just visualize her in your mind's eye. Then imagine a nuclear bomb exploding over her school. Imagine the skin on her face evaporating and her body tissues melting like butter in a frying pan. Listen to your girl's cries before they stop abruptly. At that moment you'll realize that it's our responsibility to get rid of those bastards before they can do something like that to us."

Martin realizes he's struck a nerve. He's discovered the one subject that provokes Alpha's anger, or maybe his fear. But before he can figure out how to reply, the fat man has disappeared into the passageway.

Chapter 10

Giza, Egypt
Wednesday, January 17, 2007
Late at night

The rhythm could bring you back from the dead. As for the living, they are simply compelled to join the dance. This music liberates the soul from all constraints, cleanses the psyche from every complex. Latin dancing is one continuous chain, composed of rings of interlocking pleasure. The merengue lures you to the salsa. The rumba leads to the tango. The samba seduces you all the way to the lambada. You feel completely enveloped by its unabashed sensuality. The laser beams showering you are rose pink, pistachio green, electric blue. Their playful flashes numb your senses. The spotlights drop vertical cones of pink light that intersect with the dance floor in circles, unhurriedly sliding over the parquet. Biceps and candygirl are unified in a dancers' embrace, wavering between innocence and guilt. They glide inside their own private circle that, in turn, floats—ever so slowly—across the shimmering floor.

The Cerebellum finds himself inside a magical prism of grass-green light, holding in his arms the most beautiful girl in the world. Before tonight, he has never touched a girl's hand, not even in his dreams. Now he is unable to determine whether a physiological revolution is actually fermenting deep inside his body's labyrinth, if something dangerous is happening within the mysterious glands, in the silence of the cells. After their prolonged abstinence, he wonders if his testicles have suddenly decided to jumpstart, to secrete male hormones and flood his veins with that crazy testosterone, if his soundness of mind is about to be subjugated to blind animal impulses.

Or is it that, in this alternative electronic existence, his impotence simply fades away? In this place that is free of both glands and testosterone, of pregnancy and AIDS. Here, where eternal loyalty, and even emotional fidelity, are alien concepts. Here is a form of existence that has liberated itself from the shackles of both history and geography— the two boundaries that, according to Immanuel Kant, define human perception. Could male virility have been rendered meaningless in a world of absolute security and unbridled romanticism?

Dancing girls wriggle on the giant screens that cover the walls on three sides. Their eroticism is contagious. It crosses the Cerebellum's mind that these are flesh-and-blood girls, not electronic dummies like the dancers on the floor. Their existence, however, is restricted to pre-recorded material. In contrast to avatars like Biceps and candygirl, they are deprived of free will. Their very existence is therefore uncertain. Their reality is less convincing than that of these electronic dolls. Can anyone still doubt that digital beings alone have been endowed with the gift of life in the parallel universe?

There are not many dancers tonight. On his screen, he can only see his lover and himself. The screen's limits define privacy. These are the rules of the New World. Lovers need not hide behind trees or lock themselves behind closed doors.

"With you, I am living the most beautiful moments of my life," says Biceps.

The Cerebellum never thought he would utter such words to any woman.

"I like what you're saying. Don't stop."

Is candygirl encouraging or seducing him? Right now, it does not matter.

"When I am with you, all my troubles simply evaporate," he says, with perfect sincerity. "In your presence, I am completely transformed, like a charcoal creature reborn as pure diamond. This transformation happens inside every cell in my body, in every molecule, in each electron. When I am with you, I feel in harmony with the rest of existence. For once, I feel I am an extension of the galaxies; I sing in unison with the comets and asteroids."

Candygirl stops dancing and starts to laugh in her delicious way.

"Intelligence is what attracts me most to a man. And you are, without a doubt, the most intelligent man I've ever met, and the most knowledgeable, too," she says. After a moment's hesitation, she continues: "Your intelligence arouses all my feminine instincts."

The music binds them even closer . . . crystallizes their love . . . yes . . . love!

At last he has found a woman who appreciates his genius, who even considers it a source of sexual arousal.

The song with the sizzling rhythm is followed by a sweet love ballad. And he had thought that romance was extinct. He was not even sure it had ever existed in the first place—outside the realm of dreams, that is. But today he is experiencing romance firsthand. His infatuation makes him soar. He rises above his shoebox of a room with its rusting table and shaky chair, high above the Good Lady's house, crooked in appearance, crooked to the core. Over Cairo with its pitiful slums and middle-class neighborhoods that try in vain to conceal their chaotic disposition. Finally, he feels himself floating through the infinite space of love.

Biceps spontaneously takes candygirl by the hand. Together they penetrate shimmering curtains of colored light and rush into the open air. Outside, the ground is smooth, covered with snow. A fluffy layer has even accumulated on the branches of the fir trees. Candygirl circles around a fat snowman made up of three big snowballs, with an old hat on top of its head and a carrot for a nose. Biceps catches up with his girl and bows theatrically before her. The gold chain glitters around his neck. She laughs so hard she bends backward. Snowflakes fall tenderly around them. Over here, it is possible to enjoy the dreamy snowscape without having to worry about the cold. Influenza, pneumonia, and frozen extremities pose no threat here.

He rotates his angle of vision 360 degrees. There is not a soul in sight. This paradise now belongs exclusively to the two of them. He stands before a stone fireplace with a romantic fire roaring in it. How wonderful is this world, where fireplaces are built on the outside of houses. It makes a lot of sense, actually. When you are immune to the cold, the sole purpose of a fireplace is to establish a romantic mood. And that is precisely what is required, right now.

"Let us lie next to the fireplace," he says.

She nods. When they reach the fireplace, she throws herself down on the snow, without a moment's hesitation.

"I want to make love with you," she says simply.

Her bold advance takes him by surprise. He is barely discovering his romantic side and here she is pulling him toward a completely different level, leading him by the hand to the danger zone where, he had always assumed, he would never venture. He is ashamed to admit to her that he does not know how to carry out her request in virtual reality, not to mention his ignorance in these matters in the material world. He chooses a gesture from the menu and ends up flexing the muscles of his electronic alter ego. He is not quite sure what message he is trying to convey.

"Why don't we start a private chat?"

Now she is acting naughty. Maybe she has sensed his confusion.

"My hair is cascading down over my chest. Its tips caress my full breasts." Her words reach him through the chat box that ensures their privacy.

"I'm in my pink dressing gown. It's all silk . . . feels like rose petals . . . and . . . that's right, you've guessed it . . . I'm wearing nothing underneath. I've dropped my lingerie on the rug."

The Cerebellum breathes more vigorously than before. His mouth is dry, as though he's lost in the desert. He is lost, indeed . . . in an endless desert.

"Every part of my body has been waxed and feels smooth as butter." Her words keep coming at him on the screen, relentlessly.

"Do you want to feel my body?"

Candygirl does not give him a chance to respond. She goes on, "I can feel your fingers caressing my hair . . . now they're touching my breast, ever so tenderly . . . slowly. That's right, there's no hurry."

"Ahhh . . ."

The letters appear on the screen. Her erotic groans actually ring in his ears.

His body trembles on the decrepit chair. Today it will surely collapse under his weight and let him hit the floor. But he could not care less. He feels young and strong. His body is invincible, like steel. As though his metamorphosis into Biceps is complete, or, to be more precise, as if the two forms of existence have finally fused together, making it impossible to distinguish one from the other. Finally, the Cerebellum has inhabited Biceps, as the soul inhabits the body. He can no longer tell where one begins and the other ends. They have become two manifestations of the same being, two facets of that diminutive kid with the big head, whose father named him Mustafa so that he could carry on the name of the simplest of peasants, his grandfather. But today, all that does not matter much. Nothing matters except these erotic words that bombard him across the ether, shaking him to the roots. Nothing matters except that electronic doll with the body of a woman in full bloom, lying next to the fireplace on the snow. All that has transpired in the past does not matter any more, because this is the moment of his rebirth.

Charlotte, North Carolina
Wednesday, January 17, 2007
1921 EST

Martin envisages scenes of horrific violence. Cruelty. Sadistic torture. The perpetrator is none other than himself, and the victim is always Agent Alpha.

It's not unusual for him to take refuge in fantasy to fill up his endless hours of solitude in the Ghost Center. It's quite normal, really, for someone like him, endowed with a vivid imagination. He embarks upon these flights of fancy between games of FreeCell, whose cards he now moves mechanically. These imaginary adventures, however, usual take the form of action movies. Naturally, he plays the leading role. An American James Bond parachuting out of airplanes, catapulting off speeding cars, taking advantage of hi-tech gadgets to achieve consecutive victories over an endless chain of bad guys. In the end, of course, he wins the hearts of all the beautiful girls.

Sometimes his daydreams take a romantic twist. They may even turn into erotic fantasies. On other occasions, they involve debates with Alpha, in which he shatters his shallow arguments. Then he gets to enjoy the embarrassed look in the fat man's eyes. All this is perfectly normal. Imagination usually makes up for the shortcomings of reality. But it's this bloodthirsty violence that worries him today. He never realized that he concealed such evils in the dark folds of his soul. This silent rage that he's been slowly nurturing, to the point that it has become impossible to ignore.

He understands only too well that anger is only an advanced stage of fear. A tool the body uses to trigger the production of adrenaline in order to deal with an anticipated threat, thus priming the body for battle or flight. What's essential is the will to survive. It's the mother of all instincts. They taught him all that at the academy. But he also learned that adrenaline is no longer sufficient to face the challenges of modern life. In most cases, it becomes a hindrance. An angry man is a weak man, easily manipulated to serve the purposes of intelligence agencies. His anger has blinded him, made him easy prey. The same is true for angry nations. Revolutions usually generate greater oppression. Angry men end up betraying those who are closest to them. So why did he allow his anger to take control of him to this extent? And what's the source of this latent fear that generated all this anger in the first place?

He takes a quick look at the screens in front of him. Today he hasn't put up a game of FreeCell on the big screens. Another game is taking its course. The game of life, which really is stranger than fiction. This is all insane, like a nightmare. Such is the way of modern technology. It has turned nightmares into familiar scenes on our screens. Nothing surprises any more. The interrogation is now approaching its conclusion, though its results were already obvious an hour ago. The steps will now follow each other like playing cards placed in inevitable sequence. This is a universal game that recognizes neither mercy nor pity. The process of softening up the subject has produced nothing to write home about. The torture operation, however, was successful. But by its very success, it has highlighted Martin's predicament.

Torture. . . .

Martin repeats the word to himself. But even within the security of his inner soul, thinking 'torture' rather than 'softening up' is not without risk. Liberals and human rights activists who claim torture doesn't work have got it all wrong. The tragedy is that torture does work—at least in the short run.

The game is more complex than they think.

The guard has indeed revealed everything he knows. He confessed to belonging to a criminal gang, but one that, unfortunately, is not linked to Mickey Mouse. Its objective was limited to kidnapping a girl called Didi. They later sold her to a white slavery network. So they've even lost track of Didi. As for the Cerebellum, well, the guard never heard of him. It seems that he stumbled on the scene by mere coincidence . . . a person who found himself in the wrong place at the wrong time.

Martin has no choice but to admit that all the threads leading to Mickey Mouse have been severed. He has no alternative but to restart the whole operation from square one. Luckily, Alpha left as the softening-up was starting. Martin needs time to think. The whole situation worries him. The outcome could be frightening.

The scene that is unfolding on the screen, however, doesn't give him a chance to think clearly. It forces itself on him. The male nurse in the attack team has left the room. His job is done. Martin can clearly see that the naked guard, with his head entirely covered, is sobbing quietly. The quivering of his penis speaks more eloquently than squeals of pain. The poor guy must have figured out that his fate has been sealed. Perhaps he even longs for the end, anything to take him out of the humiliation he's been living for the past few hours.

This scene reminds Martin of a confidential documentary they showed them at the academy. It was basically an interview with a torture victim—a U.S. POW from the Korean War. He was already middle-aged by the time the film was shot, over ten years after his release. But his body still shook in this very same way, ever so slightly. He too sobbed quietly whenever the painful memories ganged up on him.

"Torture is worse than death, because it's a crime extended in time. It never stops. You keep on suffering. Every moment of every day," the soldier whispered to the NSA camera. Then, grinding his teeth, he went on: "I feel like I've already been killed, but that, due to some technical problem, they let me go on living. Every moment of every day, I'm certain I'm already dead. Trapped in a new self I can't escape from."

At that moment, Martin realized that the ultimate outcome of torture is to break a victim's will, or to strengthen it. In either case, that person's soul is exchanged for another. And the original innocent self is buried away. A new being comes into existence.

Torture works. The problem lies in the extended damage it leaves behind.

"It feels like you're living in a science-fiction movie where aliens take over a human body," the unidentified U.S. soldier had said, just before the end of the documentary.

The only agent remaining in the room points his pistol with the silencer at the guard's hooded head. Martin wants to cover his eyes with his hands, but the scene is too gory to resist. For once, he appreciates the practice of hooding their prisoners. It's quite merciful, really. He wants to shout to the guard: "You're damn lucky. The end will be quick for you. At least you don't have to live the rest of your life trapped inside a science-fiction movie. Your body won't be taken over by aliens."

Martin's body shudders violently. The destruction engendered by torture goes beyond the victims. It extends to the torturers themselves. Contagion is assured. The plague of human suffering does not recognize state borders. It does not distinguish between masters and slaves. There exists no barrier that can contain it, not even these reinforced electromagnetic-radiation-proof walls.

He's sick to his stomach as the naked guard falls into a lifeless heap. What's this unprecedented feeling of disgust that shakes him from head to toe? And why? Isn't this the "dark side" that Cheney directed U.S. agencies to venture into, after September 11?

He's not sure whether these intense emotions are generated by guilt or fear of punishment. In either case, he has only himself to blame. It was understood from the very start that his organization operated outside the law. They warned him of the need for "plausible deniability": that it was necessary to allow politicians to deny any knowledge of the existence of Operation COBRA. In turn, he'd made it clear to the agents on the ground that if they got caught, they couldn't count on the government to come to their rescue. They call this organization a private contractor—or a security consultant, to use the politically correct term.

He knew all this from the beginning. The law grants immunity from criminal prosecution to the president and other senior officials. All the decisions they make within the context of the War on Terror are protected. No such immunity is given to soldiers and junior officers. If caught, they walk the plank on their own. As for people like him, who work in the shadows, there's no protection whatsoever.

Neither protection nor respect.

It dawns on him that his agitation has nothing to do with the plight of the poor Egyptian who had met a humiliating death on the screen a few seconds ago. The man, after all, was a hired killer, a thug in criminal gang. Moreover, he was an Arab and a Muslim: frankly, an enemy. Let's call a spade a spade. There's no room over here for sympathy. If it makes you feel better, you can feel sorry for them in the same way you pity a cockroach as you crush it under your heel. The crisis is Martin's own. He no longer believes that what they're doing is ethical, or that it's even working. They've crossed the line and he's not sure that they're morally any better than the terrorists they're fighting. His self-confidence is quickly eroding.

He's fallen victim to the same doubts and anxieties that Agent Beta had expressed just before he disappeared . . . almost the same words he'd uttered, except that Martin has kept it all to himself.

Who owns this organization, to start with? Who runs the show? It has enormous resources at its disposal. There's no doubt about that. But other than that, he knows nothing about it. Center COBRA receives its instructions via e-mails signed "John Smith." Now he realizes that, most probably, no one has the complete picture. Nobody really knows who calls the shots.

They've killed, they've tortured, they've destroyed, but at the end of the day, the operation is going nowhere. He doesn't know what to do now, or what to say to Agent Alpha when he comes in. He needs to think for a while. But his state of distraction only reinforces his feeling of helplessness. The operation has gone back to point zero. No, below zero. He can't even guess what their failure will cost U.S. national security, or the personal penalty he'll have to pay.

Martin can no longer feel safe. What would an organization that operates outside the law stop at? An organization that was established to do anything and everything, that recognizes no boundaries and is accountable to no one. It dawns upon him that he's now more afraid of his own organization than he is of the terrorists. He's no longer confident that Amy and Susan are not at risk. But these are poisoned thoughts. It can be dangerous just to let them pass through his mind. He must exorcise them at any cost. He's a little depressed, that's all. He needs to regain his confidence. The American empire will win, in the end. It's a matter of historical inevitability. He must be absolutely certain of that. He's a sincere patriot working side by side with other sincere patriots. Victory will ultimately be theirs.

He remembers Alpha's advice and tries to visualize Amy as the first victim of a nuclear attack, but the thought is too terrible to contemplate. If he starts to think this way, he'll lose whatever remains of his sanity. What can he do now, and who can he go to for help?

With a few quick taps on his keyboard, a new game of FreeCell opens up on the large screen before him.

Giza, Egypt
Friday, January 19, 2007
Just after midnight

Extending both arms in a wave-like motion, Biceps does the hula. Then he blows a kiss to candygirl. He is hanging out with her at her post-modern villa. She holds a strawberry milkshake while reclining against the Havana-blue velvet of her sofa. Unhurriedly, she sips on her red-and-white-striped straw. He is standing in the middle of the room, seeing the world through born-again eyes. He still cannot believe what happened last night.

"What do you think of my new dress?" She stands up and makes a full turn, allowing him a view of her shapely body from every angle. "There was a sale on today."

He cannot be bothered to think of something to say, so he responds with a pre-programmed whistle. Her new dress is emerald green. She is right: it is beautiful. He must admit, however, that his primary interest is in her shapely figure, whose eroticism he can fully appreciate today. This animal worldview is completely new to him.

"Do you know . . . ?" She stops in mid-sentence to heighten his suspense.

He puts one hand behind his ear by pressing 'listen' on the gestures menu.

"What happened between us last night was the most meaningful experience of my life," she says, then goes back to her sofa.

What is he supposed to say to that? What exactly did happen last night? He is not even sure how to describe it. As an experience, it is simply beyond comparison. Nothing that has happened to him in all of his fifty-two years can serve as a yardstick to define last night. For the first time, his mind took the back seat and his instincts took over the steering wheel. For the first time, he realized that the body has a will of its own, that its voice must be heard. And now here he is, standing in the middle of this virtual room, with no idea how to control the emotions that are sweeping him away, body and soul. Luckily, candygirl is used to his periods of extended silence. She has come to accept them within the context of this sensual/intellectual edifice they have constructed together, this unique relationship that has aroused his senses like never before.

"Every word you say epitomizes intelligence. I can even sense it in your silence," she says. "And it really excites me."

"Intelligence? The word bestows upon me an honor I have never claimed, but if it is an accusation, it is one I can no longer deny. Intelligence. I have cohabitated with it since my eyes opened up to the world. My friends at university even nicknamed me the Cerebellum . . . although I'm still not sure whether that was out of admiration, or if they were just making fun of me," he says enthusiastically.

For once, he has allowed his ego free rein. Such vanity is so unfamiliar to him. Funnily enough, it did not knock on his door by virtue of his scientific discoveries or material accomplishments. Instead, it came in the wake of a few words on the screen, uttered by an electronic doll. But no sooner does 'the Cerebellum' appear on the screen than he realizes that he has crossed a red line, transgressed against a rule of a certain sanctity, broken a universal taboo that, although incontestable, no one has taken the time to precisely define. He has opened the floodgates to his ugly pride. Now, suddenly, he realizes that the inclination to look down on others has been growing in his guts for years, a satanic embryo awaiting the chance to come out into the open. To shake up stability and spread chaos . . . a predisposition that was embedded in his soul before he was even born, an ingredient of the original seed implanted by a father who held a lifelong grudge against the world. Now, at last, the Cerebellum's eyes can see clearly. It was his mother's good nature alone that has helped him tame his inner beast. But only superficially. Ambition has always been his primary driving force. Otherwise, why would he have agreed to play a central role in a nuclear program devised by a gambler of a ruler, not to protect his own people, but to allow him to continue to oppress them with impunity? Has Dr. Mustafa Mahmud Korany—a.k.a. the Cerebellum—not been possessed, all these years, by the desire to shout out to the world, "Look at me . . . see what I'm capable of . . . witness what I have accomplished"?

But above all, the Cerebellum blames himself for allowing the barricade to crumble. That rock-solid dam that separates two worlds, two dimensions of existence. That barrier, indispensable to maintaining harmony between the external and internal domains. To protect each of them from the evils of the other. He has allowed matter to come into contact with antimatter. And all he can do now is to let loose a string of hysterical laughter, like a mad scientist in a movie . . . and to wait for the horrific explosion that will, ultimately, engulf the entire universe. But this time, it is only his inner universe. The one that is more obscure and less constant.

"The Cerebellum!" candygirl repeats after him. "Yes. That suits you perfectly. From now on, I'll call you by no other name."

"Of course it'll be out of admiration," she adds quickly. Then she lets loose an extended electronic laugh.

The possibilities flash across the length and breadth of his consciousness, rushing into his veins like a drug overdose. Rather than elate him, her playful words inflate his fears.

"No. Do not repeat that word again, I beg you. It upsets me more than I can say. I only mentioned this whole thing because I trust you. I know I can share with you my deepest secrets." He composes his sentence slowly. Every word appears on the screen hesitant and lonely, until it is followed by the next one.

"Whatever you say, honey. What do you say to a walk on the beach?"

Her words feel like a balm on his wound. But can you recall a bullet once it has left the gun's nozzle? Can you turn back the clock? Will humans be able, someday, to travel back and forth in time? Well, why not? Is time, after all, not another dimension of the universe, just like distance? Or will we discover that once an act has occurred, it gains a permanent existence, impossible to erase, even though we may pretend it has not even happened? Will the day come when science intersects with spirituality, to demonstrate that every action is engraved in the texture of space even before it happens?

"Tomorrow, my darling . . . I feel sleepy right now."

He employs the key phrase they use to indicate that the external world is calling them for an urgent matter . . . although he is not really compelled to leave her, right now.

For the first time, he finds himself taking refuge in the material world to escape virtual reality. He needs time to think. He must allow this new situation to sink into his mind. He needs to figure out the potential consequences of his slip of the tongue. But can he be over-reacting? Is this a perfectly normal panic attack, spontaneously accompanying the awakening of his animal side after its long slumber? He moves away from the computer and leaves the room.

He finds himself standing in front of Tahir's door. He cannot believe his ears. Classical music is playing inside. Vivaldi. Can this be true? The boy is listening to *The Four Seasons*. Tears well in his eyes. This emotionality is new to him. It has taken him by surprise. He cannot recall ever having allowed his feelings to display themselves in this way before. He listens for a moment, gives himself the chance to regain his composure. He is not certain that he will end up knocking, at this late hour. In any case, he will have enjoyed the violin's serenade. It is the "Spring" concerto. Instead of controlling his emotions, he allows the tears to cascade down his cheeks.

So Vivaldi's tunes have found their way to the Good Lady's crooked house, embedded, as it is, in the guts of a city that is crooked from head to toe. This, in itself, is nothing short of a miracle. But luck has, moreover, willed that he would be welcomed by none other than the "Spring" concerto. Life is stubborn. It constantly refuses to give up. It pulsates in the depths, beneath the accumulated layers of filth. Vivaldi's notes stand in the face of Bush's tanks, the neo-cons' ideology, and Israel's massacres. The music challenges the dungeons of Saddam and his fellow dictators and the sadism of their henchmen. It mocks the fanaticism of terrorists, the Vali Faqih's plots, and the Zionist Christians' financial clout. Despite all the organized plunder that gnaws at this country from above and below, despite the burglaries and muggings, the incest and the groans of street kids being raped . . . roses will rise out of the sewage swamps. Despite all of us, their fragrance will continue to challenge the rot. And it will fill the world with hope.

The door is thrown open and Tahir stands in front of him. He is wearing his jeans and the brown cashmere sweater that looks like it has just been unwrapped from a Milan fashion house package. The boy studies him in silence. The Cerebellum is certain he has not produced a sound or done anything to alert the kid to his presence. So what made him open the door at this moment?

"I am worried about Didi."

He talks in hushed tones once he is inside the room and the kid has closed the door. Finally, the Cerebellum is expressing the feeling that has been creeping into his heart, slowly but surely, ever since he met the beautiful girl in Dokki, ten days ago. Now he has become obsessed with the girl's fate. He has sent more than one message to the New Owner, confirming that he is putting together the required sum, and pleading with him not to mistreat the innocent girl. But he has received nothing by way of reply.

"What's so special about this Didi of yours? What makes you think she's any better than all those pickpockets and junkies? Was she born with an extra arm or leg to set her above Condoleezza, your partner in the prostitution business? Why don't you just let Didi sink, like the rest of the country?" Tahir snaps.

"I am responsible for Didi. As for the others, there is nothing I can do to help them."

He feels offended by the boy's reference to his partnership with Condoleezza in prostitution, but decides to let it go. The look in the boy's eyes hurts even more. But he must avoid exposing his feelings. More importantly, he needs to put off the inevitable confrontation with his own self. What is the use of regret, or even self-justification? Right now, he must focus on his most difficult and pressing task. He cannot afford to be sidetracked by secondary matters. Didi must be rescued, even if the whole country, as Tahir said, is sinking. And he knows he cannot do a thing to help her without the skinny youth's help.

The Cerebellum notices the spotless state of the Bedouin carpet under his feet. Its colors are a somber palate of browns, in perfect harmony with Tahir's other belongings. The most important thing is for a person to be in harmony with himself . . . and to be truthful.

He realizes that resolving Didi's crisis has become the most important challenge of his life.

"If you are responsible for Didi, then who am I responsible for?" Tahir mutters, more to himself than to the Cerebellum.

"Didi has been kidnapped. She is being kept against her will."

"They've all been kidnapped. And they're all kept against their will," the boy interrupts.

"No. They are free to quit prostitution if they choose. We are all free to make our own decisions, and must be ready to face the consequences." The Cerebellum's words do not sound convincing, even to his own ears.

"Mister Poet . . . Mister Mathematical Genius . . . you'll never understand because you weren't born here. You didn't open your eyes to find yourself in a place like this, and in these terrible times we live in. The problem is not poverty, or prostitution, or drugs, or crime. What's really demoralizing is that everyone you meet hates everything. They hate the world. They hate themselves. They even hate God for having created them!" Tahir explodes.

"May God forgive us all." The Cerebellum tries to hide his shock at the volcano of anger behind the young man's outburst. He is sure he did not mean it literally. After a long silence he says, "But despite all this, you are listening to Vivaldi. Does this not tell us that there is hope?"

Tahir starts to laugh. The anger disappears from his face in the blink of an eye, just like it started. Goodness is the dominant feature of his character. It shines without warning, like gold beneath the dust.

"Vivaldi's music is perfectly suited to the everyday lives of Egyptians. He composed it to be played in Venice during carnivals, where men and women would eye each other from behind their masks. As for us, we hide behind our masks all our lives. Our relationships are no less shady. And from cradle to tomb, we live in a carnival," Tahir says.

"Precisely. And the only thing we lack is Vivaldi's music," the Cerebellum says, laughing.

A sudden hush descends upon them. The Cerebellum is certain he can hear a coarse voice calling from afar. His mind tells him the words are not addressed to him. How could they be meant for his ears? But his heart says otherwise. The words carry a message of sorts, addressed to him and to others. The voice restates its desperate point. The Cerebellum can no longer bear its distinctive croak. He can no longer . . .

"The boat is sinking, Captain," the voice repeats for the third time, unconcerned about the Cerebellum's rising nausea.

"The Señor called. The sale is going ahead tomorrow afternoon." Tahir gets directly to the point. Maybe he has noticed the Cerebellum's despair, and could not help but show some pity. "I meant to tell you in the morning: the price will more than cover the sum you asked for."

"Then we must set Didi free tomorrow. I will organize the handover right away. We cannot afford to waste one second," he says quickly, although he is not sure he will even get a reply from the New Owner.

The music slows down, as if the viola were trying to emphasize that a turning point has been reached. A dog barks in the distance. The other dogs in the neighborhood immediately respond with a barrage of barking.

"Do you know what Vivaldi called this movement?" Tahir says, smiling.

"The barking dog," the Cerebellum says, and the two men share a good laugh.

The laughter relieves them of their individual burdens, if only for a fleeting moment.

Chapter 11

Charlotte, North Carolina
Thursday, January 18, 2007
1948 EST

"They call me the Cerebellum."

The statement reverberates across the farthest reaches of the parallel universe. It sends the electrons of the IT world into fits of vibrations. Electromagnetic waves pulsate with its every syllable, circumnavigating planet Earth in the blink of an eye. With its unique intelligence value, there is no way it can escape the sharp eyes of surveillance hawks. The information highway is not devoid of intersections. These are the very joints controlled by the servers of U.S. companies. They single out the Cerebellum's words from the billions of signals racing through, like a hen picking up a corn kernel in the midst of countless grains of sand. The servers transmit the magic words across miles of fiber-optic cables. They're relayed from satellite to satellite, transported on wireless waves that slice through the atmosphere. This relentless activity, carried out in total silence but with a deafening buzz of its own, takes the golden word all the way to the Ghost Center's supercomputer, which in turn displays the statement inside a red-alert box that flashes across all the screens.

Martin comes back from the kitchen with a coffee mug in his hand. He freezes for a few seconds in front of the screens. He's not sure if what he's seeing is real or if he's daydreaming, as usual. He rests the mug on the counter and runs his fingers across the keyboard. He needs to be certain. He knows 'the Cerebellum' is not a common nickname, but on the Net everything is possible. In his line of work, caution is essential. But if it really turns out to be Mickey Mouse after all, then he'll have fallen into the trap. He'll have inadvertently come to play on their home ground. The tables will be turned. Will Martin at last be able to snatch victory from the jaws of defeat?

Still, he must be certain before allowing himself to get intoxicated with victory.

Charlotte, North Carolina
Thursday, January 18, 2007
2100 EST

Alpha enters the Ghost Center through the magic corridor that opens up when the bathroom sink slides to one side. He is carrying a huge bucket of Kentucky Fried Chicken.

"Good evening, Gamma." He takes off his worn-out bomber jacket and hangs it on the hanger next to Martin's tweed, then approaches with his bucket, which holds enough chicken to feed an entire family.

For the first time in a long time, Alpha says something upon arrival. Martin, however, doesn't return the man's greeting. He struggles to contain his jubilation. He wants to extend his moment of victory for as long as he can. He's hoping the fat man will try to bully him as usual, so he can rebuff him. Martin wants to establish, once and for all, his superiority in all intelligence matters. He'll only need to say a few words, but something razor sharp that will make up for all the affronts he's had to endure throughout his career, starting from his painful expulsion from the NSA.

But he can't hold it in any longer. He's going to explode if he stays quiet for one more second, so he finds himself doing an impromptu victory dance in the middle of the room.

"They call me the Cerebellum," he chants. "They call me the Cerebellum."

Giza, Egypt
Friday, January 19, 2007
Just after the noon prayers

"If the entire Egyptian population were to march in line in front of you, the queue would never end. Can you explain why, Tahir?"

The Cerebellum wonders why he wastes his time with these useless mathematical quizzes. He turns every idea that crosses his mind into an arithmetic problem that must be solved. In his youth, he considered this habit to be another form of escape from reality. But now it dawns on him that numbers and calculations are, for him, the truest form of reality. All else is clutter. Like the buzz of the cosmic background radiation that scientists need to neutralize in order to compose a sonar image of the universe through their radio telescopes. Numbers are his only truth. He had always known this in his heart, but had been unable to accept it. Mathematics is his final destination. The day will surely come when he will rid himself of all the clutter and, through numbers, lead a perfect existence. It is just a matter of time. The sand has almost run out, and the clock is about to reverse itself.

Revolution is imminent.

"The problem can be approached through the relation between the rate of demographic growth and the velocity at which the line moves," says the youth after some thought. He bites his lower lip.

Tahir's voice is fainter than usual. His face is pale. His apparent anxiety does not surprise the Cerebellum. Today, after all, the deal with the Señor will go through. In fact, he has been expecting Tahir to drop in and pick up the rest of the gold coins, in order to accomplish his mission.

"Precisely. In other words, our women are spawning kids faster than the line can move."

The Cerebellum is not sure if this conversation is helping to reduce the boy's anxiety. He even doubts that this had been his objective in the first place. Perhaps, too scared to contemplate the possible outcomes of his next move, he has been merely putting off his own moment of decision. Rather than Tahir's meeting with the Señor to conclude the coin deal, what really concerns him is his own planned rendezvous with the gang boss who is holding Didi. The New Owner, as the criminal likes to describe himself, has given the go-ahead for the exchange to take place tomorrow afternoon.

He was not successful in arranging for Didi's liberation today. In his e-mail, the man had politely reminded him that Friday was his day off. The guy thinks he is the under secretary of the Department of Human Trafficking.

What worries him most of all is Didi's ordeal. What have they done to her? How will she cope when all this is over? What if the gang got the money and still refused to let her go?

"But you're assuming that the rate of growth of the population is constant. In fact, it must ultimately slow down," Tahir says, perhaps only to keep the mental game going. He avoids mentioning Didi, or even the reason he has come to see him today.

"So long as our sheikhs keep on preaching backwardness, it will hardly slow down." The Cerebellum pulls up his shaky chair and sits on it.

"Reason will prevail in the end . . . even over the sheikhs. People will ultimately want to fulfill their material needs," Tahir says with enthusiasm.

He relaxes on the Cerebellum's well-made bed and continues with even greater enthusiasm: "When the church forced Galileo to recant his belief that the sun, not the earth, was the center of the solar system, he acquiesced in order to save his life. But do you know what else he did?"

The self-proclaimed title 'the New Owner' nags at the Cerebellum with renewed intensity. So far he has considered the title a tragic expression, suited for a tragic situation. However, the enormity of the term begins to dawn on him. The man actually means he is Didi's new owner.

In other words, more than a century since the abolition of slavery, people are still being treated as goods. Didi's body has become subject to the laws of the market. To be bought and sold, to be chopped to pieces and sold as body parts, even to be rented out by the hour, if that happens to be more profitable. The Cerebellum is so overwhelmed by this thought that he is incapable of responding.

The young man continues: "Some historians believe he formed a secret society, the Illuminati, whose objective was to defend enlightenment and reason, and to limit the power of the clergy. These historians think that the great achievements of western civilization, its liberalism and democracy, are all the fruit of this society's efforts."

"And what has any of this got to do with our sheikhs?" In his confusion, the Cerebellum cannot grasp where this conversation is leading. He wishes the young man would limit his comments to mathematics.

"If Osama bin Laden is an ideological extension of the Khawarij, then it's up to us intellectuals to organize ourselves in a modern-day enlightenment movement—even a secret one. The Net can serve as an avenue for reform in Islam, just as the printing press was the tool for reforming Christianity." The young man talks in hushed tones, which makes him sound even more serious.

"But what has all this got to do with me?" the Cerebellum says, rising from his chair. Does he not know I am a secular Sufi? he wonders.

Tahir is right, of course. When people like Condoleezza and the cub sheikh pray to God, it is out of fear of His punishment and greed for His blessing. He, on the other hand, worships without limiting himself to any particular ritual. He does it out of love for the Creator, with no desire to achieve any benefits, whether immediate or postponed. This is true religion, because it is absolute and it considers the Creator to be absolutely good. Still, he cannot accept Tahir's solution. He will simply not agree to turn religion into an arena for ideological confrontation. In any case, he lacks the inclination to spread his thoughts or convince others to follow him. Let every person search for the essence of existence in his or her own way. Why do people not simply relegate religion to the personal realm?

He can no longer bear this pointless conversation. The title 'the New Owner' has shaken him to the roots. The New Owner . . . how obnoxious! The whole of Egypt has been kidnapped by the New Owners: the owners of power, the owners of wealth, the owners of religion.

"Let us get down to business. Here are the rest of the coins." The Cerebellum heads for his jacket and draws the coins from its pocket.

"I'd feel more comfortable if you came with me to the Señor . . . and don't let my babble about Galileo and the church worry you, Mister Poet," Tahir says. After a moment's hesitation, he adds, "It's a big responsibility . . . and in any case the place is not very far away." The boy talks without looking him in the eye. Then he stands up and smoothes the bedclothes. The Cerebellum does not know why the Doctor with the Marines sunglasses comes to mind right now. Can we call him "the Original Owner" then? Tahir is right, again. The boy has done enough already, and he expects him to shortly do even more. How can he ask him to carry such a heavy load on his own? He drops the coins back into his jacket's breast pocket and puts it on.

"All right." For a fleeting moment, the Cerebellum adopts the tone of the gangster who started this whole mess.

Cairo, Egypt
Friday, January 19, 2007
Early afternoon

"What if they grab the money, but still don't release Didi? After all, she could always identify them," Tahir says once they are off the crowded minibus that has stopped on the May 15th flyover.

The Cerebellum says nothing. Of course the boy could be right. But what choice does he have? He follows Tahir in silence down the stairs to 26 July Street. He cannot remember the last time he was in Zamalek. Cairo's chaos has not spared this posh neighborhood, which used to epitomize elegance and good taste. The heaps of garbage are no less prominent here than in the Good Lady's alley. Pools of clotted blood, leftovers from the massacre of sheep at Eid, have yet to be cleaned away. Most of the buildings are in a pitiful state. Even the ones that have been renovated seem strangely out of place. Wherever they have built additional floors, they never even bothered to adopt the same architectural style as the existing buildings. The same is true of individual apartments. The façades of most buildings are eyesores.

Chaos engulfs everything in its way. Cairo is the entropy capital of the world. In Zamalek, he is faced with empirical evidence that chaos will ultimately take over the universe. But so what? Life's tireless struggle to create an area of order amid infinite dead space is, at best, temporary. Life will ultimately surrender to death. Both the victorious and the vanquished will end up as equals. In the blink of an eye, oppressor and oppressed will exchange places. Is chaos not, after all, the ocean on which the boat of order must sail? And is every boat not destined to sink?

He lags behind Tahir, like a child being led to school. The boy's words have opened up Pandora's box, and raised the very issues he has been putting off, perhaps for too long. Poisonous thoughts strike him, like machine-gun bullets aimed at his heart. But all this is nothing compared to his fundamental worry. He is not quite sure that this depressing torrent flooding his soul is in fact the outcome of a rational thought process. That is the problem. Is he starting to slip into the same river that swept away his mother, years ago? Can this be the critical step that will set him irrevocably on his charted course?

"Don't worry, Poet. Everything will be okay," Tahir says, and gently pats his arm. The Cerebellum realizes that the expression on his face must have given away his fears.

The Señor's shop lies in a narrow side street, almost blocked by parked cars. Tahir steps in without hesitation. The Cerebellum lingers outside. It is an ancient shop, its window narrow and so dusty that it nearly obscures the stamp collections that are crammed inside it. Some rusty coins are strewn about on a shelf in the corner. He wonders if Tahir ever brought Condoleezza to visit this magical place. He tries to see this shop window through the eyes of the young prostitute. The myriad designs and colors of the stamps, the strange names of countries, most of which she had probably never even heard of. A sight to make anyone's mind dizzy. Behind the dusty glass, thousands of windows open up before his eyes, inviting him to savor the wonders of history and geography. Millions of stories, infinite possibilities. The youthful Queen Bess stares at him from under her imperial crown. Now he is starting to understand how stamps could give back Condoleezza her freedom, why they have become the life jacket that keeps her from drowning.

Before joining Tahir inside, he notices that the shop has no sign. He could have easily passed by dozens of times without noticing it even existed. Like Aladdin's lamp, this shop encompasses the whole world, but is left to rust, buried beneath the sand.

"And peace be upon you, sir," the pale-skinned man replies in the Egyptian dialect, with a hint of a foreign accent. The Señor is ancient, like his shop. He is, after all, the practitioner of a dying profession. He is wearing a three-piece suit made of warm gray wool and a gray-and-black-striped tie. A woolen beret covers his head. He brazenly studies the Cerebellum from behind his steel-rimmed glasses.

Tahir nods to the Cerebellum to produce the coins. He complies, and arranges them in three piles inside a small drawer with a red velvet interior that the Señor has placed on the glass counter.

The Señor is wearing surgical gloves. He picks up one of the coins and places it in a machine that showers the coin with intense light and magnifies it. All three of them lean forward and stare at the enlarged image. The Señor points to the words engraved on the coin in Kufic script. He passes his glove-clad finger over the three concentric legends, reading from the inner to the outer bands.

"It looks like the dinar of al-Mu'izz," the Señor says without raising his eyes.

"A Fatimid dinar?" Tahir asks with interest.

"Not just any Fatimid dinar. This is a very rare coin that was issued by al-Mu'izz and circulated for a very brief period. Then the Fatimids were forced to withdraw it."

"Why?" the Cerebellum asks. The man has succeeded in piquing his curiosity.

"Look." Tahir points to the engraved legend.

In its magnified state, the Cerebellum can easily distinguish the wording. "Ali ibn Abi Talib is the Nominee of the Prophet and the Most Excellent Representative and the Husband of the Radiant Chaste One," it reads.

"As you know, the Fatimids were Ismaili Shias. Whereas Egyptians were—and still are—predominantly Sunni," the Señor explains in his pleasant accent.

"Are you saying that this is the only coin minted by the Fatimids with this inscription about Ali?" The Cerebellum's pulse is getting faster.

The Señor nods. Then he returns the coin to the velvet-clad drawer and picks up another.

"The buyer is confident that these coins date back to the early Fatimid period. He insists that is virtually impossible to replicate these minting techniques today," the Señor says softly. Then he continues to examine one coin after the other under his magnifying machine.

The Cerebellum notices that, despite its small dimensions, the shop's interior gives the impression of being spacious. This he attributes to the high ceiling and the squeaky-clean surfaces that contrast sharply with the dusty outer shop window, which, he reasons, must have been left in this sorry state by way of camouflage.

"While we wait for the buyer to arrive, there's one thing I'm curious about. Where were the coins stored all these years? They should be darkened and dented," the Señor says calmly, while still inspecting the coins.

"Right here . . . in my pocket," a beautiful, confident voice intervenes.

The Cerebellum turns around. To his shock, the old man with the tarboosh is standing two steps behind him. The man points to his breast pocket . . . and his heart. Then he adds, with a smile:

"In here, gold will never be damaged in any way."

"Welcome, Hajji. We've been waiting for you. The coins are available . . . are you still interested in purchasing them?" the Señor asks, in his direct manner.

"Why should I pay? I'm here to collect a debt." The old man gives the Cerebellum a look that penetrates his soul.

"But you said . . . you said it was a debt you owed me," the Cerebellum says.

For the first time in his life, he feels he is talking total nonsense.

"Did you ever lend me anything, Mustafa?" the old man asks simply. His expression is gentle, despite the difficulty of the situation. Then he heads for the velvet-clad drawer, whisking past Tahir and the Cerebellum without touching them.

"You are right . . . but there is a lirg who has been kipnadded and it is my serponsibility to tes her reef," the Cerebellum says, with some hesitation. Almost immediately, he realizes that he has started to reverse his words, a speech impediment that made him the butt of many jokes in his youth. His confusion mounts. He had thought that after the immense effort he put into speaking straight, he had exorcised this particular demon for good.

"And you figure you need gold to be able to shoulder your responsibility, Mustafa?" The old man's tone bears neither anger nor blame.

As the man talks, his face is just centimeters away. But the Cerebellum cannot feel his breath on his face. The old man walks to the Señor, picks up the gold coins, and simply drops them into his breast pocket, where they belong.

The Señor turns to the Cerebellum. Seeing no objection from the alleged owner, he decides not to intervene.

"One moment, Hajji, please." Tahir extends his arm to hold the old man back before he can leave the shop. But he withdraws his hand before touching the man's arm, as if shocked by an electric current.

"I still have one of the coins," the young man says, his eyebrows raised in astonishment. Then he produces the remaining dinar from his pocket.

"People are mules transporting gold . . . they never actually own it. One mule only delivers the burden to the next one," the old man says. He does not bother to take the coin from Tahir's hand. With unexpected agility for his age, he disappears out the door.

"And you, Mister . . . are you going to sell your coin, or will I have to count the whole day a waste of time?" The man addresses Tahir in the lingo of a vendor in the fish market. Yet he cannot completely erase the traces of his old-time, foreign accent.

The young man turns the coin between his thumb and forefinger and says nothing.

The Cerebellum watches the chain of events from a distance. He does not feel the least bit embarrassed by the way the young man is staring at him—in perplexity or, perhaps, accusation.

Embarrassment . . . that giant he has spent a lifetime wrestling with. But today he has lost the will to fight. He has grown numb. What good will emotions do him when catastrophe approaches unimpeded. In his heart, he knew it was all a matter of time. How can he forget that the few occasions in which he noticed his father looking embarrassed all had something to do with Akeel? The man who could not care less what others thought when he went onto the balcony in his underwear, day in and day out, year after year . . . that very same man would blush in embarrassment, like a schoolkid who has just wet himself in class, at a mere question by someone outside the immediate family about how Akeel was doing. It was taken for granted that his idiot brother embodied shame in every sense of the word. The loss of one's mind was the only misfortune that could legitimately be described as a fate worse than death, a rule that his mother reinforced years later, when she, too, surrendered her reason.

As for the loss of the gold . . . well, as the old man said, we are all . . . mules.

"What's your decision, Poet? Shall we sell?" Tahir asks vaguely.

"Do you know the eshuaquion $z = z^2 + c$, Hater?"

I never meant to abandon you, Mother. The words permeate the Cerebellum's tired mind. Or can his thoughts be audible to Tahir and the Señor? Can his crime be evident to the entire world? To abandon you in a mental hospital and fly off to Iraq, to neglect calling to see how you were doing and to make sure you were being well treated . . . to do nothing but pay the bills from afar . . . that was inexcusable. But the only thing I ever feared was insanity. You were a reminder of what would ultimately become of me. By God, it was cowardice, Mother.

What I did was not out of cruelty or insensitivity. It was easier to risk facing Saddam's wrath than look in the mirror.

"It's the Mandelbrot set, Poet. The butterfly effect. But the Señor here is still waiting for your decision." Tahir's voice returns him to a tiny shop that extends well beyond its physical dimensions.

Wonderful . . . mathematics . . . always mathematics . . . the wonder of equations, numbers, and abstract thoughts.

The young man's reply indicates that he never actually pronounced the words that were racing through his mind. The Cerebellum is overcome by a sense of relief. He has not yet reached the point where the barriers collapse. The dam is still intact . . . his internal morass has yet to overflow into the exterior world.

His mother died years ago, but he has no idea what has become of Akeel. Has he survived, or did he join her on another level of existence, so much purer than ours?

That is not important now. Nothing is important any more. Every boat is destined to sink.

He turns to the Señor, who is staring at him. All hope of saving Didi is lost. And his own fate has already been sealed. He turns to Tahir:

"It is your decision, genius. This mule has already delivered his burden."

The Cerebellum is overcome by an unexpected sense of relief. Nothing can scare him any more. And more importantly, when he spoke this time, he did not reverse a single word.

Charlotte, North Carolina
Friday, January 19, 2007
1052 EST

With a faint smile on his face, Martin sends his fingers tap-dancing across the keyboard. His level of concentration befits a professional pianist. It has been ages since he carried a broad smile into the Ghost Center, as he did today. Alpha's subdued expression may have made his smile even wider. The fat man didn't say a word until he left. He let Martin do what he does best. The subject has come to play on their home ground. Now he will set a trap for this mouse.

Martin takes a tour of candygirl's virtual villa. At last he's succeeded in locating the place where the subject lets down his defenses and gives free rein to his emotions. People's emotions — as he's been told time and again — are their Achilles' heel. If you succeed in reaching their soft spot, you gain total control. Sometimes we're stronger than we think. But most of the time, we're weaker. Much weaker, really.

A familiar song resonates throughout the living room. The music video is being shown on the screen that occupies almost an entire wall. The decor is minimalist. There's only one two-seater sofa facing the screen. After all, this is the world of dreams, the place where people shirk all responsibility. There is no room here for families and kids. On a white pedestal in the corner, there's an abstract sculpture in black marble. It probably represents a cat. He likes it here, he must admit. It's simple and clean. The floor is made of good-quality hardwood and the walls display masterpieces by some of the world's most famous artists.

"They must all be originals," he says audibly, then laughs at his own joke.

The Ghost Center is not used to the sound of laughter.

He steps out into the swimming-pool area. The deck is enclosed by a small wrought-iron fence, beyond which a breathtaking natural vista takes up half the screen. Martin observes the rocky hill with its silent waterfall. The sight arouses his love of adventure. It is as though he's abandoned the civilized world and gone back to nature, unpolluted by human presence. Beyond the fence on the opposite side, the sea extends forever. He returns his focus to the pool. The steam it emits indicates it is heated. The water invites you to jump into its embrace, with the music emanating from the living room in the background, and leave behind all your worries. The greatest degree of liberation coincides with the highest level of illusion.

A couple of lounge chairs face the pool. They support two figures in a state of perfect relaxation. Martin zooms in on the two avatars.

Like a psychoanalyst, his job obliges him to analyze their personalities. Like a surgeon preparing for an operation, he must inspect their bodies. He must get inside their skins, know them as he knows himself. No, even more profoundly than a man can possibly get to understand his own self.

The avatar that Mickey Mouse chose as an alter ego is in a state of electronic hibernation on the deck chair nearest to his angle of vision. His body is unnaturally tall. Beneath an unbuttoned red shirt, his well-shaped muscles are visible. To make his point, Mickey Mouse has named his alter ego Biceps. Martin contemplates the subject's real-life photographs, still displayed on the left-hand wall screen. They've just added the ones they recently shot. He's a man of slight build who always wears oversized clothes. Although middle-aged, he still has a child's body. Martin starts reviewing all the available information about him.

"Perfectly predictable . . . a desperate attempt to make up for his physical deficiency," Martin says out loud and nods confidently.

Then he starts to study the well-formed electronic body the subject has chosen to compensate for all his life's disappointments. He's intrigued by the thick gold necklace Biceps is wearing and his almost shoulder-length cascade of black hair.

"An unusual choice for a Middle Eastern man. But then he emphasizes his masculinity by the thick mustache and the goatee." His fingers tap on the counter.

He could use some coffee right now, but he's too engrossed in his work to leave his chair. A treasure trove of information is on the laptop screen. He decides to shift the world of virtual reality onto the central wall screen. If it were humanly possible, he'd physically walk into candygirl's home.

He now turns his attention to the young woman who owns this house. She's wearing a green dress that reveals her curvaceous figure. Her orange hair spreads over her perfectly rounded breasts and bare shoulders. A delicate and sensuous Cinderella lying on the lounge chair, waiting for Prince Charming to rekindle her dormant sexual energy. Candygirl . . . her name floats in the air above her head.

Martin's fingers resume their magical dance on the keyboard. In a matter of seconds, the face of a woman in her fifties occupies the left-hand screen. Beneath the photo a few lines sum up her life history. The picture doesn't show her body, but her round face and double chin leave little doubt that she's quite obese.

"A library assistant in Nebraska." He starts to laugh, but the pangs of guilt in his chest stop him short. There's no denying that he's now invading the privacy of an innocent U.S. citizen.

With quick taps on the keyboard, he brings candygirl back to virtual life. Gracefully, she rises from her pool chair. He studies her contours. No woman alive can ever hope to compete with her measurements. By simply striking a few keys, he's deprived Pamela—Pamela Schwabsky is the fat librarian's full name—of the most beautiful aspect of her bleak life. He's stolen candygirl away from her, thus limiting her existence to this childless, husbandless woman with the cheap hair dye, whose only company is a bottle of cheap liquor. Having taken over her sumptuous villa, he's left her no safe haven in the world other than her crummy apartment that smells of sneakers and last night's Big Mac.

He can't even imagine how she'll react when she fails to resume her virtual existence. He tries to avoid picturing the expression on her face when she discovers she's unable to perform her daily reincarnation in the form of her avatar. Will she create a new avatar and go looking for candygirl? And what will she do when she finds her alive and well, leading a perfectly normal life with Biceps? He decides to send a deadly virus to Pamela Schwabsky's PC. It'll take some time before she realizes what's going on.

But in whose name is he doing all this, and to serve whose interests? All this premeditated destruction . . .

Strangely enough, defending democracy is the only excuse he can come up with to justify his crimes. As if he can only defend Pamela by invading her privacy, sabotaging her property, shattering her dreams.

Martin needs to heed the call of nature and get himself a mug of coffee, but before he can budge, Biceps suddenly comes out of hibernation and stands up. At last, Martin has come face to face with his genius nemesis. It's showdown time, like in a Western. Only the one who's fastest on the draw, the man with the steadiest hand, will make it today. This time, however, the agent of death will be no bullet, but rather sheer brainpower. To boost his confidence, Martin reminds himself that no matter how superior Mickey Mouse's mental capacity may be, his human weakness will spell his downfall.

Biceps said: I missed you, my darling.

You said: I always fall for your sweet words, Cerebellum.

Martin feels uncomfortable impersonating a woman, and not just any woman, but a woman in love.

Biceps said: Please don't call me that . . . I told you, it upsets me.

So, Mickey Mouse realizes that he's made a big mistake. He's even trying to undo it. It's too late, genius . . . can't you see that? Still, Martin needs to tread carefully. The subject is clearly on his guard.

You said: Anything you say, honey. Won't repeat it again. I was thinking maybe it's time to take our relationship to the next level.

Biceps said: After our latest experience, I don't know what other level we can attain.

Martin has no idea about this latest experience he's referring to, but he needs to keep the conversation going.

You said: Actually, it's that very special experience that got me thinking.

Biceps said: Then you have changed your mind about
the absolute freedom that the parallel universe
affords us?

Martin hesitates for a moment. If he makes a wrong move now,
the victory at hand will turn into a final defeat. He touches the keyboard gingerly:

You said: Love is all that matters.

A general statement, whose vagueness hides the fact that he hasn't
a clue what the other man is talking about.

Biceps said: How true . . . love is all that matters.

Martin takes a huge breath of relief. The subject has swallowed the
bait. Emotions . . . time and again, emotions will prove to be people's
Achilles' heel. Gathering his courage, he takes it a step further.

You said: I have found the perfect place for our first
meeting in the real world. It won't be that different
from virtual reality, because you won't be physically
present. But I'll still order you a drink and I'll
imagine you sharing my table.

Martin's euphoria, soaring since he heard the magic words "they call
me the Cerebellum," has now reached its peak. Here he is, outsmarting
a brilliant mind who for years has managed to evade the world's best
intelligence agencies. He's making a fool out of a full-fledged genius.

Biceps said: The real world? What can the real world
give us that we do not already have . . . besides
conflict and heartache?

You said: It's my way of taking our relationship to the next level. Guess what? I've made myself a real dress identical to the one I'm wearing now.

Candygirl makes a 360-degree turn, showing off her beautiful dress and her formidable figure. Then Martin goes for the jugular.

You said: Think about it this way: if you were present at that café, you'd recognize me immediately.

Biceps said: But I won't be present at the café . . . how could I possibly be present at that particular café?

Martin's heart starts to pound violently. He's just revealed his plan. If the subject fails to see through it right now, he'll have walked right into the trap, no doubt about it.

You said: It doesn't matter. What counts is that you'll know we spent a wonderful day together in a different kind of fantasy world.

Biceps said: And where will this rendezvous take place . . . in romantic Vienna or magical Venice?

You said: Let the musicians go to Vienna and the romantics to Venice. Me, I've always dreamed of going to Egypt. When I'm at the pyramids I'll pretend you're right there next to me, telling me all about their mathematical secrets. After all, you're my genius.

Biceps said: Egypt . . . but that's so far away. The only way I can be with you is if we make believe.

The subject is lying. Is it just caution, or has he seen through the plot? Is he getting ready to disappear off their radar forever? Martin's bladder is about to explode. He hesitates for a second before typing in his next move. But Mickey Mouse saves him the trouble. With a few magical words on the screen, he provides the most eloquent possible answer to his question.

```
Biceps said: Why don't you tell me where this meeting
will be? Maybe I can locate it on Google Earth.
```

Martin rushes to the bathroom before completely losing control over his bladder. He reappears in a few seconds, without bothering to flush the toilet. For the second time in twenty-four hours, he does a victory dance.

Then he controls himself and goes back to his computer.

chapter 12

Cairo, Egypt
Saturday, January 20, 2007
Around 4:30 p.m.

A few minutes ago, inside Ataba Metro station, the Cerebellum split with Tahir and Condoleezza. The plan requires each of the two parties to hit the street from their designated exit.

The moment the Cerebellum forsakes the relative security afforded him by the bowels of the earth and comes out into daylight, the sun's rays wreak havoc on his eyesight and he loses concentration. The physical sensation of being off balance is made worse by the moral burden laid squarely on his shoulders. At least he has freed himself of any remaining hesitation or fear. After a lifetime of disorientation, the goal is, at last, crystal clear. His mission is to liberate Didi.

For a reason he has been unable to clearly define, this mission has come to embody the sum of his life's ambitions. The specter of failure is the only thing that can instill fear in him today . . . especially now that Tahir and Condoleezza have volunteered to play an active role in the operation, thus doubling the cost of failure.

The distance that separates the Cerebellum—at his exit point at the corner of Adli Street and Opera Square—from Groppi, the designated venue for the exchange, cannot be more than a hundred meters.

But each step is laced with danger. Some of the threats are obvious and clearly defined in his mind. Other perils remain uncharted, which opens up an endless range of possibilities. The risks they pose have come to encompass all the world's nightmares. Yet all the world's nightmares seem harmless right now, defanged. He has recently discovered that the specter of death is a paper tiger. To be more precise, it has become clear to him that he is already a dead man walking. All attempts to cling to life have turned into a nuisance, an annoying illusion.

He proceeds with caution, walking at a regular pace so as not to attract attention, keeping close to the shop windows under the cover of other pedestrians. He makes no attempt to check if he is being followed. It is nearly impossible to detect some of these modern surveillance techniques anyway. And even if he were to ascertain that he was, indeed, under surveillance, what good would it do him?

Condoleezza came to his room last night, and for the first time ever, she brought Tahir along with her. Although he had already guessed that their relationship had developed lately, it suddenly became apparent just how far things had gone. They walked into the room and sat on the bed, side by side. The Cerebellum was a little surprised when she made no objection to shutting the door, but he made no attempt to seek an explanation. He had had enough of her religious rambling. Instinctively, he headed for the teakettle. But before he could immerse it in the water barrel, she produced, from a pocket inside her gown, two stacks of cash, each bound by a rubber band. Without a word, she handed them over to him. For the millionth time, the Cerebellum cursed her damned veil. At that instant, he really needed to try and read her face, particularly as Tahir's features revealed nothing. He just sat there and looked straight ahead, as if the whole affair was no concern of his. Yet he seemed relaxed. The Cerebellum thought he could even detect a hint of pride in his eyes. Tahir was not only in love with the dark-skinned whore, he was actually proud of her. He must surely have seen in her what others could not see.

"What is this?" The Cerebellum was left with no choice but to ask bluntly.

Her answer felt like a slap on the face. It came to him as a revelation, engendering nothing less than a paradigm shift. He was another Christopher Columbus peering into the horizon at the silhouette of a new continent, a Louis Pasteur contemplating a new world, hidden from the naked eye, throbbing with vitality under his microscope. Condoleezza, the whore, was not only handing over to him the money Tahir had obtained from selling the remaining coin to the Señor, she was actually giving him her life savings. This was the stash she had put aside to open a hair salon for veiled women, her passport out of this business, her only chance to repent of all her sins.

This act went well beyond kindness. It was an act of sacrifice. She was sacrificing her future, her very salvation, for a young woman she had never even met. But why? What had the world ever given either of them, that they would repay with such nobility of spirit?

It took the Cerebellum a few minutes to regain control of his emotions. No matter how long you have lived, how much you have learned, life will take you by surprise. Life will always maintain the prerogative to shake the temple of human knowledge to its very foundations; to bring down, in the blink of an eye, the structure of mathematics that he once believed was unassailable. The Platonic number, the triangular numbers, the pyramidal numbers, the cattle problem, the four-color problem, scientists' efforts to discover the God particle, the Higgs boson: suddenly they are no more than games we like to play, ploys we resort to, to distract ourselves. They can never reach the level of one real action . . . an action like the simple one taken by the dark-skinned whore, without the slightest hesitation.

He had become accustomed to begrudging her the respect she so richly deserved. Like the rest of the world, he had misjudged her. But yesterday, he finally learned his lesson. Then the three of them put their heads together in order to perfect the plan.

Today, as he avoids colliding with young men strolling shoulder to shoulder down Adli Street with a show of insolence that only the ignorant can afford, trying as hard as he can not to brush against the women in full veils hurrying by, shielded by their culture of defiance, he reiterates to himself the wisdom of selecting this particular branch of Groppi for the handover. For one thing, it is close to a Metro station with multiple exits, which should facilitate their escape. The café can also be accessed from two parallel streets. He will use the Adli Street entrance himself, while Tahir and Condoleezza will slip in separately from Abdel Khaliq Tharwat Street, the same exit through which Didi, when the time comes—he hopes—will make her escape.

The Cerebellum has worked out the entire operation to the minutest detail. After all, when it comes to plans and calculations, is there a man alive who can surpass him?

The choice of venue for the meeting—the two meetings, to be precise—was his and his alone. If the plan falls apart, if all hope is lost, there will be no one else to share the blame. It was he who decided that the café suggested by candygirl for their first—and definitely last—rendezvous, in this overcrowded, dusty, exhaust-polluted world, was also the most suitable location for his plan to liberate Didi.

But did he tailor his plan to fit the specific location that his electronic idol had chosen for their meeting? Could it be that, despite his determination to set Didi free at any cost, he could not bear to waste the opportunity to exchange glances—fleeting though they may have to be—with his beloved . . . no matter what risk it may entail?

Charlotte, North Carolina
Saturday, January 20, 2007
0940 EST

When the subject's slim form appeared on the central screen as he left the Metro station's exit, Martin jerked in his seat and jumped in the air like a sports fan whose team has just scored a valuable goal. He wished agent Alpha were present right now, so he could see with his own two fiendish eyes Martin's predictions materialize, one by one. He'd be left with no choice but to give Martin due credit for the success of one of the Ghost Center's most important operations. But the fat man left at the end of his shift without a word of appreciation, without even mentioning, out of common courtesy, that he was leaving. For the thousandth time, he exhibited his mean nature.

The subject walks slowly, pretending to be window shopping. What a pitiful attempt to make yourself invisible, Mickey. Little does the poor man realize that their cameras are zooming in on him from every angle. Nor does he imagine that the WASP and his team are already in Groppi. The WASP is calmly sipping his cappuccino, waiting for him to show up. The net is tight and the fish is almost in. All the fisherman needs to do now is to show some patience.

Martin sips his coffee. It tastes more bitter than usual. Perhaps his senses are more alert than at any other time in the past. The subject approaches, slowly. But it's a short distance, anyway. Success is at his fingertips. It's only a matter of minutes.

Suddenly, two men obstruct the subject. The mug shakes in Martin's hand. The subject is now only steps away from Groppi . . . but something fishy is going on. The subject is having some sort of argument with the two men in the middle of the crowded sidewalk. They're hefty types, one with a big belly, the other more athletic. Martin's fingers race across the keyboard, but the computer is unable to locate a file for either of them in its database. They're both wearing fancy suits but they've got bad news written all over their faces. Could they be gang members, or is this another one of the subject's tricks? Is Mickey Mouse part of a larger scheme, an operation their agencies know nothing about?

"All units, full alert!" Martin shouts into the mike. A meaningless statement, really.

What's Mickey Mouse doing with these guys, anyway? He must be involved in something ugly. Something really shady. One thing's for sure: Command is right in making his elimination a top priority. Martin regrets his recent doubts. Beta was an idiot, whatever happened to him. Even if Mickey Mouse and his ilk are innocent, no one should risk the future of civilized societies for a bunch of barbarians. If it's necessary to sacrifice someone, let it be these bastards, rather than Amy and their own innocent people.

The subject produces a stash of banknotes from his pocket. After a quick count, the athletic gangster pockets the money. What's happening? What does this transaction involve? The guy with the belly is talking on his cell phone. Could he be calling for a vehicle to once again snatch the subject from their grip? If that proves to be the case, Martin's instructions to his agents will be decisive. Why couldn't Alpha wait a little longer today, like he's done so many times before? The son of a bitch could, at least, bear some of the responsibility. Right now, Martin doesn't know for sure what's happening. The picture in front of him is not at all clear. He can't just sit on his hands and wait, while the situation is quickly taking a dangerous turn. But at the same time, he mustn't lose his nerve and disrupt his well-made plan.

After all the effort he's put into this . . . could the fish get off the hook?

Cairo, Egypt
Saturday, January 20, 2007
Almost five in the afternoon

The Cerebellum takes a deep breath. Today he is determined to avoid using the inhaler. Until a second ago, he was not sure if the two men would be willing to show flexibility. At first they rejected his proposal outright. They wanted to get their hands on the full amount beforehand, then would release Didi at their leisure. Their demand came as no surprise to the Cerebellum, but he insisted that the remainder be delivered simultaneously with Didi's release. He had nothing to lose. He simply did not possess the required sum. He made it clear that he and poor Didi were not close at all. In reality, the whole matter was no concern of his. He was just acting like a gentleman, doing a good deed, with no thought of personal gain. To prove he was serious, and to get them drooling, he showed them one of Condoleezza's two stashes. He wanted them to smell the money. When they saw the cash, they relaxed. Then the muscular gangster produced his cell phone to relay the Cerebellum's offer to his boss. At that point, the Cerebellum knew they had swallowed the bait.

He could not catch the boss's reply over the man's phone. Neither of the two men bothered to explain anything to him. They just froze in their steps, waiting for some predetermined event to happen. The Cerebellum can now see Tahir on the other side of the café. This restores some of his confidence. He must be waiting just outside the ladies' restroom. Condoleezza should already be inside. She will have an extra set of her clothing, face veil and all, so that the plan can work.

The café's patrons are a mixture of Egyptians and foreigners. They all talk in loud voices, the conversations punctuated by the consumption of food and drink. A few cats are busy snatching the leftovers from the tables. There are children playing hide-and-seek between the tables. One of them, its eyes radiating a naughty vitality, reminds him of Antar from the Tower of Happiness. How old would Antar be today? He quickly scans the cats, and finds one that is the spitting image of Mishmish, Antar's kitten. A waiter with an overloaded tray skillfully maneuvers between the tables. This is an ordinary scene from a Cairo café. The people here are oblivious to the game of life and death being played around them.

A black Peugeot parallel-parks just behind him. The man with the belly opens the door and pushes him inside. A familiar situation. This sort of thing no longer scares him. Familiarity has milked the venom from this snake. Situations are like emotions: they will come and they will go, then they will come just so they can go. It does not surprise him to find Didi in the back seat next to him. The sight of her cherubic face instills a sense of joy in him that he has not felt since childhood.

"Hello there," she says with a faint smile that is, nevertheless, full of warmth. She is wearing a man's shirt that is too big for her. What have the bastards done with the red sweater that he saw the monster rip on the screen?

Despite some scratches and a small lump on her forehead, Didi is still Didi, beautiful and strong, confidently smiling at him. Unbroken. He can hardly believe it. Despite all they have done to her, they have failed to tame her. Freeing you is worth any sacrifice, Didi.

A lump in his throat keeps him from returning her greeting.

"So you think you can take possession of the merchandise before I make sure you aren't playing any tricks on me?" a man with an insolent voice says. As soon as he hears that voice, the Cerebellum is swept away by an unprecedented wave of hatred toward its owner. The man is not even looking at him. He is sitting in the front seat next to the driver— where the Doctor was sitting in the Pajero. Yet the back of his fat, bald head seems familiar. From repeatedly playing the recording he received via e-mail, the Cerebellum has memorized the image of the back of this man's head. This is the New Owner, in the flesh.

He gulps, struggling for breath, but cannot get it. He digs his fingers into his trouser pocket, looking for the inhaler, but only feels the ivory dice. He must quickly control himself. He cannot allow this emotional surge to paralyze him.

"The cash is sitting there, waiting to be picked up, but I, too, need to make sure you'll release the girl. Don't forget, I've already demonstrated my good intentions. Your friend over there has the down payment." The Cerebellum speaks slowly and deliberately, perhaps only to be sure his voice will not quiver under the weight of his emotional deluge.

"What about the rest of the money?" the man says, without turning his head.

The two gang members the Cerebellum spoke with earlier are still on the sidewalk. They watch the passersby suspiciously.

"Do you see the young man in the brown sweater on the other side of the café . . . the one with the bag? You can deliver the girl to him and collect the cash," the Cerebellum says, resisting the urge to put his hands around the man's thick neck.

"Oh yeah?" The man seems to be considering the Cerebellum's proposal.

"I'd have no problem if you wanted to hold me as collateral until you're completely satisfied," the Cerebellum says quickly, trying to sound self-confident. Maybe this way he will be able to influence the New Owner's decision.

"No offense, Mister, but this beauty is ready merchandise, worth a good price. You, on the other hand, wouldn't fetch one piaster."

It takes a few seconds for the man's words to sink in. He may have a point. But the counterargument is simple and clear in the Cerebellum's mind. However, when he opens his mouth to speak, the words do not flow out as usual. Instead he produces a growling sound, like the snarl of rabid dog. He can no longer absorb the precise meaning of what he is saying. His perception of the surrounding environment is blurred. It is as though the different dimensions of existence have fused together, stripping things of their precise meanings. His father is present in front of him, in his underwear, hanging the laundry on the balcony, staring down the world. His mother, in her fancy blue dress, is cleaning the living room with a feather duster. She smiles at him from beneath her full makeup. He is at his desk, inventing an equation the algebra teacher will be unable to solve. Akeel has crept into the kitchen, opened the fridge, and is digging his teeth into a raw chicken. . . .

The Cerebellum watches himself—an engineering student who looks no older than a kid in primary school—as he debates with the most prominent professors about three-dimensional geometry. At that very instant, he is partying with a group of friends in the apartment they call "the Blimp," reading one book after the other, amid a cloud of blue smoke that is getting thicker with every puff. Yet here he is again, conjuring ghosts in a high-class séance, on the thirteenth floor of the Tower of Happiness.

One part of his mind realizes he has been talking for minutes, explaining to the man how simple it is to put together a nuclear program these days. For a determined country, it is only a matter of time and money. The only problem is how to protect the installations. How to build reinforced structures buried under mountains that can withstand the superpowers' bunker-busting munitions. Thus Mustafa Mahmud Korany—a.k.a. the Cerebellum—is the most dangerous man on the face of the planet, as far as these great powers are concerned. More dangerous than bin Laden and his clowns.

If the bald human trafficker had realized that some intelligence agencies would gladly pay a fortune for information about his whereabouts, he would have understood that he is worth something on the market.

An explosion shakes the car.

The Cerebellum comes out of his stupor to see the shock on Didi's face. The driver has rushed outside. The fat man in the front seat is looking nervously in every direction. Part of the Cerebellum's mind realizes he has just recited, to the gang boss, the proofs of some of the most complex mathematical problems. Except that everything he said came out in reverse. Totally incomprehensible. He smiles in embarrassment. What is the use of talk, anyway?

The slave trader overlooked all the sacrifices made by his father, the man's courage in challenging the world so that his son could one day become the country's leading scientist. He ignored the torture his mother must have gone through, just to remain lucid long enough to accomplish her life's mission: bringing up her son. Perhaps the man never even considered the sacrifices generations of Egyptians had to make for the country to sail out of the sea of darkness, so that we could at least have the capacity to live in the modern world.

Does this fool not understand the scale of the investment a nation has to make, the resources it must deprive its most needy citizens of, in order to produce one scientist of his caliber?

But what enrages the Cerebellum most of all is that the criminal is right. Enough. He has had enough of knowledge and polemics and dreams and talk so big it cannot fit into a meaningful sentence any more. What matters right now is: what the hell has happened to this car?

Charlotte, North Carolina
Saturday, January 20, 2007
1003 EST

"COBRA 1, shoot out his tire." Martin barks into the mike.

The moment the subject got into that vehicle, he crossed the red line. Martin is not going to wait around for a repeat performance of last time's fiasco. The left-hand screen shows the same girl with the long black hair. All he needs now is the old man with the funny red hat and all the ingredients will be there. But he's learned his lesson. Should he have reminded the sniper to screw on his silencer? Why is it taking him so long to pull the trigger, anyway?

"WASP unit, proceed immediately toward the black Peugeot."

Change of plan; he's not going to wait for the subject to walk into the café. He'll be eliminated on the sidewalk or even inside the vehicle, if necessary.

"Sting at will," he adds quickly.

He's done it. He's given the order to bring down the subject. Despite these apparent setbacks, the operation is heading in the right direction.

The Peugeot suddenly leans to one side. The sharpshooter has targeted one of the front tires. This vehicle won't be giving them a hard time today. No more ridiculous car chases in this overcrowded city. The driver cautiously gets out of the car. He studies the blown tire, then inspects the other three tires by pressing his shoe against them. He reports to the front-seat passenger through the window the man has just opened.

The passengers start to get out of the car. The driver, a fat, bald man who was sitting in the front passenger seat, and the girl are now outside. But Mickey Mouse waits inside the Peugeot. The two guys who were on guard flank the girl. The athletic one holds her firmly by the arm. He's making sure she can't escape. The WASP unit is now only feet away from their target. But they need to neutralize the gang before they can get to him. Martin can afford to wait a little longer, but if they bring along another vehicle, he'll have everyone killed on the spot. He hopes he doesn't have to resort to such extreme measures, because it would call into question the success of the operation. The requirement is to eliminate the subject quietly, without raising any suspicions that it's an assassination.

The athletic bodyguard is pulling the girl through the café to the other side. Martin doesn't know what the hell is going on, but he can see that Mickey Mouse and all the others are following the progress of these two with interest. They approach a skinny young guy with a sports bag. The two men exchange a few words, and the young guy opens his bag. The gangster looks inside, zips it shut, and takes possession of it.

He sets the girl free, then turns and heads back. The young guy pushes the girl into the ladies' restroom.

This is a kidnapping, no doubt about it. All along, Mickey Mouse was trying to get together the ransom money. So this is how he fits in with the gang. Martin has at last understood the subject's motives. He's not part of some satanic conspiracy . . . he's a victim of one. But who's the girl, anyway . . . maybe his daughter?

Could the man be the father of a beautiful daughter, just like Martin? He too would be willing to do anything to save his daughter.

Doubts are again starting to buzz in the back of Martin's mind. He thought he'd gotten over his misgivings, but Agent Beta's disquieting questions are again imposing themselves on him.

The action on the right-hand screen leaves him no time to think. Two stocky men pounce on the young guy and the girl. One of them tries to stop her from getting inside the ladies' restroom. The other blocks the young guy's escape route to the street. So the gang hasn't kept their word. They want to take the money and hold on to the hostage, too. What's worse, they succeeded in duping the genius engineer. What's Mickey Mouse going to do now?

Martin's eyes are glued to the central screen, the one that shows the subject inside the car. The image is slightly fuzzy, yet Martin can see rage in his face. Mickey throws the car door open and rushes out. The picture shakes violently. Martin understands that the WASP is moving toward his target. Now that he's out of the car, Mickey is within range of his special weapon. Martin can still track the movements of the WASP unit on the satellite image.

The WASP himself is approaching the target, while two agents of his team block the two gangsters who are about to restrain the subject.

The operation has entered a decisive phase. Everything will be settled in a matter of seconds. All he can do now is take a deep breath and wait.

But it's also within his power to call the whole thing off. To spare a human life. By simply whispering one word into the microphone, he can set his conscience at ease.

Will he take the life of an innocent man just because he's been instructed to do so by a Command whose intentions he isn't even aware of? What would he say in his own defense, if he stood accused before a judge and a jury? What is there to distinguish him from members of a criminal gang? More important, where have all the principles that his government is proclaiming, day in and day out, gone? In which waste-basket have they discarded the Constitution of the United States?

It is within his power to stop this operation, right now.

"How can democracies defeat the terrorists when they start to act like them?" Beta's words still linger in the Ghost Center's stagnant air.

How will Martin act in these critical seconds?

Cairo, Egypt
Saturday, January 20, 2007
A quarter past five, more or less

For a second, the Cerebellum thinks the two men who charged at Didi and Tahir are plainclothes policemen. The government cannot possibly be oblivious to all these evils. It must take surgical action to remove this cancerous tumor before it spreads over the whole of society. The law will ultimately take its course, but only when the time is right . . . did you not know that? Then he notices the devil smiling. Triumph is written all over the New Owner's face. He must have started to grasp the truth.

The two men belong to the gang. The whole thing must be part of their scheme. But there was no way they could have suspected that the money in the bag was less than the required sum. The newspapers had been carefully cut to size and each stack contained enough real bank-notes to be convincing. They had used all the money the gold dinar had fetched. The New Owner must have intended to betray him all along. He wanted to put his hands on the ransom money, but he could not bear to part with Didi.

Simply put, they have been betrayed. All is lost now. Life is nothing but loss and degradation.

But that was only to be expected. After all, this beauty is ready merchandise, worth a good price. Or perhaps the New Owner had taken it personally. Didi has this effect on men sometimes. Her cherubic beauty arouses their basest instincts. The New Owner had not succeeded in breaking her yet, and he would never voluntarily relinquish such a pleasure.

This lowlife has fooled you, genius. You came here to trick him, but he did it to you first.

His rage breaks loose. The rage he has accumulated over the years. The rage of a lifetime. Now it has been permanently set free. Rage follows on the heels of despair. Well, he has reached the lowest pit. The cumulative despair of generations who have wasted their lives to bring about some sort of transformation in this country, the despair of millions of Egyptians suddenly materializes in the Cerebellum's soul . . . and so does their rage.

The time for equations and mental games is past, Professor.

Like a raging bull, he charges out of the car. For the first time, his vision of reality is blurred. But he could not care less. His only concern is to get to the fat slave trader, to fasten his hands around his throat, come what may. But someone is blocking him. Someone strong and well-trained. The Cerebellum just cannot get him out of the way. Who could it be? How did he appear out of thin air, at precisely the right moment?

A sharp pain in his back. The sting of a scorpion from hell. Instinctively, he turns. The man's body is twisted as he changes direction. This is not the same guy who blocked his advance toward the gang boss. This one is carrying an umbrella. There is not a cloud in the sky. Who carries an umbrella in Egypt? He must have stuck its tip in his back. Maybe it was an accident. A momentary pinprick, nothing serious. Yet, beneath the sunglasses that cover half his face, the man's expression is intense. Why does he need sunglasses when the sun is about to set? The expression he caught on the man's foreign face, as he melted into the crowd, was anything but innocent. His expression was not hatred or anger, but the look of a man in deep concentration . . . a man totally alert. This is not a man who has gone out for a walk.

He is a professional doing a job. Could it be? Have the demons at last caught up with him?

He has read about creative methods to assassinate people, including using the tip of an umbrella to inject poison. Within minutes or hours, the victim suffers a deadly heart attack. A murder that makes use of top-notch technology, to make it look like death was due to natural causes. This is the perfect crime that the world's criminals have long dreamed about. Does he happen to be today's victim?

Tricked by a local gang, killed by foreign agents, while all he ever wished for was to save innocent Didi. He never asked for a million dollars or the Nobel Prize. Only to free Didi, and to get a fleeting look at candygirl. All he ever wished for . . . and now he is dying . . . a genius thrown to the dogs . . . a life wasted from beginning to end. You can ask one man to sacrifice himself, but what is the use, when desperation is gnawing at the entire nation's skeleton? He is overtaken by sorrow, a living palpable sadness.

There is a battle of sorts raging around him. He is unable to figure out its specifics. What use are battles, anyway, for one who has been killed and is waiting around for his death certificate to be formalized? But it is a muted battle. It produces neither shout nor groan. There are no threats or calls for vengeance. It is just professionals going about their business. But there is yet another perturbation in the making. A distur-bance originating from inside the café. Can candygirl have realized what is happening to her lover and decided to intervene to save him?

Get real, Cerebellum. Even when dancing in the arms of death, you cling to your imaginary world.

Nevertheless, he is determined to act, to take advantage of what-ever time he has left. He is just not sure on whose side to intervene in the ongoing battle. He tries to get to the gang boss, who is wrestling with an unknown foreigner, but finds himself face to face with the muscular bodyguard as he rushes to his boss's rescue. He is still holding the bag with the ransom money in it. The Cerebellum remembers the stash of banknotes, which is the sum of faithful Condoleezza's life sav-ings. The guy must still have it. He will now get it back. The moment the bodyguard turns his back on him, the Cerebellum digs his hand into his inner pocket.

The man turns to him in surprise. As the Cerebellum pulls out the stash, he grips him by the throat with one hand.

A thump is accompanied by the ringing sound of glass breaking. The man's grip on his windpipe feels like steel. He knew the waiter had overloaded his tray. He thinks of his fingernails as talons, and digs them into the muscular guy's face. The man's eyeball is moist and tender between his fingers. He is not sure who will surrender first. If the man would only let go of the bag he is holding in his other hand, he could easily finish the Cerebellum off. As for him, he will not let go of Condoleezza's money, no matter what.

The man pushes him away with both hands. He has let go of the bag. Now the brute will finish him off. His eye is bloodshot, like a boxer in the fifteenth round. A cat yowls in panic. Then it hisses and jumps high in the air. The man retreats a few steps. He cries out. Its claws leave crimson lines on his chin and neck. The Cerebellum suddenly feels his chest clamp. The poison is starting to act. He does not doubt that his end is near. Death will snatch him from the gang's hands. He tries to control his pain. He picks up the bag and heads for the café.

He has recovered all of the money. He will give it all back to Condoleezza and Tahir. He will quickly scan the women at the tables . . . and then what?

The voices intermingle. There is too much chatter. He cannot distinguish any of the words. Then that coarse voice reaches him from somewhere in the background . . . faint . . . faraway . . . yet clear as the voice of fate: "The boat has sunk, Captain."

The Cerebellum shakes his head. He is deeply sad . . . but not for himself.

The words repeat themselves, silent, crystal-clear from the depths of the sea. Traveling distances so vast as to defy human imagination, their echoes reverberate in the farthest corners of the universe. Their significance is visible in the darkest void. The instant the lights are switched off or on, Dr. Mustafa Mahmud Korany—a.k.a. the Cerebellum—can

sense them as they fill up the cosmos. This is the moment when existence metamorphoses. Just before the equations of mathematics melt
into the cauldron of infinite numbers. He can see clearly now. And he
can grasp the meaning of these words. In contentment, he welcomes
the unknown.

"The boat has sunk, Captain."

chapter 13

Charlotte, North Carolina
Saturday, January 20, 2007
1021 EST

Only one move spells the difference between success and disaster. The lesson he's learned from the game of FreeCell spins in Martin's mind. The problem is, the player can rarely see the full picture when he must make his critical decision. He has no choice but to depend on his instincts, his gut feelings, luck, or all of the above. The difficulty he's been facing in the past few moments, just to figure out what exactly is happening from his vantage point in the Ghost Center, has raised his level of anxiety. The central screen is dark. It is fed by the cameras in the eyeglasses of the agents in the café. But their sudden, sometimes violent movements cannot provide the minimum required stability for a clear image. He can only follow the events on the two side screens: one coming from the satellite, the other from the sniper in his window overlooking Groppi's Adli Street entrance.

The satellite image is the one that allows you to trace the movement of individuals with maximum precision. In the past few minutes, he had to review its recording more than once. As the events were unfolding, it was simply impossible to be certain of their exact sequence.

Those were tense moments. At first glance, it seemed like everything was happening simultaneously. All of a sudden, several individuals were in motion in different parts of the café: the athletic bodyguard who headed back toward his boss carrying the sports bag with the rest of the ransom money; the skinny youth who wrestled with the other gang member; the pretty girl who managed to set herself free and escaped into the ladies' restroom; the waiter who'd overloaded his tray; the cat that was prowling among the tables, then shot out like a missile to avoid the falling tray; the three kids who just wouldn't stop trotting around the café; the fat lady who jumped out of her chair to save her little boy; the gang boss, who felt he was losing control of the situation; the driver who stood in puzzlement next to the tire that had blown— from his perspective—inexplicably, then rallied, together with his big-bellied colleague, to the aid of their boss; Mickey Mouse, who rushed blindly out of the Peugeot; and of course, their own WASP unit, who wasted no time in carrying out their mission.

Each of them was an independent actor. But at the same time, each was influenced by the actions of others and, reciprocally, affected them. This is truly perplexing. He needs to determine the correct sequence of events, in order to write a precise Mission Report. But, for him, the matter has taken another dimension. It's become personal. He feels that understanding the correct sequence is not in itself without significance. To be precise, he now needs to decipher the actions of his nemesis, the Cerebellum.

Martin's anxiety did not ease until the WASP inserted the tip of his umbrella into the subject's shoulder. Then he started to analyze things more calmly. However, his analysis was marred by a different kind of anxiety.

He was shaken by the sight of the poison being injected into the victim's body. He did not suffer from a guilty conscience; it was more a sense of anticipation than anything else. The awareness that a new load had been added to his lifetime burden, the knowledge that he would have to carry a heavier weight till the very end. He's come to understand that people who commit crimes are rarely plagued by a guilty conscience, but rather by a powerful desire to avoid punishment, any kind of punishment. He has nothing to worry about, however. Who is ever going to think of punishing a nameless man with no history, an invisible resident of North Carolina, for the death of an unknown Egyptian scientist, apparently of a heart attack? Even if the whole thing were to come out into the open, he'd be looked upon as a hero, to be decorated, not punished, a national icon in whose honor statues should be erected.

Hitting the target would go down as a success in anyone's book. What's important now is to get the agents out, especially as the situation with the gang is getting more and more complicated. He needs to focus his energy into finishing the operation successfully. His victory would turn sour if any of his agents were to get hurt or, worse still, fall into enemy hands. He's not about to let such potential catastrophes snatch victory away when it's finally within his reach.

The two members of the WASP unit were only trying to keep the gang away from Mickey Mouse long enough for the team leader to finish the job. But obviously, the gang felt threatened. They may have even thought that the WASP unit was working for Mickey Mouse and that they'd fallen into a trap, particularly when it looked like Mickey Mouse was trying to attack the fat, bald man, who was obviously the gang boss.

A really stupid move on your part, Mickey.

Until now, everything you've done has been perfectly rational, well thought out, as if planned by a chess grandmaster. Then you had to charge at the bald man. . . .

What happened?

After carefully reviewing the video recordings, he has established that it was Mickey Mouse's blind rush out of the car that sparked the commotion. Almost immediately, the pretty girl tried to break free, which prompted the skinny guy to come to her rescue. Was this a pre-agreed signal? But what really complicates matters is that neither the girl nor the young man stood a chance of escaping. That is, not until the two members of the gang were distracted by the scuffle that flared up between the agents of the WASP unit and the gang boss and his bodyguard. Is it possible that Mickey Mouse had anticipated COBRA's plan from the very start?

But what about the kid who was hiding behind the car, and was knocked down by the door when Mickey threw it open? If the subject hadn't flung the door open so violently when he rushed out, the kid wouldn't have been thrown onto the pavement. His fat mother wouldn't have jumped up inside the café, the waiter's tray wouldn't have been overturned, and the yellow cat wouldn't have sped away in terror. Could this whole chain of events possibly be part of Mickey Mouse's plan? Or did he, at the very last moment, decide to entrust his fate, and that of the kidnapped girl, to chance?

The WASP unit's agents have at last managed to extricate themselves from the situation. They're off on their motorbikes, leaving the gang to try to figure out what hit them. Martin instructs all units to return to their safe houses, except the sharpshooter in the window, who'll stay put for a few more minutes. He must continue to film the scene of the operation. It's the only way to make certain that the operation has been an astounding success, from beginning to end. Martin is determined not to give anyone the chance to raise doubts about his achievement in the future.

He takes a sip of his coffee as he follows Mickey Mouse's progress on the image coming from the sniper's weapon that is pointed at him. The coffee has gone cold and sour. The subject has actually managed to stagger all the way to the middle of the café. But now he stops. He looks all around him.

The poor man is looking for his imaginary lover.

Martin suddenly starts to sob. His emotions have taken him by surprise, and just when he least expects it. His crime is apparent to him in all its dimensions. But he's not crying over Mustafa Mahmud Korany—a.k.a. the Cerebellum—whom they childishly code-named Mickey Mouse. He's crying for himself. Over the innocence he's lost, forever. He's crying over the dark, lonely world he's helping to create that will ultimately be the legacy he leaves his beautiful, innocent Amy. He cries like he's never cried before.

He doesn't stop crying until the subject sways, then falls to the ground for the last time. At that instant, the sobbing freezes in his heart.

Martin catches a glimpse of an old man in a red Turkish hat. Sharing his table is a sexy young woman with—strangely enough—orange hair. Is it the same man? His image is completely blurred. The shooter's lens is focused on the subject, not the people at the tables. Nevertheless, it seems like there's a mist surrounding both the old man and the girl . . . could it be her?

Martin wipes the tears from his eyes. Then he starts to rub them. Impossible!

The crowd that has gathered around the subject obstructs his view of the old man and the girl. Martin puts the blame on himself. A professional intelligence officer must never indulge in such fantasies. Exhaustion and emotion have affected his judgment. He must get a grip on himself.

Finally, Martin gives the shooter the order to disengage. Before the image disappears, he rises, stands up straight, and raises his hand to his head in a military salute. He pays his respects to the subject, as more and more people crowd around him on his deathbed, on the café's dusty tiles.

Is there an end more appropriate for a scientist of his caliber than to be killed by means of the world's most advanced technology?

Cairo, Egypt
Saturday, January 20, 2007
Just before the sunset call to prayer

The old man with the tarboosh smiles at him from behind his table. He nods to emphasize his greetings. Candygirl is sitting next to him. She toys with the tip of her striped straw as she positions it between her lips. Then she takes a long sip from her strawberry milkshake. The Cerebellum freezes in the middle of Groppi. Has he lost touch with reality? Is he now starting to hallucinate? Perhaps he is already long dead. But there she is, right in front of him, in the flesh. Her hair cascades over her bare shoulders like an orange curtain of thick velvet. She is wearing the emerald-green dress she just bought that shows off her firm, ripe breasts. She has actually recognized him. Her face lights up. Her smile comes from deep within. She waves eagerly, but half coyly. She beckons him to her.

She promises to recapture all their special moments.

The old man smiles in encouragement. But again, that invisible steel fist grips him by the chest. Its impact, this time, is more decisive. The pain does not exceed his tolerance threshold. The specter of death evokes no panic. The problem lies in the mechanics of breathing. He feels like an entire ocean is flowing into his lungs. . . .

Surrounded by all the air in the world, he is drowning.

Just like that.

The impact of the fall is soft. As though the café's tiles were padded with spongy rubber. The sky above him is a surrealist painting. The blue fuses with the orange, like molasses mixed with tahini. He is mentally aware of the tang of cold, but cannot sense it. There are voices in the background. Faces are starting to block the sky. The red of the old man's tarboosh emits warmth, pulsates with the living breath of the galaxies, the grinding swirl of black holes. Yet the convulsions become more violent. Can the world be trembling, sobbing for him . . . or is it only his frail body, shedding life, like a captive fish in a merciless fisherman's net?

The old man picks up the bag containing the cash. He waves it to make sure the Cerebellum can see what he is doing. He smiles. Then both tarboosh and smile vanish. Only the glum faces of strangers remain.

"People are mules transporting gold . . . one mule only delivers the burden to the next one," says the Cerebellum. He is not sure that the words have actually left his mouth. He is not sure that he even managed to return the old man's smile.

His eyesight is foggy. But his vision is crystal clear. His mind contemplates existence, serene till the end. Is that not a victory of sorts?

Two bloodshot eyes stare at him from the blackness. It is Condoleezza. A surge of emotion. He is not sure if he is being shaken by emotions, or if the poisoned body is resisting, foolishly clinging to a life that has already purged it. Someone violently pulls the veil off her face. Her sexy features are frozen in astonishment. She turns and slaps the man. The crack of her slap restores sound in his ears. It is the bald man, the only human being he has ever hated . . . the New Owner, who really is as ancient as the pyramids. He must have thought she was Didi in disguise, after putting on Condoleezza's extra set of clothes inside the ladies' restroom.

Then Didi has been saved. She is inside a Metro train by now, speeding in a tunnel toward . . . toward the future.

Precisely . . . the plan has worked, Cerebellum.

The gang boss takes a step back, repulsed by the angry human mass. He mutters apologies, then, like a hunted jackal, slips away.

The Cerebellum remembers the stash he is still holding in his hand. It is the fortune Condoleezza entrusted him with, her ticket to freedom. He must now raise his arm. His final mission . . . his greatest challenge. He grits his teeth. He can distinguish the lone tear that has escaped her eye. He has done it, delivered what he owes. Tahir's good-natured face is next to hers. Didi has been saved and Tahir is right here, next to Condoleezza. What good would al-Mu'izz's dinars do them anyway?

All they need are their stamps of Queen Bess.

Candygirl smiles calmly. She has gone down on her knees to get closer to him. Together they glide around the dance floor in a sensuous tango. . . .

When it is over, they stop. She laughs.

"Did you know, my darling, that the merengue is my favorite, because its rhythm is the closest thing to a heartbeat?" he says.

"I'm no stranger to your taste in music, honey . . . of course I know it's your favorite." Her smile is all honey and hot peppers.

"The plan has worked," he says to her, feeling happier than ever before.

"Life is more complex than any plan, honey," candygirl replies in a voice that encompasses the songs of all the world's nightingales. She comes closer, whispers something in his ear. Her hair caresses his cheek, but her words make him think.

"And?"

Of course she is right. He can feel his ivory dice digging into his left thigh . . . at last he understands.

"Yes, honey . . . $d(f^T(x), f^T(y)) > \delta$ . . . you've got it right," says candy-girl. Then the lights go out.

www.candygirl-thebook.com

glossary

Abdel Wahhab: iconic Egyptian composer and singer who dominated the Arab music scene for over half a century. He also starred in musicals in the 1930s.

Ali ibn Abi Talib: the fourth Muslim caliph (656–61) and the Prophet Muhammad's son-in-law.

Antar: a lively child who used to live in the Cerebellum's last hideout; a refererence to the author's novel *Murder in the Tower of Happiness*.

camarera: Spanish for 'housemaid.'

"Did you pull a lion or a hyena?": Arabic expression: Did you succeed, or have you come back empty-handed?

Dokki, Manial, Mohandiseen, Bulaq: Cairo districts.

Fayza Ahmad: a popular singer in the 1950s and 1960s.

fuul: a paste made from mashed fava beans; a traditional Egyptian food.

gallabiya: an ankle-length, long-sleeved robe; a traditional Egyptian garment for men, especially in the countryside.

Gamal Hemdan: (1928–93) a prominent Egyptian geographer and thinker.

Hajji: a respectful form of address to an older man; literally, a person who has performed the pilgrimage (Hajj) to Mecca.

Halim: Abdel Halim Hafez, a popular Egyptian singer and movie star of the 1950s and 1960s.

Khawarij: a group that rebelled against the chosen ruler in the early days of the Islamic empire. The term is sometimes used to describe groups trying to disrupt the unity of Muslims.

al-Mu'izz: the first Fatimid caliph to rule Egypt (969–75).

Munufiya: a governorate of Egypt.

Nancy Agram: a Lebanese pop star.

Qur'anist: a member of a denomination of Islam that holds the Qur'an to be the only canonical text in Islam, rejecting the catalogued narratives of what the Prophet Muhammad is reported to have said and done. Mainstream Muslims, both Shi'a and Sunni, consider them to be a misguided sect.

Shadia: a popular Egyptian song and movie star of the 1950s and 1960s.

"The son of a duck is a floater": Arabic expression meaning that a child resembles or takes after his or her parent.

takfiri: a hard line-Islamist who considers any understanding of Islam other than his own to be apostasy.

Umm Kulthum: iconic Egyptian diva of the mid-twentieth century, popular throughout the Arab world; her recordings are still listened to today.

Vali Faqih: Guardian Jurist, the Supreme Leader of Iran.

WASP unit: A type of special-forces unit, a direct translation from the Arabic name.

Zaynat Sidki: Egyptian movie actress of the 1940s and 1950s who frequently played the role of a jovial housemaid.

Modern Arabic Literature
from the American University in Cairo Press

Bahaa Abdelmegid *Saint Theresa* and *Sleeping with Strangers*
Ibrahim Abdel Meguid *Birds of Amber* • *Distant Train*
No One Sleeps in Alexandria • *The Other Place*
Yahya Taher Abdullah *The Collar and the Bracelet* • *The Mountain of Green Tea*
Leila Abouzeid *The Last Chapter*
Hamdi Abu Golayyel *A Dog with No Tail* • *Thieves in Retirement*
Yusuf Abu Rayya *Wedding Night*
Ahmed Alaidy *Being Abbas el Abd*
Idris Ali *Dongola* • *Poor*
Rasha al Ameer *Judgment Day*
Radwa Ashour *Granada* • *Specters*
Ibrahim Aslan *The Heron* • *Nile Sparrows*
Alaa Al Aswany *Chicago* • *Friendly Fire* • *The Yacoubian Building*
Fahd al-Atiq *Life on Hold*
Fadhil al-Azzawi *Cell Block Five* • *The Last of the Angels*
The Traveler and the Innkeeper
Ali Bader *Papa Sartre*
Liana Badr *The Eye of the Mirror*
Hala El Badry *A Certain Woman* • *Muntaha*
Salwa Bakr *The Golden Chariot* • *The Man from Bashmour* • *The Wiles of Men*
Halim Barakat *The Crane*
Hoda Barakat *Disciples of Passion* • *The Tiller of Waters*
Mourid Barghouti *I Saw Ramallah* • *I Was Born There, I Was Born Here*
Mohamed Berrada *Like a Summer Never to Be Repeated*
Mohamed El-Bisatie *Clamor of the Lake* • *Drumbeat* • *Hunger* • *Over the Bridge*
Mahmoud Darwish *The Butterfly's Burden*
Tarek Eltayeb *Cities without Palms* • *The Palm House*
Mansoura Ez Eldin *Maryam's Maze*
Ibrahim Farghali *The Smiles of the Saints*
Hamdy el-Gazzar *Black Magic*
Randa Ghazy *Dreaming of Palestine*
Gamal al-Ghitani *Pyramid Texts* • *The Zafarani Files* • *Zayni Barakat*
The Book of Epiphanies
Tawfiq al-Hakim *The Essential Tawfiq al-Hakim* • *Return of the Spirit*
Yahya Hakki *The Lamp of Umm Hashim*
Abdelilah Hamdouchi *The Final Bet*
Bensalem Himmich *The Polymath* • *The Theocrat*
Taha Hussein *The Days*
Sonallah Ibrahim *Cairo: From Edge to Edge* • *The Committee* • *Zaat*
Yusuf Idris *City of Love and Ashes* • *The Essential Yusuf Idris* • *Tales of Encounter*
Denys Johnson-Davies *The AUC Press Book of Modern Arabic Literature* • *Homecoming*
In a Fertile Desert • *Under the Naked Sky*
Said al-Kafrawi *The Hill of Gypsies*
Mai Khaled *The Magic of Turquoise*
Sahar Khalifeh *The End of Spring*
The Image, the Icon and the Covenant • *The Inheritance* • *Of Noble Origins*
Edwar al-Kharrat *Rama and the Dragon* • *Stones of Bobello*

Betool Khedairi *Absent*
Mohammed Khudayyir *Basrayatha*
Ibrahim al-Koni *Anubis* • *Gold Dust* • *The Puppet* • *The Seven Veils of Seth*
Naguib Mahfouz *Adrift on the Nile* • *Akhenaten: Dweller in Truth*
Arabian Nights and Days • *Autumn Quail* • *Before the Throne* • *The Beggar*
The Beginning and the End • *Cairo Modern* • *The Cairo Trilogy: Palace Walk*
Palace of Desire • *Sugar Street* • *Children of the Alley* • *The Coffeehouse*
The Day the Leader Was Killed • *The Dreams* • *Dreams of Departure*
Echoes of an Autobiography • *The Essential Naguib Mahfouz* • *The Final Hour*
The Harafish • *Heart of the Night* • *In the Time of Love*
The Journey of Ibn Fattouma • *Karnak Cafe* • *Khan al-Khalili* • *Khufu's Wisdom*
Life's Wisdom • *Love in the Rain* • *Midaq Alley* • *The Mirage* • *Miramar* • *Mirrors*
Morning and Evening Talk • *Naguib Mahfouz at Sidi Gaber* • *Respected Sir*
Rhadopis of Nubia • *The Search* • *The Seventh Heaven* • *Thebes at War*
The Thief and the Dogs • *The Time and the Place* • *Voices from the Other World*
Wedding Song • *The Wisdom of Naguib Mahfouz*
Mohamed Makhzangi *Memories of a Meltdown*
Alia Mamdouh *The Loved Ones* • *Naphtalene*
Selim Matar *The Woman of the Flask*
Ibrahim al-Mazini *Ten Again*
Yousef Al-Mohaimeed *Munira's Bottle* • *Wolves of the Crescent Moon*
Hassouna Mosbahi *A Tunisian Tale*
Ahlam Mosteghanemi *Chaos of the Senses* • *Memory in the Flesh*
Shakir Mustafa *Contemporary Iraqi Fiction: An Anthology*
Mohamed Mustagab *Tales from Dayrut*
Buthaina Al Nasiri *Final Night*
Ibrahim Nasrallah *Inside the Night* • *Time of White Horses*
Haggag Hassan Oddoul *Nights of Musk*
Mona Prince *So You May See*
Mohamed Mansi Qandil *Moon over Samarqand*
Abd al-Hakim Qasim *Rites of Assent*
Somaya Ramadan *Leaves of Narcissus*
Kamal Ruhayyim *Days in the Diaspora*
Mahmoud Saeed *The World through the Eyes of Angels*
Mekkawi Said *Cairo Swan Song*
Ghada Samman *The Night of the First Billion*
Mahdi Issa al-Saqr *East Winds, West Winds*
Rafik Schami *The Calligrapher's Secret* • *Damascus Nights* • *The Dark Side of Love*
Habib Selmi *The Scents of Marie-Claire*
Khairy Shalaby *The Hashish Waiter* • *The Lodging House*
Khalil Sweileh *Writing Love*
The Time-Travels of the Man Who Sold Pickles and Sweets
Miral al-Tahawy *Blue Aubergine* • *Brooklyn Heights* • *Gazelle Tracks* • *The Tent*
Bahaa Taher *As Doha Said* • *Love in Exile*
Fuad al-Takarli *The Long Way Back*
Zakaria Tamer *The Hedgehog*
M. M. Tawfik *candygirl* • *Murder in the Tower of Happiness*
Mahmoud Al-Wardani *Heads Ripe for Plucking*
Amina Zaydan *Red Wine*
Latifa al-Zayyat *The Open Door*